MAFIOSA PRINCESS- TRUST

LIZA MALLOY

CHAPTER 1

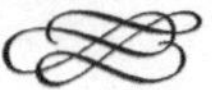

Giada

I paid the driver and gazed up at the neon pink sign above the solid black door. It identified the popular nightclub as Oro, the pride and joy of none other than Salvatore Marino. Of course, Sal wasn't the Marino I was hoping to see. Unless I'd botched my research, Sal was still in Sicily, which left his sexy son overseeing the family's clubs in Rome.

My breath hitched as I thought about finally seeing Luca again. Aside from one brief phone call, my last contact with him had been that fateful day in my yard, where he kissed me with so much passion that I nearly keeled over. Then, he promptly ditched me to fly to Italy. I'd spent weeks pouting over the separation from my home in Connecticut before convincing Matteo to let me tag along on his trip to Rome.

Even once I'd reached Italian soil, I'd waited another two weeks for Luca to swap locations with his father, unwittingly joining me in the Eternal City. Despite the time I'd had to think, I still didn't know exactly what I wanted to accomplish at Oro. I hoped not only to see Luca, but to talk with him, touch him, and ideally convince him to run away with me. But at this point, I'd settle for any contact at all.

I walked around the lengthy line of patrons hoping to gain entry and flashed the bouncer my sweetest smile, tilting my head downwards in a seductive manner. Just in case my skimpy outfit and pouty lips didn't do the trick, I also offered him roughly fifty dollars in Euros. Giada Conti did not wait in lines, especially on nights like this one. No, I had a mission.

Once inside the club, I stood near a wall, my best fuck-off expression plastered to my face, and I continued to watch for signs of Luca. I was just starting to get discouraged when the crowd parted, allowing two burly guys to pass. They strode straight to me, and before I could even formulate my protests, their hands were on me. They nudged me towards the bar, then down a hallway labeled PRIVATO.

Part of me yearned to scream or fight back, but self-restraint —and the realization that no one in the club could possibly defend me against Sal Marino—kept me quiet. The men opened the door to a room bathed in darkness, holding me still in the entry.

"Leave us," the familiar voice commanded. My heart fluttered as they nudged me into the room, shutting the door behind me.

The light switched on, and our eyes met. *God*, how I had missed those deep, chocolatey brown eyes. I stepped forward as if pulled by a strong magnet, then stopped an arm's length away. I let my eyes dip to his soft, full lips, which were currently set in a straight line. His expression was intense yet unreadable. Meanwhile, I probably looked like I was about to pass out from excitement.

The only indication whatsoever that Luca was even remotely affected by me was the rapid movement of his chest. I inched forward again, and this time, my movement broke the spell. His eyes left mine, traveling slowly down my body then back up again.

Luca looked the same as I remembered. He wore black suit pants that flattered his strong, masculine physique and a dark gray button-down that I yearned to slowly unbutton while he squirmed against my hands. His dark hair was slightly longer, barely grazing the tops of his ears, and he was cleanly shaven. His shirt clung to the cluster of muscles along his chest as he inhaled slowly and with restraint.

Everything about him screamed power and control. I desperately yearned to tip the balance, to watch him come undone at my hands.

"You're here," he finally said, his voice level and calm.

I tried to come up with a snappy response, but instead, I croaked a lame "yes."

He stepped forward, clutching my face in his hands. He held me still as he inspected me then leaned closer and inhaled sharply. I was close enough to feel the heat emanating from his body but not close enough to touch him in the way I wanted. I held my breath in anticipation of a kiss that never came. After a moment, his hands fell to his sides.

"Where's Matteo?"

I shrugged.

"You came here without him? Why would you do that?"

"I saw your car outside. I knew you were here."

"It's not safe for you to be at a place like this alone."

"It's a club, Luca. People come here for fun."

"People come here for drugs and sex," he replied.

"Well, I came here for one of those, but if I can't get my first choice, I suppose I'd take the other at this point."

Luca stared at me for a long moment, like he just couldn't figure out what to do with me. I stepped closer, hoping to hasten his decision, but he held me at a distance.

"Your brother is going to wonder where you went."

"He thinks I'm in bed. As long as I'm back by tomorrow morning, no one will ask questions."

"Giada, this is my papà's club. If he reviews the security footage, or if anyone sees us together…"

I peered around us, realizing that must be why he had someone bring me into the office. It was probably the only place outside of the bathrooms with no security cameras. There was plenty of room on the desk…

"No," he said, always the mind reader. "You deserve more than my papà's office."

"Okay, but I've waited weeks for you to make some progress on figuring out how we can be together, and you've gotten nowhere."

"Not for lack of trying. I need to get in my papà's good graces again, let him see I'm capable of whatever he throws my way. Then, I'll tell him I want you back. I just need you to wait for me a little longer."

I bit the side of my cheek, hating the feeling that the person I needed most in the world was rejecting me again.

Luca bent his head down and cupped my face in his hands. My eyes fluttered shut in anticipation of a slow, romantic kiss, but instead, he pressed his forehead against mine. "Amore mio," he sighed.

I inhaled the familiar scent of his aftershave and smiled. Everything about Luca was familiar to me, yet he was still so mysterious. I could spend years getting to know him and still not understand the way his brain worked.

I shifted my head so I could kiss him, brushing my lips against his with a light, feathery touch.

Luca neither reciprocated nor pulled away, but when I finally ended the kiss, he yanked me closer, devouring my mouth with his own.

I moaned into him, his tongue sending jolts of pleasure through my entire body. Luca ended the kiss too soon, as always.

"I need to finish some things here. Go get lost in the crowd, but don't accept any drinks from anyone but the bartender. In exactly sixty minutes, come look for me," he growled.

I shivered at the prospect, then licked my lips, savoring his taste.

CHAPTER 2

Four weeks earlier...

Luca

I arrived in Italy with determination and a bad attitude.

I did what I was supposed to do—again. I said goodbye to Giada, left her crying at her house so that I could do my papà's bidding. Again. I promised Giada the separation was temporary, that I'd prove myself to my papà and then go a step further and convince him that she was an asset to me, not a liability.

But even she couldn't have been naïve enough to buy that. I'd spent my entire life trying to earn the approval of my papà with limited success. Surely that wouldn't change now.

Alessio promptly passed out during the flight, so I finally let myself ruminate. Pressing the pad of my thumb to my mouth, I traced every place Giada had been. If I closed my eyes, I could still taste her on my lips. The heat from her breath still warmed my cheeks. The neediness of her tongue clashing against my own still accelerated my pulse.

I was so screwed.

Every time Giada and I were apart, it was harder to find my way back to her. I told myself I'd never stop trying, never give up, but I wasn't sure that mattered. The longer I went without her, the darker I became— the more like my papà, or at least, more like he wanted me to be. And every time Giada returned to me, I was less deserving of her.

Eventually, the lapse would be too great. There would be no bridging the gap between her innocent perfection and my guilt-ridden, tarnished soul, not with the countless misdeeds I'd committed. Not after the ones I hadn't yet committed but would soon.

At least I'd been a hero the last time we were apart. Now I was just the asshole that broke her heart. Again.

I'd fully intended to tell Giada not to wait for me, but I'd caved as soon as she'd resisted. Selfishly, I wanted her to stay loyal, to put her life on pause until we could enjoy it together. In my mind, I framed the next couple of months as a hiatus from reality. I would serve as the loyal foot soldier my papà desired. Once my deployment ended, I'd return to the woman awaiting me. Not seeing or touching Giada for so long would be challenging, but not talking to her would be even worse. What would I start to forget first—the refreshing sound of her voice, the tickle of her silky hair on my chest, or her spicy-sweet scent?

Alessio eyed me warily as the plane thunked along the runway in the least smooth landing I'd experienced. "You could call her from my phone whenever you want," he said.

Alessio knew as well as I did that I couldn't do that. My papà had spies everywhere, and they'd figure it out if I was talking with Giada. The more I thought about it, though, the more ridiculous it all seemed. Why was I letting this man control my life? I was an adult. He didn't get to dictate what I did and didn't do.

Well, except a certain blood oath I'd sworn nearly a decade before sort of said he did.

I was fucked.

I stayed quiet as Georgio collected us from the airport. As we neared my apartment, I unfastened my belt, eager to be on my way.

"We're just dropping off Alessio here. Your father thought you'd stay at the house with him."

I couldn't suppress my grimace at the thought. "No thanks. We can both stay here."

"He didn't make it sound optional," Georgio said.

I groaned, but said goodbye to my friend. I'd have to deal with my papà sooner or later. And the quickest path back to Giada was to simply do what the asshole wanted. I needed to make him trust me, and fast.

~

Giada

I spent two weeks at home, pining over Luca. I bought a disposable phone and called him, leaving a nondescript message when he didn't answer. Thankfully, he called me back. He sounded tense, unhappy, and oh so far away. Luca tried to reassure me, but he'd made no progress with his father. Worse yet, he told me not to call again, claiming we couldn't have any contact if we wanted to convince his father we'd broken up.

Luca encouraged me to stay busy, to keep looking for an internship, but for what? I certainly wasn't moving back to New York with Gabriella now, and I didn't want to get a job in Connecticut when there was little chance Luca would return there.

My situation was hopeless.

"I'm having serious déjà vu," Matteo said, interrupting my pool-side siesta.

I ignored him and tugged my blanket higher. After weeks of being unseasonably warm, the weather had cooled drastically, hampering my daily routine of lounging by the pool. Still, I spent my mornings in a punishing workout at the gym, then piled on the layers to enjoy a post-lunch nap by the pool. Most afternoons, I headed to church. In the evenings, I'd drink at home with my cousins or brothers or anyone else who was there. In part, that was to gain intel on Angelo, but also I didn't have anything better to do. Having attended boarding school and college out of town, I didn't have local friends who weren't either related to me or employed by my father.

"This is how you acted when you thought he was dead, Giada. Except Luca isn't dead," Matteo said, explaining his comment.

"He might as well be," I replied, wincing with regret immediately.

"Angelo tried to reach Adrian. He seems to think that would cheer you up."

"It wouldn't. I'm not interested in Adrian, and I'm sure he's not interested in me now. We don't even talk anymore."

My brother blew out a sigh. "Well, this is depressing. You need a hobby or some purpose. You can't just lounge around all the time."

I rolled my eyes at the irony, since my entire family seemed to want me to live my life as an heiress. Every time I attempted to attain any measure of independence, they found a way to ruin it. But that was beside the point. Right now, I had a purpose. I had a noble mission, really. I just couldn't tell anyone what that was.

Luca said it was my brother—my *other* brother—who told his father that he killed a man for me. And we both knew Angelo did that just to get Luca shipped across the country, away from his business. Luca somehow didn't think that merited vengeance, but

I felt differently. Thanks to Angelo, I was spending the next three months away from the love of my life. I wasn't about to let my asshole brother get away with that.

So when I spent my days at the gym, it wasn't just to look good. I was toughening up, training, so that I wouldn't have to worry about assholes like Tony in the future. And when I went to the church, I wasn't just silently praying like I had before. I was researching. I was tracking Angelo's movements, trying to figure out what he could be up to and why.

And at night, when my family thought I was reading sappy romance novels and sleeping off my evening drink, I was on the computer. I scoured every news article I could find about the mafia, meticulously noting every detail I could learn about my family or Luca's.

What I didn't yet know was what to do with this information.

"How's that sound?" Matteo asked.

I gazed up at my brother. I sensed he'd already asked me at least one other question from the look on his face, but I hadn't heard enough to even piece together clues.

"Sorry, how does what sound?"

"Italy. With your favorite brother," he added. He was probably teasing, except everyone knew he really was my favorite brother. Not that Angelo even tried to be decent competition.

"For vacation?"

He shrugged. "For a month or so. Dad asked me to check in on some of his contacts in Rome, and we all thought the change of scenery might help your mood."

I considered that. Being in the same country as Luca was so tempting. But if I couldn't see him or talk to him anyway, it probably shouldn't matter how far apart we were. And while I couldn't very well spy on Angelo from across the Atlantic, I hadn't actually made much progress on that mission locally.

"I'm in," I said. "But we should at least stay through the holidays, you know, like we used to when we were younger.

Christmas in Italy is just what I need," I added, already feeling the unfamiliar sensation of my cheeks widening to a smile. Now all I had to do was figure out how to ditch Matteo and get to Luca without Salvatore Marino finding out.

~

Adrian

I'd told myself at least a dozen times over the past year that I should block Angelo's number, but of course I hadn't. I wouldn't have answered if he'd called me, but when he sent the ominous message, I had to call him. My last class had just ended, and I was walking back to my apartment anyway, but I didn't need the heart palpitations his message gave me.

"Something happened to Giada. Call me ASAP," was all Angelo had said.

Of course, he didn't answer when I called. I hung up and immediately called back a second time, failing to reach him again. I tried a third time, planning to leave a message. To my surprise, he answered.

"What?" he growled.

It took me a moment to remember why I was calling. "What happened to Giada?"

"What?" he repeated, this time sounding more confused than annoyed. "Patras?"

"Yes. You just texted me that something happened to her."

"You called me three times in a row. Is someone dying?"

My head fell backwards, letting me silently curse the heavens. Why was this awful man in my life? "I don't know, Angelo. You're the one who sent the mystery text. Is she okay?"

"Hang on," he mumbled.

I clenched my jaw so hard I could've chipped a tooth, but I reasoned that he wouldn't be so cavalier if his sister truly were in danger. I heard him talking to someone else in a vastly different tone than what he used with me. I assumed it was his girlfriend.

After a minute, I lost my patience.

"I don't have all day," I shouted into my phone.

"Jesus, Patras. Learn some patience," Angelo said a moment later.

"You didn't expect me to have some questions after the message you sent me? What's going on with Giada? Is she okay?"

Angelo sighed. "She will be. She was attacked, nearly raped, thanks to Luca. Oh, and then they broke up, but now—"

"Giada was raped?" I stopped dead in my tracks, nearly dropping my phone as the guy behind me slammed into me. I mumbled an apology to him then focused back on my call.

"No, she got away, but she could've been, and the whole thing really shook her up, and—"

Suddenly, the rest of his earlier statement caught up to me. "She and Luca broke up?"

"Yeah."

"For good?"

Angelo's chuckle reminded me of the devil. "That probably depends a little on you. Look, you weren't my first pick for her initially, but she's not safe with Luca. If I have it my way, they'll never get back together."

I agreed with Angelo, which was disturbing, but at least I had the presence of mind to clarify something. "I am never getting back together with your sister. No matter what."

Angelo was silent, so I pressed forward with a question.

"Who attacked her? What happened?"

"The guy's dead now. Luca killed him—literally beat him to death in front of Giada. She'll obviously need therapy. But the whole thing was Luca's fault. He stole some business from the wrong guys, and one of them came after her for payback."

"Jesus," I mumbled. None of what Angelo was saying should've been surprising. That sort of shit happened to people who ran in a crowd of criminals. Except Giada didn't deserve to be involved in any of that, no matter how flighty or naïve she was.

"Look, I gotta go. I just thought you should know she's single, and that if there's anything you can do to keep Luca out of her life, I'm on board."

I winced at the implication, but Angelo disconnected before I could respond. I walked the rest of the way to my apartment, then called Giada. As much as I didn't think I could handle hearing her voice again, I had to check in on her. If a monster like Angelo was worried about her, she must be in bad shape.

Giada answered on the first ring.

"Adrian?" she sounded breathless and confused.

"Yeah. Am I catching you at a bad time?" I heard a rustling sound and then silence.

"No. I was just packing."

"Packing?"

"I'm moving to Italy."

I felt my jaw literally drop.

"Well, not forever," she clarified. "I'm going with my brother till the new year."

"Angelo called me," I said.

"Not Angelo. I'm going with Matteo. Wait, Angelo called you?"

"Yeah. He said you and Luca broke up, again. Told me some pretty heavy stuff. Said you were struggling. He wanted me to check in on you."

"Wow. And you actually did," she said, sounding surprised and impressed.

"I still care about you, Giada. As a friend," I quickly added. "I don't want to be involved with your family anymore, but that doesn't mean I want you to be miserable."

She exhaled loudly into the receiver. "You are a great guy, Adrian. Seriously, the best. I'm glad we can stay friends after everything. Honestly though, you don't have to worry about me. I'm fine. I'm going to be, anyway."

I had to admit she sounded good. I didn't get the impression that she was just pretending, either. "I'm relieved to hear that. Angelo seemed to think you were taking the break up badly."

Giada didn't answer right away. Usually, that meant she was debating whether to tell the actual truth or some alternate version of the truth. I hadn't a clue which one I was about to hear.

"Look, I'm only telling you this because I still care about you, and I don't want to lie to you. Luca and I didn't really break up. Luca's father doesn't want him to see me now, so we aren't exactly together, but he's working on it."

"His father doesn't want him to see you?" That seemed completely backwards.

"He thinks I make Luca reckless," she explained. "Either way, it doesn't matter. I'm going to Italy, and if Luca doesn't figure out a way to get his father off his back, I will."

Wow. So that was her plan. It took me a minute to formulate a response to that foolhardiness. I debated being the neutral moderator but instead opted for complete honesty.

"That's a terrible idea, Giada. Your family has its share of problems, but as long as you stay away from the Marinos, they can—and will—keep you safe."

"It's complicated, Adrian. And I don't want to get into the details…"

"Angelo said Luca murdered a man for you."

Her soft gasp was barely audible. It took her a minute to respond. "I'm surprised he told you that, and for the record, that's not exactly what happened. But even so, the point of all that is that Luca was the one who protected me."

"Luca was the one who put you in danger in the first place."

"No, that was Angelo."

I rolled my eyes, not surprised she put a different spin on the facts than her brother had. "Either way, you're a good person Giada. I realize you have some connection with Luca I don't understand, but this isn't you. You aren't the type of person to seek revenge on someone else or to physically beat a man until he dies. You shouldn't be with someone who is that way."

"If I want to be with the kind of man who would do anything for me, that's none of your business."

"You're right," I agreed. "But the Giada I knew wouldn't want anything to do with a man who would kill for her. That Giada would've wanted a man who loved her enough to at least try to be a decent person. That Giada still has morals."

Her voice was different when she finally spoke. "I don't think that Giada exists anymore."

I had no response for that. I'd said my piece, and she'd acknowledged it. So that was that.

"I should finish packing. I appreciate the concern, Adrian."

"Yeah, whatever," I mumbled.

"Hey Adrian?" she paused, apparently concerned I'd already hung up. "Be careful. Angelo is up to something. You shouldn't trust him. He's on some sort of mission, and he doesn't care who he hurts along the way."

"Duly noted. Have a good flight." I hung up before she could say anything else.

I clenched my phone in my hand, trying to decide my next move. There were two logical options—drinking or exercising. I gazed at the dog as if he'd voice a preference, then texted Ryan. It was seven p.m., and I'd already aced my last exam. There was no reason to choose the gym over the bar. Luckily, Ryan agreed, so I took Scruffy on a short walk then changed to meet my friend.

Our favorite bar was a few blocks from my apartment, and on nights like tonight, the frigid blast of air on the walk home was sure to sober me up enough to get a good night's sleep. I spent the walk there ruminating about Giada, since I didn't want to bore Ryan with more complaints about my ex.

Ryan had lived through the soap opera that was my relationship with Giada almost as much as I had. He was a great confidant—the type of guy who'd listen when I vented, then would pay me a compliment before promptly distracting me with a different topic. He was fantastic as a wingman, too.

I tried to run the conversation we'd have through my mind as I walked. Ryan would tell me—as he often had before—that Giada was toxic. According to Ryan, I didn't want to be with Giada. I just wanted to save her. In his theory, I was practically a hero. In reality, I wasn't so sure. Yes, I wanted Giada to be safe and happy. But not with Luca.

Just because I didn't want to be with Giada didn't mean I wanted Luca to be with her, either. Maybe that was selfish, but it was also keeping her safe. As much as I didn't like—or trust—Angelo, he was not the bad guy in this scenario. Luca was. Giada, as always, was just too willfully blind to see that.

I could've called Angelo or even Marco and let them know what Giada told me, how the breakup was simply a sham, and let them take things from there, but that felt wrong. She'd confided in me out of respect for our history. I didn't want to punish her for that.

Right as I reached the front entrance of the bar, it hit me. I didn't care about winning Giada back. I wanted to make sure Luca never got her back. And the only way to ensure that didn't happen was to show Giada his true colors, once and for all. With all the bad shit Luca was into, it couldn't possibly be hard to find enough proof to convince Giada to stay away from him for good.

I swung open the door to the bar, already bopping my head to the beat of the music.

CHAPTER 3

Luca

My first week in Italy was miserable, but then I settled into a routine. I hated living under the same roof as my papà, but I had forgotten there were a few perks. Papà had people handle our shopping, cleaning, cooking, even the laundry. In my free time, I rediscovered how relaxing it was to watch television in my native tongue, to truly binge on a show without having to think. And I enjoyed the finest food and drink available.

My papà began our time together treating me like a bumbling idiot, but after I'd completed a few menial tasks for him without complaint or mistake, he dialed back the condescension. Within weeks, Alessio and I were working the town like a well-oiled machine. We'd always made a great team, but the last time we'd been together in Rome for more than a few weeks was high school. Despite the odds, we'd both matured considerably since then.

"Think fast!" Alessio said abruptly.

I gazed up just in time to see a highball glass of whiskey slide right past me along the bar. It smacked into Lodovico's hand and a little splashed over. Lodovico scowled at Alessio, then stood up and sulked out of the bar towards the restrooms, holding his hand like it was coated in toxic waste.

Alessio and I both burst into laughter.

Possibly, we hadn't matured as much as I thought. Although, maybe it was just Ludovico's presence that brought out the childishness in us. As one of my papà's more mature men, Lodovico often filled the unofficial role of babysitter for Alessio and me.

I reached for the wayward glass and poured the rest of the amber liquid into my mouth. It wasn't the best whiskey; the crap at this club never was. But it would suffice to get me through the night.

"How are we both here tonight anyway?" I asked, suddenly worrying that one of us had missed a meeting.

"You want me to explain the space-time continuum?" Alessio replied.

I quirked a brow. Maybe it wasn't intentional, but my papà had done an excellent job so far of separating me from Alessio. Not only had my papà made me stay with him at the house while letting Alessio crash at my apartment, but he'd arranged the schedule at the clubs so Alessio and I were never both at the same one on the same night.

"I'm covering for Tomasso," Alessio said, long after I'd forgotten the question I'd posed.

"He have a hot date or something?"

We both laughed. Tomasso was roughly the same age as our parents, but he'd never married. As far as I knew, he hadn't had any serious girlfriends. The only woman he ever spent time with was my mother.

Tomasso was one of my papà's most trusted captains and had been since before I was born. My papà used him for everything from security and transportation to actual business deals and management. During my teenage years, whenever my papà seemed sick of the parenting gig, he'd delegate disciplinary duties to Tomasso, too. If my papà weren't so damn possessive, I wouldn't be surprised if he tried to delegate some of his marital duties too.

"Porca puttana!" Alessio exclaimed suddenly, roughly translating to 'holy shit.'

I followed his surprised stare to the door, where a leggy brunette had just sauntered in. Once she was in earshot, Alessio switched back to English.

"Well, look what the cat dragged in," he said, just as some random patron whistled.

The woman ignored the whistle, clearly welcoming the attention, and raised an eyebrow at Alessio before leaning slightly closer and offering her cheek to him. He made a face only I could see, then pressed a quick kiss to each of her cheeks.

"Chiara," I said, greeting her by name. Surprisingly, I was happy to see her.

"Ciao Luca," she replied, offering me her cheek but lingering much longer than she did with Alessio.

Behind her back, Alessio gagged, then returned to his inventory check. It was only eight o'clock, so while the club was open for business, we didn't have a full crowd yet. I debated inviting Chiara back to the office so we could catch up, then thought better of it. Nothing good could come from me being alone with her.

"Can I get you a drink?" I offered, sticking to the language of the land since Chiara didn't speak a word of English.

"Sure. I'll have an Americano," she said to Alessio, knowing damn well he wasn't the bartender. He passed the order along, and I tried not to read into the fact that she'd requested a drink with the same name she'd used as my nickname as of late, since she seemingly found it hilarious that I spent so much time in America.

"Aren't you going to compliment my necklace?" she asked, leaning forward.

A small silver chain dangled between her impressive cleavage. I turned away quickly before the deluge of happy memories involving those breasts hit me.

Chiara was trouble. From her glossy brown hair to her ridiculous high heels, she was everything I needed to stay away from if I wanted to get back with Giada.

She was also the woman I hooked up with every time I was separated from Giada.

Right after Giada and I had broken up the first time, when we were still teenagers, I'd gotten involved with Chiara. Our relationship was mostly physical, but I supposed we were friends, too. It just never had amounted to love. Years later, when Giada left me for Adrian, Chiara was there to comfort me.

My parents loved Chiara. On the surface, she was everything I needed in a partner. She was wealthy, attractive, and obedient. She didn't ask questions, and as long as her needs were met, she wouldn't have any moral qualms about anything I did, in the unlikely event she actually noticed what I was up to.

I could envision a long-term relationship with Chiara, but the idea didn't excite me. Without a doubt, we'd bore of each other quickly. We didn't challenge each other and we wouldn't grow with each other like Giada and I could. Chiara wouldn't force me to question the world around me, and she certainly wouldn't encourage me to be better than my papà.

"You look sad," Chiara said, interrupting my thoughts.

I opened my mouth, then closed it. She was right, but I couldn't exactly tell her that. The second she learned Giada and I had separated, she'd pounce like a hungry jungle cat. Except, maybe that was the point. Maybe she'd already heard, and that's why she was here.

"What brings you into the club tonight?" I asked.

She cocked her head to the side and extended her finger, her long acrylic nail pressing into my chest. "You," she said.

"How'd you know I was in town?"

Chiara shrugged and tossed her hair over her shoulder. "I hear things," she said. Then she laughed and added, "Your mamma said you were lonely."

I cringed at the thought of my mother worrying about my sex life.

Chiara continued after a sip of her cocktail. "She's obviously right, though. It was never going to last with you and that American girl, but I'm sorry you're hurting."

I still didn't speak. From the moment she'd entered the club, I'd known what was on the table if I chose to partake. I just didn't know if I should. On the one hand, a night with Chiara would solve several of my problems. It would get my papà off my back and convince him I wasn't still so hung up on Giada. It would dispel some of the tension that was undercutting my ever move after nearly a month without a partner, and it would, at least for a night, distract me from my obsessive thoughts about Giada.

On the other hand, I didn't want to sleep with Chiara. I wanted Giada. And the two were so different in bed that there was no way I'd be able to pretend I was with Giada while actually with Chiara. Besides, I already had enough secrets from Giada. If I was going to find a way back to her eventually, which I was, I shouldn't screw myself over by hurting her.

"Luca?" Chiara's brows pinched together as she again tugged me out of my daydreams.

I exchanged a look with Alessio, then nodded.

"Why don't we grab a drink somewhere else?" I suggested. "Maybe in an hour? Give me a chance to finish some things here and then you and I can catch up."

Her lips curled up into a smile. She named an upscale bar a couple kilometers down the road, then quirked an eyebrow. "Unless you'd prefer my place?"

My abs clenched, and I forced a smile onto my face. "Let's start with the bar," I said. "See you soon."

I watched her saunter out of the bar—it was impossible not to, with the tight little dress she wore, then turned back to Alessio.

He raised his hands defensively. "You don't have to explain yourself to me."

"I'm not going to sleep with her," I said, switching back to English and keeping my voice quiet so only Alessio could hear me. "But it'll get my papà off my back if he thinks I am."

Alessio nodded in appreciation of my brilliance, but I still sensed his skepticism. I didn't blame him. I, too, questioned my willpower when it came to Chiara.

~

Giada

Aside from packing, the only other tasks I absolutely had to tackle before leaving for Rome were saying goodbye to Gabriella and visiting the church one final time to chat with Father Ryan. Luckily, my favorite chauffeur was willing to facilitate both of those outings, back to back. We arrived at the church a few minutes before the late afternoon mass, and I was surprised when Enzo parked the car instead of dropping me off at the door.

I must have given him a funny look, because he laughed.

"I thought I'd come with you today," he explained. "Is that okay?"

My surprise quickly gave way to joy. "Of course! That's great. I always enjoy company."

We walked towards the front entrance, where Father Ryan stood greeting parishioners upon arrival. When we'd almost reached the steps, my ankle twisted in my stupid high heel, and I stumbled backwards. Enzo, with his cat-like reflexes, caught me, then kept his hand against my lower back as though anticipating another fall. Having been touched before by Enzo in many platonic—and a few not-so-platonic—ways, I didn't think anything of it. Nor did I think twice about the odd expression on Father Ryan's face as we reached his post.

He extended his hand to Enzo, introducing himself and welcoming him. I was about to tell him he'd already met Enzo, since surely he must have. But Enzo was already smiling and shaking the priest's hand.

"Lorenzo Alfonsi," he said. "Nice to meet you." He returned his hand to the small of my back and nudged me into the sanctuary, dipping his head down to whisper while we walked. "Tell me you're not bringing those shoes to Italy."

We stepped into a row about a third of the way back and sat. "The shoes aren't the problem. My legs are. All those kickboxing classes are giving me calf muscles, and it's throwing off my balance."

Enzo gazed down at my legs then chuckled. "So, are you all done packing?"

I nodded, glancing around the church and waving politely at anyone I recognized.

"Think you'll see Luca any while you're there?"

My abs clenched at the mention of his name. "I doubt it. His place is in Palermo."

From the way Enzo watched me as I spoke, I got the impression he suspected I wasn't being altogether forthcoming.

"You're sure he won't be in Rome any?" he continued.

I chose my words wisely. I hated lying inside a church, period. And I hated lying to Enzo, but his loyalties lay with my father first of all. But there was no reason I should inform my family that Luca wasn't at his place in Palermo.

"I wouldn't know. We haven't exactly spoken since he dumped

me. But at the time, he told me he was returning to Sicily. Now can you stop bringing him up?"

Enzo offered a slight dip of his head, then turned forward right as mass began. When the service ended, he stood slowly and stretched.

"Are you going to talk with the priest now, or are we heading out right away?" he asked.

"I need to say goodbye to Father Ryan. Can you give me ten minutes?"

"Take your time."

I scurried off, but as expected, Father Ryan didn't return to his office until all the other parishioners had left. I knew the priest was hesitant to meet with me in private after Luca accused him of flirting, but I hoped he'd make an exception today. He paused by his office door and nodded to acknowledge me.

"I just have a couple minutes, and I wanted to ask you a question. If you're more comfortable talking in the confessional, we can," I offered.

He glanced into the hall outside his office. "Your, um, boyfriend doesn't want to join us?"

I must have looked as confused as I felt because Father Ryan pointed towards the sanctuary. "Mr. Alfonso, was it?"

"Alfonsi," I corrected, "And no. I mean, he's not my boyfriend."

"Oh."

"And he doesn't want to join us," I continued. "He's my driver. Luca and I…" I paused and stared pointedly at the door.

Father Ryan closed the door but kept a wide berth as he walked around me to the other side of his office.

"Luca and I are still together, but no one can know that. I'm headed to Italy through the holidays, and—"

"Are you in danger?"

I blew out a sigh, sick of people asking me that. "Luca will never hurt me. And I'm going to Italy with Matteo, so I'll be fine.

My family has an apartment in Rome, so I'll just do some shopping and exploring while Matteo works."

Father Ryan relaxed in his chair at this news, so I continued.

"Angelo is up to something. I don't know what, but it isn't good, and I'm worried he's dragging Father John into it."

"Your brother Angelo?"

"Yes. You've seen him coming to church more lately and talking with Father John. He's a loose cannon, and he can't be trusted. I just need you to watch him, maybe let me know if he does something suspicious."

"You want me to spy on your brother?"

"No, just keep an eye on him."

"Giada, your brother never comes to see me. He always speaks with Father John. And even if he did come to me, I would hold whatever he said in the same confidence I do with everything you tell me." Father Ryan stood and started towards the door.

I followed him with my eyes, noticing Enzo loitering in the hall outside the office. The priest smiled at him and opened the door before turning back to me.

"I hope you have a fantastic trip. Let us know if you need any help finding a church there," he continued.

I rolled my eyes then tried to send him a telepathic message once his gaze locked on me. When his expression didn't change, I resorted to actual words. "Just keep in touch with me, okay? Please? You don't have to pass along any information that violates your oath or whatever, but simply mentioning if he was here isn't confidential, right?"

Enzo laughed out loud. "Time to go, Giada." Then he turned to the priest. "Have a nice night."

"I can't believe you were asking him to spy on your brother," he muttered as we headed back to the car.

"Oh please, like you aren't curious what Angelo is up to," I said. "Speaking of which—"

"Not happening, Princess."

"Oh, come on. He's up to something. I know it."

Enzo chuckled and shook his head. "I'm relieved that Matteo is taking you out of the country. I think you'd get yourself—and me— into a lot of trouble if you stuck around longer."

"Oh, like you weren't hoping we'd catch Angelo there, up to some no good business with Father John," I said. I could've sworn Enzo's eye ticked, essentially confirming my statement, but I didn't want to push it, so I switched topics. "And speaking of trouble, can we stop at the liquor store on the way to Gabby's?"

"No."

"It's not for drinking. Well, I mean, not for me. I want to get Gabby some champagne for New Year's Eve, in case I'm not back by then."

He huffed loudly but agreed.

I cranked up the radio and treated the rest of the drive as one last hangout with my friend, who happened to also be my driver. If everything worked out with Luca as I hoped it would, it might be the last time I'd have a long drive alone with Lorenzo.

Luca

A few days later, Alessio and I were cruising down the Autostrada del Sole in the Maserati, headed south to pay a visit to some guy who failed to pay Papà on time. The sky was clear and bright, causing us all to forget the bitter chill that had begun to settle over the region now that winter had arrived. Still, I wasn't about to complain. Out of all the ways to spend my day, behind the wheel of my favorite car with my amico at my side wasn't the worst.

"Hey, you never told me how it went with Chiara," Alessio said, knocking down the volume on the music so he didn't have to shout. "Did you meet her for drinks?"

I wasn't sure if he was asking if I stood her up or if we just skipped the drinks and went straight to bed. Either way, the answer was the same. "Yep. We met up. We drank. We went home."

Alessio quirked an eyebrow. "Alone?"

I nodded. We'd talked, laughed, and flirted for over two hours, and then we went our separate ways.

"Wow. Your willpower is enviable."

I snorted.

"Seriously, man. I'm assuming she offered…"

I shrugged. Chiara never made any explicit offers, but it was clearly on the table. "I told her I'm not quite over Giada yet, said that I wanted to spend time with her as friends. She was fine with that."

Alessio cackled. "Yeah, because every other time you've said let's be friends, you end up in her bed a few days later."

He wasn't wrong, and Chiara probably assumed this time would be the same. But it wouldn't. "Listen, I made sure Iacopo and Lodovico know I went out with her, but if you could just casually comment on it in front of some of the other guys, I'd appreciate it."

"You'll have to see her again if you want your dad to believe you're over Giada," Alessio said, understanding my plan.

I nodded. "I will. As her friend."

I gazed at Alessio long enough to read the skepticism in his face before turning back to the road. We both fell quiet for a moment, which was unusual for Alessio.

"Everything okay with you?" I asked.

He blew out a sigh. "I have to tell you something, and I don't know how you'll react."

Based on his tone alone, I was certain I wouldn't react well. I took a deep breath, then waited for him to speak.

"Lorenzo called. He said Matteo is headed here for a few weeks, or maybe through the holidays."

"Here?" I glanced out the window as if that would remind me what town we were in at the moment.

"Rome." Alessio paused, exhaling hard. "And he's bringing Giada with him."

I would've sworn I stopped breathing for a minute. "Why?"

"I don't know. Lorenzo said Matteo felt bad for her, and you know he probably wants the company. And if she asked him, there's no way he could say no, especially when that would mean leaving her behind with Angelo."

"How did he know we were in Rome?"

"That's the thing. He doesn't. He thought we were still in Palermo. I said you might be in Rome sometimes for some business, and he promised to remind Giada to stay away. I think he was just calling as a favor, but he seemed to think she's not over you."

My lips twitched at that. Selfishly, I was relieved she wasn't over me. But the awareness that we'd soon be in the same city filled my bones with unease. My papà had been right. Without Giada, I'd been focused, efficient, and precise. My behavior was always controlled and calculated. I'd meant what I told her—I wanted to be with her, and this time, I was going to wait until I could.

It was obvious from our clipped, infrequent conversations that Giada didn't believe I was trying to change my papà's mind about our relationship. But I was. And despite having no real measure of progress, I didn't doubt my success. I was proving myself to my papà, and I was earning his trust. He spoke to me like one of his other respected captains, occasionally even asking my opinion on business matters. And each day he delegated more responsibilities than the one before. Less than a month from my arrival, he announced that he was headed to Palermo until the new year. He left me in charge of his nightclubs and other local business. He took his favorite guys with him, of course, but left

Tomasso, Lodovico, and Iacopo to help—or spy on—me. Still, it was progress.

The ringing of Alessio's phone snapped me out of my thoughts.

"It's your dad," Alessio mumbled, quickly accepting the call. "Pronto," was all he said into the receiver before he fell silent. After a lengthy pause, he spoke again. "Si. Certamente. Ciao."

I turned to Alessio as he disconnected the call and nearly laughed out loud at the prominent scowl on his face. "What did he say we should do?"

Alessio shook his head. "Doesn't fucking matter. I'm not doing it. So I might as well not even tell you."

I chuckled, mostly at the fact that literally all he'd said to my papà aside from the basic greetings was "yes" and "certainly." But then nausea washed over me. If a task was too grisly for Alessio's low standards, there was no way I'd be able to stomach it.

"Cazzo," I swore. "Does it have to do with children?"

"No. Worse."

I tried in vain to think of something worse than hurting a kid for the parent's fuckup.

Finally, Alessio spoke. "Your dad is one sick fucker. You know that, right?"

"Yep."

"He said the guy has a dog. We're supposed to kill the dog and shove a note in its mouth with our message."

"What's our message?"

"Jesus Luca, I don't know. Pay up or you're next? You're the scholarly one. You think of something. I'm not doing it. Any of it. I'll wait in the damn car."

"Not a chance." Even if I were up for the task, it wasn't safe for me to do it alone. Papà claimed the guy wouldn't be home now, but if he were wrong, or if someone else was there, I'd want backup. Besides, if he found out Alessio sent me in alone, that would be very bad for my friend.

I slowed as we exited the highway. Alessio shuddered and danced around like bugs were attacking him.

"This is bullshit. I thought we were just going to bust some things up or poke holes in his condoms and shit. I didn't sign up for cruelty to animals. What did that fucking dog ever do to your dad?"

I bit back a laugh. Yeah, it was messed up, but Alessio's reaction was amusing.

"I hope it's a chihuahua. I can't stand those little yappy things."

My laughter escaped. "Why would a gangster have a chihuahua? He needs a guard dog, not a lap dog."

Alessio waved his hand at me. "Just stop talking to me. I'm gonna be sick."

When we arrived at the address my papà had given us, we saw a nondescript brick building. Judging from the condition of the exterior of the apartments, the residents weren't exactly rolling in dough. We jogged the stairs to the correct unit. Then I pulled out my gun as Alessio knocked on the door.

No one answered, but more surprisingly, no one barked.

"Maybe he took his dog with him," I said.

Alessio looked hopeful as he pulled out a wire and began working it around the lock. I leaned back against the wall beside the door, looking casual while also scanning for any witnesses. It was late morning on a cold Wednesday though, so I wasn't surprised that we seemed to have privacy.

I turned as the lock clicked, and Alessio nudged the door open a few inches. I braced myself for an attack by a Doberman or Pitbull, possibly even a German Shepherd, but nothing came. We shut the door behind us, then looked around.

Alessio quickly spotted a notepad—decorated with Christmas trees, no less, and tossed it to me. "Write your damn note," he said.

I wasn't so sure about the legitimacy of a death threat written on decorative stationery, but I wanted to get back to the car fast.

So I did it. Just as I recapped the pen, we heard a high-pitched howl from the back of the apartment.

"Fuck," Alessio mumbled. He trekked back to the closed door, paused till the howling repeated, then swung open the door. A blur of curly golden fur pounced.

I flew back, but Alessio crouched down to meet the beast at its own height.

"Hi baby. Oh, you're a friendly one, aren't you? Yes, you are. Uh huh," he cooed.

I cringed as Alessio shook hands, or paws, with the dog.

"Yes, you are a sweet boy. Your human is a dickwad, but you don't need to worry about that," he continued. The dog licked all over his face, and then Alessio turned to me.

"Luca!" he scolded, bolting to his feet. "You're not shooting the dog!"

His panic confused me until I realized my gun was still poised in my hand. I sighed and wedged the weapon in the waistband of my jeans. "I wasn't going to shoot the dog unless it attacked."

Alessio scowled. "Do what you need to do. I'll watch the dog."

I suppressed an eye roll, walking around them to check the bedroom. Judging from the contents of the nightstand, the stupid dog was the guy's best—and possibly only—companion. I found a little cash in the back of the sock drawer, then checked my watch.

"We should go," I said. "What's your plan for the dog?"

Alessio gazed up as though he'd put zero thought into it.

Christ. "Why don't we take off its collar and let it go free? We'll tell my papà it escaped."

"He could get hit by a car, Luca," Alessio said, his brows furrowed. "We'll take him with us."

I snorted at that. "Over my dead body. A Maserati is no place for a dog."

"I'll hold him on my lap. It'll be fine."

I cringed at the thought. "He'll claw at everything. He'll scratch the leather. And what if he pees?"

"He's obviously housebroken," Alessio said with a dramatic eyeroll. He stood and rummaged around in his coat pocket. He pulled out a few yellow pills. "I'll give him these, and he'll sleep the whole drive."

I wasn't even going to question why my friend carried around enough drugs to knock out a dog. I hated the idea of the animal in my car, but I didn't see any other options. "Where are you going to keep a dog anyway? It isn't staying at my apartment."

Alessio grinned. "Mamma would love a pet."

I rolled my eyes and moved to the kitchen. "Fine, but you're taking my car to get detailed the second we get back," I mumbled. I began opening cabinets and knocked a bunch of stuff onto the floors, letting some of it shatter. I shook out a box of cereal all over the couch, then returned to check the freezer for cash. By the time I was done, Alessio had fed the dog the pills with a handful of food.

"Let's roll," he said.

We dropped the dog directly at Ms. Rizzo's house then called Papà to say we'd completed the task. We told him the dog escaped. He was disappointed, but seemingly comforted himself with the thought that it probably got hit by a car.

I had him on speaker phone, and Alessio flashed the finger at the phone when my papà said that.

That night, after Alessio returned my newly cleaned car, I drove to the club. I made a few calls and took care of a few other debts my papà had been asking about, then I arranged a new shipment back to the States and negotiated a lower rate with one of the club's suppliers. When I called my papà to update him, I could tell he was genuinely impressed. And even more than that, he was proud. He admitted it.

Well, not in those words exactly, but he said "ben fatto." *Well done.* The last—and only—time he'd ever said that before was over a year before, when he learned I'd won Giada over from Adrian, the first time. This time, I felt like I truly deserved the praise, but the mere memory of the previous compliment made me think of Giada again.

I was so close I could taste it. And truly, I could taste her, that wonderful mixture of tangy sweetness I'd been dreaming of for a month now. It was maddening, and I figured it was just a natural response to going for so long without sex.

But then, I saw her.

At first, I thought I was hallucinating. I hadn't slept more than a handful of hours the previous night. Though I was generally accustomed to the onslaught of noise, vibrations, and smells of the crowded club, that night, I was more sensitive to all of it. From my office in the back, I was relatively sheltered, but sometimes, that almost made it worse. To feel better, I had to embrace the chaos, fully immerse myself in it for a moment, rather than fight it. It was similar to the way that peering out a window in a moving vehicle reduced motion sickness.

I had a waitress bring me a club soda with lime, my preferred drink as of late, then I made my way up the back staircase of the club to a small private room overlooking it all. From there, I could see the flashing of the lights, hear the pulsing beat of the music, and see the slew of people clamoring over each other like a herd of wild animals.

It was nearly one o'clock in the morning, so the patrons were fully inebriated by that point, and in many ways, the movements of the masses reminded me of zombie apocalyptic scenes. Their faces blurred together as their bodies mashed into one another on the darkened dance floor.

From this vantage point, I could survey my entire kingdom. I didn't need to do so, since I wasn't in charge of the running of this club. That was Lodovico's job. But since we'd been using this club as the home base for some of our other business operations, I'd gotten in the habit of coming up there to think.

I tipped my glass, letting the ice clink against my teeth as the cool liquid spilled down the back of my throat, the fizz soothing my nerves and the sharp citrus scent perking me up ever so slightly. I stretched my neck, tilting my head to one side, then the other, and then rolled my shoulders. It had been a long day.

I was just deciding to head home when a flash of red caught my eye. I honed in on it just as the slick glass slipped out of my hands. It shattered against the concrete floor, sending ice cubes skidding in every direction, but no one heard the sound. I stepped closer, unable to stop my lips from curling upward as I saw her, even though her appearance was bad news.

The red flapper-style dress was too dressy for this club, but Giada wore it confidently, and rightly so. It looked like it was made for her. Perhaps it had been. Her back was to me, but it was her. I was certain. The way she shimmied her hips, the thick, lustrous dark hair swaying across her back—that was my Giada.

She was surrounded by men, but they didn't appear to be fawning over her, so I assumed they understood who she was. I'd have expected a heads up if multiple guys from another family were heading onto my turf, but if they weren't here for business…

A waitress came and offered to clean up the broken glass, and I dismissed her with a wave of my hand. A man leaned towards Giada, placing his hand possessively on her back, causing every muscle in my body to tighten painfully. If I'd still been holding my drink, I likely would've crushed the glass in my hand at the nauseating sight.

But then he turned, and it all made sense. The man was Matteo. Giada was here with her brother, and, judging from the way the guys around him moved, those were friends of his, not associates of his father or brother. Matteo looked bored, and I wondered how long they'd been here. I could easily see Giada passing hours dancing in the center of all the action, and part of me hoped she would. As exhausted as I felt, I could gladly stand here for hours and watch her from afar.

Still, the longer she stayed, the greater the risk of her seeing me, and that would not be good. Nor would it help matters if my papà learned of her presence in his club, even if it were simply coincidental.

She twirled in a circle, offering me a precious glimpse of her face. I couldn't make out the details, but she looked happy. That was good. Her brother leaned in to say something to her, though I doubted either of them could hear anything where they stood. A moment later, he walked away. I frowned at the thought of her alone in such a place, even for a brief moment, but she immediately tugged the hand of one of Matteo's friends. He was clearly more than willing to dance with her, but the reserved way he approached her comforted me. This man realized who she was and was smart enough to treat her appropriately.

Matteo had no real rank in his family, not being the firstborn and not having earned anything of the sort on his own accord. But as the son of the boss, and brother of the future boss, he was respected and known. Someday, he could progress up the ladder and reach a position of relative authority, but I doubted he would. Matteo, though smart and loyal, had none of the traits necessary to truly succeed in this world.

I watched Giada until her brother finally returned and ushered her off the dance floor. It was apparent she wasn't ready to leave, and as she glanced around the room, I could've sworn she spotted me at one point.

She froze, and I could almost make out the hint of a smile from across the room. But then she turned, and I decided I'd imagined it all.

CHAPTER 4

Back to the present...

Giada

*M*atteo was easy to ditch the following night. He didn't even question it when I showered then claimed I was headed to bed. Instead of sleeping, I styled my hair, applied my makeup, and chose the slinky top and skirt sure to bring out that sexy, awestruck look of Luca's when he saw me in it.

When Matteo left, I wasn't far behind. I was so excited at the prospect of seeing Luca again, up close this time, that I didn't even notice the nervousness flooding my system until I reached the line outside the door. I was tempted to skip the madness and tell the scary-looking guy manning the front entrance that I was there to see Luca, but I couldn't risk his father finding out. I was fairly confident the elder Marino was back in Palermo today, but I didn't want to bet my future with Luca on my intel.

After finally talking with Luca in person, I happily made my way back to the dance floor. Moments before, when I'd been there, I'd felt so alone, surrounded by a sea of people but without the one person I wanted. Now, knowing Luca was nearby and that I'd be alone with him soon, I was in heaven. Still, the sixty minutes dragged along.

As soon as I reached Luca's car, I felt complete. When he wasn't shifting gears, his hand tightly clutched mine. He didn't tell me where we were going, but instead of asking, I made a suggestion.

"You could just keep driving forever. We'll run away together."

"We'd need money."

"You could sell this," I said, eying the expensive leather interior of the Maserati.

"Hard to unload a hundred and thirty thousand dollar car without raising some eyebrows."

He pulled into an underground parking garage and killed the engine.

"Is this your place?"

"No, it belongs to a friend. I've used it as a safe house," he said. "I'm staying at the villa, and some of my papà's men are there too."

I was willing to accept anything, as long as it offered me a few hours alone with Luca.

He gripped my hand firmly, tugging me along at a brisk pace until we were inside the apartment. Luca switched on a lamp, poured himself a club soda, then offered me a sip. I accepted, not realizing how dry my mouth had become. I swished the liquid around my mouth before swallowing all but the ice cube, which I then sucked.

Luca smiled, eying my lips hungrily. He helped himself to another gulp, then set the glass on the counter. I hadn't even checked out our surroundings when he pounced, capturing my mouth like he feared I'd run away.

I dug my fingers into his hips, wishing the silky shirt wasn't between us. His hands skittered along the back of my skirt then up my back, leaving a trail of goosebumps in their wake. Luca's kiss grew more forceful, more demanding, and as much as I wanted to undress him, I couldn't concentrate on anything but the consuming power of his silky sweet tongue.

Luca pulled back after a moment, giving me space to maneuver his buttons through the miniature holes. He unzipped my skirt, his lips curving up as the garment dropped from my hips to the ground, revealing lacy black panties. Apparently frustrated with the speed at which my fingers worked at his shirt, Luca nudged my hands out of the way, shucking his own shirt a moment later.

His eyebrows dipped as he took in my top, a thin, slinky piece of fabric with crisscrossing straps across the back. The shirt contained a half liner to serve the function of a bra, but was otherwise, virtually nonexistent. Luca looped his finger under one of the thin straps holding the material together as though toying with ripping it. I eyed him mischievously, daring him to tear through it, baring my chest to him. I had nothing else to wear though, so I should've been relieved that he instead chose to slip the top up over my head.

"You will burn that scrap of fabric," he whispered, his tone serious.

I beamed with pride. I'd worn the shirt solely for attention and earned precisely that.

Luca tugged his belt free but left me to unfasten his pants. I did so eagerly, pausing to pet his hardened length through the stiff material. He groaned sharply, cupped my butt cheeks, and lifted me. I let my legs fall around him and kissed him hungrily.

By the time he set me on the back of the cool leather couch, my body was on fire, sensitive to every slight touch and desperately demanding more. His strong arm supported my back, preventing me from falling backwards as his lips dipped down to my breasts, tugging and sucking until I shrieked at the intensity. Luca's hand fell to my thigh, slowly tracing its way upward, searing a path along my skin until he reached the lace shielding me from the rest of his delicious onslaught.

His fingers stroked me through the material before sliding beneath it. "God you're wet," he moaned against my neck as his finger traced along my slick epicenter.

"Luca," I begged. I'd needed this for weeks, and I couldn't wait another minute. I yanked his pants down blindly, searching for his lips. Our mouths crashed together again, and as the hand disappeared from my back, I tightened my legs around his hips. I felt both of his hands near my groin, then a rush of air accompanied the sound of fabric ripping.

I barely registered the fact that he had literally ripped my panties before he thrust roughly into me. I was ready, beyond ready, really, but he stilled nonetheless while my body adjusted to the intrusion. I was made for him, I thought, but it had been several weeks, so the slight twinge of pain as I stretched to accommodate him wasn't entirely unexpected.

By the time he withdrew then pulled me onto him a second time, the pain was gone, replaced completely with a pleasure so intense that I could barely see, let alone think. I had no choice but to let him control the movement, my position on the back of the couch leaving nothing for me to brace myself against. But that was fine by me. Luca knew how I liked it, and he never failed to satisfy.

I felt the tension growing in my core, and I wished I could hold it at bay a little longer. But it was futile. As Luca thrust into me again, he hit that tightly coiled bundle of nerves, and I exploded around him, convulsing in wave after wave of exquisite pleasure. Luca shouted my name, slamming fiercely into me two more times before releasing warm spurts deep into me.

Luca didn't move for a moment, and I relished the sensation of his breath pounding against my neck. Then he gently lifted me, walked around the couch, and placed me on my back over a blanket that had been draped over one arm. He disappeared for a moment, but I was too dizzy from the post-orgasmic haze to protest. When Luca returned, he held a warm cloth which he dabbed gently across my thighs before scooting beneath me on the couch.

Neither of us spoke for several minutes. When Luca did break the silence, his words were unexpected.

"Tell me you're still on birth control," he said.

"Yes." I laughed. "Although, I'd tell you anything you wanted to hear right now."

He turned to me, panic filling his eyes.

"I am, promise."

He settled back. "Tell me you'll leave Rome in the morning."

Okay, maybe I'd misspoken.

"You have to leave Rome. My papà will be suspicious if he even finds out you're in town."

"I don't like being away from you," I said.

"But we're old pros at separation now."

"At least when you were dead, I could still see you sometimes."

Luca frowned. "I just don't know how to sneak around here. My papà has spies everywhere. He has Alessio staying at my apartment with Georgio, and I'm stuck at the house with Tomasso. Any missteps will be reported directly to my papà. And even if I don't get caught, it won't be good if he learns you're in town. Unless you're dating someone else, my papà will assume you're here for me."

I didn't say anything, but he just gave me an idea.

Luca

*A*s much as I wanted to relax with Giada, to fall asleep to the rhythm of her pulse only to wake and sink into her over and over again until we were both dizzy with satisfaction, I needed to focus. It wasn't just about my papà anymore. Now that Giada was here, physically present in my life again, it was time that I prove to him—and to myself—that I could seamlessly run the Marino empire without distraction.

Giada might have been my weakness, but she could be an asset. I just needed to figure out how. And fast. All of those years when our families pushed us to be together, there was a reason for that. There had always been talk of a merger, so to speak. Combining my family's hold over Sicily and Rome with the Conti's control of Connecticut, we wouldn't just be the largest family. We'd be the most powerful. And while my papà perhaps had shifted his sights to a full takeover rather than a merger, I could work with that. I just needed to remind him of the benefits and convince him I could still behave rationally with Giada in my life.

Her finger traced soft circles along the faint scar on my chest. It wasn't meant to arouse or tease me, but I felt every touch from Giada deep in my groin.

"You don't have to worry about me, you know?" she said. "I don't need you to always be my knight in shining armor."

I was smart enough to keep my mouth shut.

"Just because you saved my life once doesn't mean—"

"Twice," I interrupted.

She lifted her head and giggled, apparently amused that she could somehow forget the other time someone had shot at her. Her hair, still messy from our lovemaking, cascaded around her face. She was gorgeous, framed by the dark hood of her luscious locks, but I wanted to see more. My fingers swiped her hair to the side, and I gazed into her espresso eyes.

"Anyway, I'm not helpless," she continued, one corner of her lips quirking upward.

"No. You're tough. You're smart. And you're resourceful. I pity the man who underestimates you."

"Wow. I think that's the nicest thing you've ever said about me."

"Hmm, well, if you charm me again with that magical pussy, I might really sweep you off your feet."

She thwacked me gently, her eyes sparkling. "Now there's the Luca I know and love." Giada shifted slightly, but I roped my arms around her tighter, holding her to me. I may not be able to keep her the whole night, but I wasn't letting her go just yet.

My phone buzzed a minute later. I intended to ignore it, but it was my papà. "Che palle!" I swore under my breath.

Giada quirked an eyebrow as I shifted her off of me.

"It's my papà. I have to answer."

"I'll be quiet," she promised, sitting up enough so that the blanket fell away, flashing me an unobscured view of her beautiful nipples.

For the first time in my life, I was smiling as I answered my papà's call.

He skipped the preliminaries, immediately asking if I was okay.

"Of course. Why wouldn't I be?"

"Tomasso said you left early tonight."

My stomach clenched. I hadn't noticed Tomasso when I was leaving. Hopefully, he didn't see Giada. "I finished everything I needed to do at the club before I left. I'm just tending to some personal matters now."

Just then, Giada sneezed. The softest, most delicate squeak escaped her lips as she did, but of course, my papà heard. She mouthed an apology just as he chuckled.

"Are you with Chiara?" he asked. "I heard she came to see you at the club last week."

"I'm not answering that," I replied. "So do you need anything, or—"

"No, get back to your woman."

I tossed my phone to the coffee table, but when I gazed up at Giada, ready to rejoin her on the couch, it was obvious something was off. She looked tense and unsettled.

"Who is Chiara?" she asked.

I cringed, then dropped to my knees on the floor in front of Giada. Better rested, I probably could've thought of a response that wouldn't stress her out, but as it was, I went with the truth. "She's an old girlfriend."

Giada nodded, clearly having remembered that already. "Why would your dad think you were with her?"

"Because he doesn't know you're in town, and because I've done nothing but work since I arrived here, except for when I've met up with Chiara." I kept my eyes locked on hers so she'd believe me, but still, her eyes widened.

"You're dating her?"

"No. She came to the club one day and had a drink. We met up later that night for drinks, as friends. Nothing happened. Nothing ever will. I made sure my papà heard about it so he'd think I'd gotten over you." I squeezed Giada's thighs, offering a gentle massage. "I'd be fine if I never saw Chiara again, but I think she's a good decoy. My papà is less likely to suspect I'm sneaking around with you if he thinks I'm seeing her."

"So you want to keep dating her?"

"Not what I said. We aren't dating. I told her I wasn't over you, and she's fine with staying friends."

Giada snorted.

"Even if I just have her drop by the club once or twice, that'll help," I continued. "But I'm fine staying away from her, too." I dropped my lips to her thighs where my hands had been, tasting her salty-sweet flesh.

"Does she know we're still—" Giada began.

"No. I don't tell her anything about my personal life that I wouldn't tell my papà. I don't trust her the way I trust you."

Giada sighed. "Can we talk about it later? I feel like I'm keeping you from a very important mission," she said.

Our eyes met, and I understood exactly what she meant. I dipped my head back down where she wanted me and smiled at the soft moan that escaped her lips.

CHAPTER 5

Giada

*I*t didn't take me long to decide who I should use as my fake boyfriend. Since arriving in Italy, countless random guys had hit on me, but only one had been brave enough to flirt—Nicolo Cotroni. At the time, I thought he was just being nice, since he was friends with my brother. But as I replayed the conversation back in my mind, it was obvious he'd been trying to ask me out.

I brainstormed a variety of ways I could try to get Nico's phone number, then decided to start with the easiest. I called Enzo, and after a few minutes of pleasantries that likely had him wondering why I'd called, I outright asked if he had it.

"Why do you want his number?"

"He kind of asked me out the other day."

"He *what?*" Enzo's tone was incredulous. I wished I could've seen his expression. It would've been priceless.

"Yeah."

"Does he have a death wish?"

The slightest twinge of guilt hit me. Nico seemed like a nice guy, and not to be totally cocky, but being seen with me would probably help his prospects with other girls. I was fine with leading him on and using him to get time alone with Luca, but I didn't want him to be physically hurt by my games.

"Do you think my dad would hurt him if I went out with him?" Surely Matteo wouldn't.

Enzo didn't answer.

"Is there some rule against dating me?" I supposed I could just fake date a stranger if I had to. Surely the "rules" only applied to guys who worked for my father or brother.

"Not exactly," Enzo finally replied. "As long as he's respectful and takes care of you, I guess your father and brothers wouldn't hurt him even if they object to the relationship. But Luca is a different story. Just because he broke up with you doesn't mean he'll tolerate other men…in the business dating you."

"Luca is not a problem. Number?"

He sighed. "I'll ask around."

I thanked him and hung up. When Enzo called back with the number, I immediately dialed Nico. I was relieved when he didn't answer.

"Hi Nico, it's Giada. Um, Giada Conti. Anyway, Matteo has been busy lately, and I'm kind of bored, so if that offer still stands to show me around town, I'd love to take you up on it."

Twenty minutes later, I had myself a date scheduled for that very night.

Nicolo was a true gentleman, walking me around a few of the touristy spots in Centro Storico, a historical section of town, before buying me dinner at a café. He wasn't my type of man, honestly. He was too unsure of himself and almost too polite. But we made it all the way to the end of dinner without any too awkward pauses. He made no attempt to touch me during the first part of the date, and while that was more than fine since I had zero interest in him, it would've been a huge turn-off had it been a real date. I needed a man with some confidence, one willing to take a risk to make me his.

I'd mentioned my love of dancing several times during dinner, hinting that we should return to the club where we'd met. I couldn't tell if he realized Salvatore Marino owned that club or not, since he kept changing the subject. But then, when he outright asked about Luca, my entire body stiffened.

"So, um, you went out with Luca Marino for quite a while, huh? Weren't you guys engaged when he got shot?" Nico asked, picking at his food.

I tightened my abs but made no effort to conceal my discomfort. "Actually, we broke up shortly before that."

"Oh. He was kind of a legend around here."

I shrugged. Did Nico think sharing his man-crush on my ex would somehow win me over?

"When did you find out he wasn't really gone?" he continued, clearly oblivious.

I nudged my plate away as the waiter brought the check. "I'd rather not talk about him."

Nico nodded but looked more intrigued than before. An awkward silence ensued as he clearly couldn't think of anything but Luca to discuss.

After he paid the bill, I took the lead with our plans. "So, what do you say? Do you have some energy still for dancing?"

He grinned. "If that's what you want."

"It is. Club Argento is close."

In a flash, Nico's expression transformed to more of a grimace.

"If we want to dance, it's the best place in town." Despite its name, which translated to 'Silver,' Argento was the best club in the area. Ironically, it was even better than the Marino's other club, Oro, which meant 'Gold.'

Nicolo still looked skeptical.

"Matteo won't be there tonight if that's what you're worried about." I suspected that wasn't his primary concern, but he shrugged and stood.

"Alright then, let's go."

I spotted Luca's car when we parked, but saw no sign of him when we entered. We ordered drinks first, which was good since I was way too sober to dance with Nico. He'd been with us the last time we'd gone, but unlike several of my brother's other friends, Nico had made no attempt to dance with me that night. I chugged my drink, relieved that the club was too loud for more pointless banter. Nico took his time and sipped his own drink, so by the time he finished, I was beginning to feel the effects of the alcohol.

I led him to the dance floor, and by the second song, I was enjoying myself. In my mind, though, it wasn't Nico dancing with me, but rather Luca. Nico was too timid to grope me or even touch me at all, which was fine by me. After one more song, I nodded towards the edge of the dance floor.

I mouthed the word "bathroom" then motioned that I'd be right back. And then I squeezed through the crowd, disappearing in a surge of people. By the time I reached the private hallway, I was confident Nico couldn't see where I'd gone.

I didn't know the names of the guys outside Luca's office, but before I even addressed them, Luca's office door swung open, and he yanked me inside. I barely got a look at him before he launched into me.

"Seriously? Are you here with Nicolo Cotroni?"

I shrugged, demurely raising my gaze to meet his. His expression was intense, from his full, pursed lips to his hooded stare. "It was your idea for me to date someone else."

Luca's eyes widened. "He's your *date*?"

"He's a nice guy."

"He's not your type, Giada. Besides, he's an idiot."

"Maybe I actually like him. You don't know."

"Not happy unless you have two men, huh? That sounds about right."

Wow. That was so not where I had expected this conversation to go. Suddenly, I was regretting the whole dumb plan.

"So I'm either a tease or a slut? I can't win with you."

Luca snorted. "I don't know. Let's ask Adrian."

I slapped him, barely making contact before he grabbed my wrist.

"Admit you're only trying to make me jealous," Luca said, his lips dangerously close to mine.

I *was* using Nico, but not to make Luca jealous. He was my decoy so that I could be with Luca and not rouse suspicion. Still, I felt my mouth curving upwards into a smile. I had forgotten how fun it was to argue with Luca. He was ridiculously sexy when his temper flared. His skin flushed, and he licked his lips. Plus, seeing how bothered he was by the sight of me with Nico confirmed that he still wanted me all to himself.

"You're hot when you're jealous," I said. I brushed my hair off my shoulders and let my hand linger on my chest. He opened his mouth to spew out some angry retort but froze as my hand drifted lower, grazing the top of my breast.

"When I was getting ready for my date tonight, I was thinking about you. I wore the perfume you like, the earrings you like, the shoes you like…" My voice trailed off as I reached for the hem of my skirt, slipping my other hand beneath it. "But not the panties you like."

I could tell by the pronounced increase in Luca's breathing that he understood exactly what I meant, but he waited a full minute before acting on his desires.

"Fuck, Giada," he finally growled, roughly pulling me towards him and devouring my mouth with his. He kissed me like he owned me, and it was exquisite. It was everything I'd been dreaming about since our last encounter. His taste, his smell, even his heat—every aspect of his assault was perfect in every way.

Luca unzipped his pants but didn't bother pulling them down before yanking my skirt up, bunching it at my waist. He crouched before me, using his fingers to spread my damp folds before licking me once, then twice. I groaned loudly, the heat in my core building already. Luca rose suddenly, swiveled me towards the wall, and angled me downward.

I pressed my palm against the wall, bracing myself for what would come next, but Luca wrapped his arm around my chest, supporting me. He didn't hesitate, thrusting to the hilt all at once. I cried out at the suddenness, but really, I welcomed the abrupt intrusion. It stung for a moment, then all I felt was a delicious fullness as he started to move.

The music from the club poured in under the door, the bass throbbing through the walls, but I was oblivious to all other external sensations. I was breathless and shaking from the tightly coiled tension that was starting to unfurl deep in my belly.

Luca whispered my name, and that was all it took for me to combust, with wave after wave of heat rolling through my body. Luca's hands shifted to my hips, holding me in place while he thrust into me several more times before groaning loudly. His release filled me as he kissed the side of my neck, just behind my ear.

He held me tightly for a moment, which I appreciated since I wasn't sure my legs would support me yet. Then, Luca stood me upright and broke all contact between our bodies. I leaned into the wall, still dizzy and shaky. Luca handed me a few tissues before tucking himself back into his pants.

"Sorry," he mumbled as I tried to clean up then shift my skirt back into place. "I bet you're regretting omitting my favorite panties now."

I breathed a laugh. "I have no regrets right now."

Luca reached for my hand, tugging me so suddenly that I

practically stumbled into him. A bemused grin appeared on his face, then he simply stared at me for a moment. Then he dropped my hand and smoothed his palms over my hair, wiped his thumb under my lip, and handed me my clutch.

"You should get back to your date. He's going to wonder where you've been."

"Long bathroom line," I said, having already prepared my excuse. I retrieved my lipstick and compact from my clutch and quickly reapplied lipstick, checking the damage with the small mirror. I didn't look nearly as freshly fucked as I felt, which I supposed was a good thing.

"Well, until next time, Luca," I said, trying to seem casual.

I brushed past him towards the door, but he stopped me, pressing his hand against the door.

"I can't live without you, Giada," he said, his dark eyes locked on mine.

I squeezed my eyes shut, savoring every syllable of his statement. It was all I'd ever wanted to hear from him, yet more than I'd ever expected him to admit.

"Then don't," I said, nudging his hand to the side and returning to my date.

~

Luca

As much as I'd enjoyed my brief encounter with Giada, the rest of the night made me uneasy. I hated seeing her with Nicolo. The thought of him touching her, even innocently, and even after I'd so clearly marked my territory when we were alone, made my stomach churn. And just knowing the things he probably thought about her made me want to kill him. When Nicolo showered, Giada surely filled his fantasies. When Nicolo dressed for his next date with my girl, he had to be hoping this finally was the night where they'd get physical.

I gagged just thinking about it.

"What's wrong with you?" Lodovico asked, sauntering into the kitchen looking every bit the role of a nineteen fifties gangster.

"Nothing," I snapped. "Where is your shirt?" He wore dark trousers, a white, sleeveless ribbed undershirt, and suspenders. His shoes were already tied as if he were about to head out for the day.

"I don't want to spill coffee on it," he explained, scowling at me like it was obvious.

I sighed, then scrolled through my texts to see if I'd missed anything important. I finished the last bite of my croissant, then stood.

"Hey, your dad wanted you to ride along with Tomasso today."

"Why? He can handle himself. I've got my own shit to do."

Lodovico shrugged. "He likes things done in pairs."

Obviously, I already knew that about my papà. "Alessio will come with me. Tomasso can take you. Or Iacopo."

"Iacopo and I are busy, and the boss said it's you. So, guess what, kid. It's you."

I flipped him my middle finger, but he was right. As if on cue, Tomasso rounded the corner into the kitchen then.

"You ready?" he asked.

I shoved my phone into my pocket, wedged two guns in place, then followed him out to the car. Lately, Tomasso was always chatty when we were together. I supposed he was lonely or whatever, but it was weird. He didn't seem overly friendly with anyone else, just me. I'd always got the sense that he felt sorry for me, being raised by the world's biggest asshole, but maybe that wasn't it. After all, Tomasso was best friends with the asshole.

And because of that friendship, I shared as little as possible with him. I didn't need any information getting back to my papà.

We drove for about a half-hour, then stopped off to collect payments from a few different businesses. Nobody gave us any trouble, and they all seemed to be friends with Tomasso, so I wasn't sure why I had to tag along. We did some business at a bank next, then headed over to the main port. Lodovico and Iacopo were already there, overseeing some shipment that had just arrived. Tomasso left me with them while he went to "chat" with the government security guys doing random checks of shipping containers.

Papà's shipping business was a well-oiled machine. There was no one in Rome, Naples or Sicily who would insist on a true or accurate inspection of Salvatore Marino's crates. Most had been bought off, but those who couldn't be were replaced. I didn't dare ask how, but my papà relied on less savory methods of dealing with people who wouldn't bend to his will.

When Tomasso wrapped up his work, the four of us went out for a late lunch. I hoped my work with Tomasso was drawing to a close, but instead, he said my papà had one more task for us.

I followed him back to the car, and something about his uneasy posture or the way he held back the details reminded me of high school, when my papà would make him drive me back to school after his men beat the shit out of me for whatever dumb thing I'd said or done last. It wasn't like Tomasso to be so quiet.

"Where are we headed?" I asked.

"Just down the road a few minutes."

"Okay, why? What are we doing?"

He hesitated. "We need to pay someone a visit."

My abs clenched, and my throat tightened. In our world, paying someone a visit didn't involve friendly chitchat or shared baked goods. When we paid someone a visit, it was to teach them a lesson. Sometimes, the point was to scare them so they'd follow through with whatever we needed them to do. Other times, we'd visit to punish them for not completing a task.

"What did they do?"

"Guy from the docks. Can't keep his mouth shut. Told his girlfriend about a big shipment that was arriving, and she told her brother, who's a cop."

"So?" Obviously blabbing key details to a girlfriend was against every rule, but in Italy, the cop thing wasn't the big deal one might imagine. The cops here depended on my papà almost as much as he did them.

Tomasso shrugged. "Guy's new to the force, wants to play by the rules. It's a hassle we don't have time for."

"Okay, so what are we doing about it?"

"Your papà wants them both dead, but I figure we take out the rat, and the cop will get the message. He might even be more helpful then." Tomasso paused, rummaging around in the center console until he found a pack of gum. "But if not, we could get rid of him then."

No part of that plan sat well with me. I hadn't directly promised Giada I wouldn't personally kill anyone, but it felt implied when I'd told her I'd try to hold myself to higher moral standards. Giada aside, I still didn't like the idea of killing people who didn't keep their mouths shut.

As we pulled to a stop at the next corner, Tomasso was eying me.

"You okay with all of that?" he asked.

I turned to the window, buying myself an extra moment to think. There wasn't a doubt in my mind what would impress my papà most. He'd want me to stride in there, shove a gun in the rat's mouth, and shoot him seconds after telling him he should've kept quiet. Then again, my papà wasn't here. And if he was going to set up stupid traps for me like he used to, plying me to see how cruel he could force me to become, I was screwed anyway.

"No. I think it's a dumb plan. The guy blabbed to his girlfriend, right? To me, that says he's proud. He was bragging about this new 'in' he's got with our family, and that means he values the association. We can use that to our advantage. It doesn't make any sense to kill a guy who's already on our team but just hasn't figured out how to play the game. What we need to do is teach him the rules in a way he'll remember."

Tomasso quirked an eyebrow and appeared to consider the suggestion. Finally, he nodded. "Alright, you take the lead. But if he doesn't seem to value our little teachable moment, kill him. Okay?"

"Sure," I said, rolling my eyes towards the window as he parked in front of a small cottage-style house. The front lawn was well manicured and a row of potted plants decorated the porch. "Does he live with his mom?" I asked.

Tomasso chuckled. "Girlfriend. She shouldn't be home now, though."

"What's his name?"

"Mario."

We walked up the front path, and I knocked on the door. The dumbass actually answered, looking like he'd just woken from a nap. Tomasso stood behind the door, and the guy clearly didn't recognize me, so I introduced myself.

Once the last name slipped my lips, Mario's eyes widened. But before he could slam the door in my face, Tomasso kicked it wide open.

"I didn't say anything!" he shouted, stumbling backwards.

"So your brother-in-law is psychic?" I countered.

"We're not married. She's just my girlfriend."

"Not the point," I mumbled. I was about to say something else, Mario lunged for an end table drawer. Before he could grab whatever object he'd stashed there, I tugged my gun from my hip and cracked it over his head. He crumpled to the floor, instinctively shielding his hands over his head. I kicked him once for good measure, but not hard.

I turned to Tomasso, but he seemed content to let me take the lead.

"You should know better than to blab to your girlfriend, or anyone else," I said.

"I do. I'm sorry," the man replied.

He was crying, which really pissed me off. I was going easy on him—way easy. If it weren't for me, he'd be dead. Now, he probably wouldn't even have a headache after some aspirin. He should be kissing my fucking shoes and thanking me, not cowering in terror and bawling.

"My papà wanted you dead. He thought that would let your girlfriend and her brother know that we mean business."

"No, please no, don't—"

"I think you might still be of some use to us alive, though," I interrupted. "Can you do that? Follow the rules and be helpful?"

Mario began mumbling his stupid promises, and I gazed around to see Tomasso had wandered off through the house. I groaned internally. I had nothing left to say to this moron and wanted to just get out of his fucking house. I needed a shower and new shoes.

"So if I let you live, you'll get your shit together and be the best, most loyal man my papà has ever met, right? Because if I have to come back here again, it won't be to talk."

Tomasso flashed me a photograph of Mario and an attractive blonde. I nodded my approval to Tomasso but didn't have a clue what he was asking.

"Maybe we should pay your girlfriend a visit, too," Tomasso said. "Make sure she understands not to talk so much. This is her, right?"

Mario lifted his head to the picture and nodded. His eyes were bloodshot, and snot had begun to trickle out his nose, so when Tomasso pressed his foot onto Mario's upper back, holding him down to the ground, I didn't mind.

"No, you don't need to visit her. I'll make sure she understands. I swear," he mumbled.

Tomasso smiled, then held out a butcher knife. It was easily eight inches long, making me wonder how I hadn't noticed it in his hand when he showed me the photo.

"We need to make sure he remembers us," Tomasso said softly to me. "Your papà would expect it."

I took the knife, despite having no idea what I was supposed to use it for.

"Are you right-handed?" Tomasso barked.

Mario tried to lift his head to nod, but Tomasso shoved him back down and gestured for me to cut off Mario's fingers. Bile churned in the back of my throat, but I told myself I could do this. It would take two seconds, and then we'd be on our way. It was not a big deal.

I shifted the knife in my hands, wiping my damp palm on my jeans. I tried to picture something else, to pretend I was somewhere else or someone else. Tomasso gestured wildly at Mario's left hand, splayed on the ground for the taking. He motioned for me to hurry up.

I crouched down, poised the knife, then froze. I could already picture the blood spurting, could already hear his screams. I was already traumatized, and I hadn't even done it yet. *Fuck*, my papà was a monster.

I shifted the knife again, trying to focus on my internal pep talk, then Tomasso nudged me out of the way. He snatched the knife from my hands so abruptly it almost cut my palm, and before I could even blink, he'd brought the knife down on the man's hand.

Mario cried out louder than I'd imagined, and as soon as Tomasso released him with an annoyed kick, he rolled onto his side, clutching the remnants of his hand and writhing around.

"If you get to the docs fast enough and tell them you're a

clumsy cook, they might be able to reattach those," Tomasso said. "And if we have to come back, you'll lose more than your fingers."

He dropped the knife, made a show of tucking the photo into his pocket, then we left. I could still hear Mario's cries until I was safely ensconced in the car with the doors shut.

Tomasso climbed behind the wheel, wiped his hands on a rag, then stared straight ahead, grimacing. After a moment, he started the car and pulled away from the curb.

"Sorry," I mumbled.

"You can't hesitate like that," he snapped.

"I know. But I'm not used to carrying out someone else's business. I had no beef with that guy."

"That's not how this job works, kid." Tomasso sighed. "Tell your papà you were the one who did that. He won't believe it was me, anyway."

I appreciated him offering to give me credit, but it still confused me. "Why wouldn't he believe you did it?"

He turned to me. "Because I don't do things like that. I don't have the stomach for it. I'm never the muscle."

I paused, my next inquiry lingering on the tip of my tongue when he jumped ahead and answered my question before I posed it aloud.

"I did it so you wouldn't have to," he said.

He switched on the stereo, and neither of us said another word.

For once, I was grateful that I wouldn't see Giada that day. I couldn't handle being around her after doing something so atrocious. I didn't deserve the calm joy she brought to me, not after what I'd done.

CHAPTER 6

Adrian

After my last exam of the semester, I packed up my bags, then drove towards the city. I'd planned to fly out of JFK to get home for winter break, so it wasn't far out of my way to stop by Giada's hometown church. I'd looked online to confirm that Father Ryan Wilson still worked at the church since he was the priest she always talked about.

When I arrived at the church, its familiarity comforted me. I made my way to the office where a kind, middle-aged woman greeted me then motioned me towards Father Wilson's office. As he gazed up to me, I regretted coming. Why had I even thought this was a good idea? The man clearly didn't remember me, and he probably didn't know anything about Luca, either.

He smiled, but there was no recognition in his eyes as we shook hands.

"My name is Adrian Patras," I said. "We met a while back—"

"Ahh yes. You're Giada's friend, right?"

I nodded, then sat when he motioned for me to do so.

"What brings you in today?" he asked.

"I, well, I was just worried, honestly. And Giada always told me how much you helped with her anxiety, so I thought it would be worth monopolizing a few minutes of your time. If you're not too busy, that is."

"Of course."

I hesitated, having hoped for more of an obvious intro to what I wanted to ask about. I started rambling. I told him how I was headed home to Chicago and how my mom had cancer. Once I'd garnered his sympathy, I admitted that I was also worried about Giada.

The realization washed over him. "Ahh, so that's what brings you here today," he said. "I wondered why you didn't head to your local church."

"She's in Italy," I said. "And I'm worried she may be in danger."

The priest offered a false smile. "Well, her family is probably able to offer more insight about her wellbeing than I am, but I can tell you I spoke with her before she left. She asked a small favor, but she seemed fine."

That was news to me, but I went with it.

"Was she asking for help because of Luca?"

"Luca?" he repeated, visibly confused.

"He's her ex, but I'm sure they're involved again."

"Yes, I know who Luca is. We've met a couple times," he said, without hinting at whether he already knew Giada was back together with the monster.

I cringed. "Sorry. He's not a nice guy, is he?" I didn't pause long enough for him to reply. "He's dangerous for Giada. He almost got her killed, and the list of others he's hurt just keeps growing. Her family is trying to keep them apart for her safety, but…" I shook my head. "I just don't know what to do. She won't listen to me. She thinks I just want to get back together with her." I paused. "We used to date, but that's all in the past. I don't want to be involved with her or her family ever again."

"I see."

"But I also don't want her to get hurt."

Father Wilson remained quiet.

"Maybe if you could tell me what exactly she was worried Luca would do, I could figure out how to help her. Or at least how to convince her family she's at risk."

A frown crossed his face. "She wasn't worried about Luca. She shared some concerns about her brother, Angelo. I can't divulge exactly what she confided in me, but she assured me she was safe."

"Giada blames Angelo for a lot of things that are, in reality, Luca's doing," I explained.

I paused, watching the priest for any hint that he would give me more, but instead he simply gazed at the door.

"Well, you might be in luck. Angelo has been stopping by to meet with Father John on occasion, and I think he's here now."

My stomach dropped, and I tried in vain to think of an excuse to leave. But the more I thought about it, maybe this was perfect.

The priest led me to the lobby, and within a few moments, Angelo appeared as if summoned. He appeared shocked to see me. Father Wilson told him I'd dropped by to share some concerns about Giada and that he thought we should speak. Then, he left us alone.

I reiterated to Angelo that I wanted nothing to do with his sister but that I feared she was somehow involved with Luca again. He assured me that wasn't the case, but promised to look into it.

I suppressed a smile. That was exactly what I needed, someone on the inside spying on Luca and reporting back to me. Maybe I would find some dirt on Luca after all.

Giada

*F*or my second fake date with Nico, he invited me to a movie festival featuring films from the mid-twentieth century. I couldn't muster any fake enthusiasm for watching old black and white movies in a crowded theater, so we compromised with dinner at a local café instead.

I glanced down at the menu, immediately honing in on the caprese salad and bruschetta appetizer. But when the waiter came to the table, Nico ordered for both of us and omitted any appetizer. I silently cursed myself for nearly flunking my Italian classes, since it left me unable to call back the waiter and order for myself.

I took a deep breath, sipped my wine, and reminded myself I'd get to see Luca soon. The mere thought of that brought a smile to my lips.

"So who's handling everything at the church when you're here in Italy?" Nico asked, interrupting my daydream.

"Hmm?"

Nico made a face, then relaxed and laughed. "Oh, right. We probably shouldn't discuss business matters here."

I was already annoyed with him over the appetizer thing, so I was barely listening anyway, but something about his tone gave me pause. I glanced around and noted no one was within earshot and even if they were eavesdropping, it was unlikely they'd garner any top secret info from a moron like Nico.

"I'm sure it's fine to discuss here, actually."

"Well, I think it's great how it really is a family business for you guys," he said. "I can't talk to my brother about anything I do for work, so it must be nice how you guys can all just talk openly with each other."

"Not all of us," I said pointedly, annoyed that he was so willing to pretend my brothers and father didn't exclude me from everything even remotely related to the family business.

"Well, yeah," he said after a pause. "Although Angelo doesn't think your father will be too mad about being kept in the dark about it all."

I cocked my head to the side, unsure why Nico seemed to think my dad, and not me, was the excluded one. Suddenly, I realized Nico was telling me something important. I focused on his words, hoping he'd continue without any response from me since I didn't want him to know I had no clue what he was talking about. Luckily, he did.

"I mean, I know Angelo doesn't want your father to find out until it's all set up and going, but he's convinced that once Marco sees how successful it is that he'll be proud."

"And you don't agree?" I asked, desperate to prod him into continuing.

He shrugged. "Your father doesn't strike me as the forgiving type. And he was pretty clear that he didn't want anything to do with chiva."

"Hmm?"

"You know, heroin," he whispered.

"Oh, right. I'm not used to you guys calling it that," I said lamely.

He nodded casually, signaling I hadn't just blown my chance to find out more.

"My father generally thinks anything Angelo does is wonderful," I said.

"Yeah. That's what Angelo says too. He's got balls going against your old man, that's for sure." He sipped his wine and then frowned. "You don't think you'll get in trouble for helping him out, do you?"

I reached for my wine, buying time to think of a response. "I'm not helping much."

"Is that why Matteo brought you here, to get you away from it?"

I shrugged, having no idea what the right response might be for that question.

The waiter delivered our food before we could delve further into Angelo's mysterious treason, but I was too eager to learn more to eat much.

"So, what were you asking about the church earlier?" I said casually.

"Oh, I was just curious who was monitoring that end of things now that you're here."

"How much do you know about what I was doing there to start with?"

He grinned and leaned forward as though we were truly in cahoots. "Well, I for sure know you weren't just praying that long every day. No one goes to church that often."

"I don't know, the priests there are so nice," I said, still not certain which church he was talking about.

"Father John is the one helping Angelo, right?"

My stomach clenched. Suddenly the memory of my brother arguing with the priest flashed back to me with a new possible meaning. "I wouldn't say he's helping, but…" I said, forcing a bite of food into my mouth. I didn't know Father John as well as Father Ryan, but I couldn't believe he would willingly get involved in any of the crap my brother would think up.

"Angelo never said anything about you helping. We all just assumed you were in charge of monitoring the storage and repackaging, since you were always there when it was being done." He chewed a bite while talking. "That's pretty cool that he wanted to protect your image or whatever."

I gritted my teeth together, wishing I could drown Angelo in a vat of holy water. I'd always known he was a monster—but this? Involving the church in his crap? Unacceptable. "Angelo is a dick," I said, unable to even pretend to feel otherwise.

Nico chuckled. "You kind of got to be to get where he is, right?"

I kept Nico on the discussion as long as I could, slowly plucking details about my brother's illicit escapades from Nico's comments, hoping I could thread it all together later into some coherent understanding of it all. I wasn't sure exactly how I could use this information to benefit me yet, but I was confident this material was gold.

After dinner, I faked a headache so Nico would drop me off at the apartment. By some miracle, Matteo wasn't home. I reached for my phone to call Alessio, certain Luca needed to hear this information. But then I paused. Luca wasn't the reason we'd been together twice so far—I was. His efforts hadn't made any progress as far as I could tell. So why would I pass on my precious intel to him rather than take the opportunity to show him once and for all that I was a capable partner?

I confirmed that it was mid-day back home, then called Father Ryan. Not wanting to risk talking with anyone else, I dialed his personal cell phone as opposed to the church switchboard. To my surprise, he answered.

"I hope I'm not catching you at a bad time, Father. It's Giada Conti," I began.

"Is everything okay?"

"Yes, Matteo and I are fine. I just, well, I learned some disturbing news. Are you alone at the moment?"

He hesitated before confirming that he was. I pictured him in his office, probably with a mug of chai tea.

"One of Angelo's business associates told me that Angelo's gotten himself involved in the drug trade. Heroin, to be specific."

"Your brother is using heroin?" The priest's shock was audible.

"No," I began, then I realized I didn't know that for sure. "Well, I don't think so. But he is selling it. Or making it, or something. And I have reason to believe he's storing it at the church. I think he's involving Father John."

"Giada, I don't—"

I cut him off before he could reiterate his unwillingness to spy on his coworker. "I'm not asking you to go to the police or anything you're not comfortable with. I just thought you should be aware, so you could stay safe."

There was a long pause, almost as if he was debating telling me something.

But then, he basically changed the subject. "I appreciate the concern, Giada. I'll keep my eyes open for anything out of the ordinary. Have you found a church home in Rome?"

I had, actually, but I'd only gone the weeks that Matteo was free to accompany me. Not speaking the language, I wasn't entirely comfortable attending alone. I didn't mind not understanding the mass itself, since I still absorbed the spirit of the service and could simply say the prayers in English in my head, but I was nervous about other interactions with the clergy. To my surprise, none of the priests seemed to speak English. I guess that meant I was off the hook for confession at least.

I talked to Father Ryan for a few more minutes about the churches, then we hung up. While I still felt chatty, I called Gabriella to catch up, and by the time we hung up, I was tired and just went to bed.

~

Luca

My next two weeks were a mixture of work and Giada. I threw myself into the family business, doing everything my papà wanted and then some. He was still in Palermo, so I was supervising his clubs and checking in on his shipments at Civitavecchia. None of it was particularly challenging, and I found myself with more free time than I was accustomed to. No one asked me to maim anyone else, nor did I do any more ride-alongs with Tomasso. I also didn't see any more of Chiara.

Meanwhile, Giada was still "dating" Nicolo Cotroni. Their

dates were always in public places where any spies from either of our families could see them, but I suspected she couldn't keep the ruse up much longer. Giada claimed Nico wasn't pressuring her for more, that he bought her story about wanting to take it slow because she'd been hurt in the past. But I couldn't imagine him lasting too long without ever tasting what she had to offer.

Luckily, she used the holiday as an excuse to avoid him for a couple weeks. She attended Christmas eve mass with Matteo, then faked a stomachache and insisted on heading home while he went out to dinner with the rest of their friends and extended family in Rome. Holidays had never been a big deal at my house growing up, but for Giada, they were. So for her to blow off her brother and spend the entirety of the holiday with me was huge.

Alessio was celebrating the holiday with his mom, so Giada and I had my apartment to ourselves. It was probably the only time of year when my dad's men were all so preoccupied with their own families that I could steal a whole day with Giada, without anyone noticing.

We'd exchanged gifts before bed on the twenty fourth, and when we woke the next morning, I made her breakfast. We spent the majority of the day in bed, doing very non-Christmassy activities. I had worried Giada would miss the decorations, the traditions, her family, and the loud, overcrowded, overblown affair that the holidays often became at her house. But she'd simply clutched my cheeks in her hands and kissed me.

"You are all I need today. There's no one I'd rather be with on Christmas," she said.

"Maybe next year we'll spend it with your family," I suggested.

"You and me both?"

I nodded, and she beamed wider than when she'd opened the gifts I'd bought for her.

"I would love that," she squealed.

Giada had told her brother she was spending the day with a girlfriend just outside the city, and being the gullible chump that he was, Matteo didn't question her plans. That left us with a second, consecutive night together.

It truly was a Christmas miracle.

The next morning, Giada clutched the mug of coffee in her hands like it was the holy grail, wandering around the room with a dazed look in her eyes. "I don't understand. This is your apartment. So, why haven't you been staying here?"

"Alessio has been living here. He's just at his mom's for the holiday."

She turned to face me, her eyebrows still tightly wrinkled. "There's two bedrooms. You wouldn't have had to kick him out."

"My papà wanted me to stay at home with him. And until he left for Palermo, he had one of his other guys staying in the spare room anyway. Hopefully, I can move back in here now that Papà is returning, though." My papà should be back in Rome the next day. I planned to tell him I was moving back into my old apartment, then I'd give him a few days to observe my success at running his businesses. Once I'd exceeded his expectations, I'd tell him I wanted to rekindle things with Giada.

Giada sunk onto the couch beside me, and I sighed. Even though we'd spent nearly forty hours alone together in my apartment, I still wanted more of her. We only had another hour or so before she needed to leave, and we couldn't waste it discussing my living situation. I kissed her gently, waiting until I felt her relax to start prying the mug out of her hands.

Without breaking the kiss, I placed her drink on the table, then shifted my body over hers. Right as I began to slip my fingers under the hem of the shirt she wore, Giada abruptly shoved me off her.

"This isn't working," she said.

I bit back the first comment that came to mind and opted for humor instead. "It worked pretty well on you last night. Twice, if I'm not mistaken."

Giada shot me a look that killed any hopes I had of seeing further action of that kind.

"I need more than sex," she said.

"Okay." I snuck a sip of her coffee, certain I'd need more caffeine for this discussion. But as the sickly sweet, creamy concoction hit my tongue, I decided it was worth a walk to the kitchen to get my own black coffee.

"At least when you were dead, we could talk."

"We're talking now," I pointed out.

"You know what I mean, Luca." She stomped into the bedroom and began dressing.

"We just spent two nights together," I reminded her. "You said you were happy."

"I was. But now I realize that was stupid. I don't want to be thrilled over two nights with you. I want every night." She paused and stared at me. "I want a real relationship."

I opened my mouth to speak, but she cut me off.

"Meeting for sex whenever you can sneak away does not count as a relationship," she continued. "I miss having you there to talk to any time I want. I miss touching you on a daily basis in a non-sexual way. I need human contact and affection. I need someone who can comfort me when I'm having a shitty day."

"I thought that's what Nico was for," I said.

"Fuck you, Luca!"

Shit. Perhaps I'd misjudged how pissed she was. "Giada, come on. I was kidding. I want all that too, and I want it with you. And I told you I'm working on it. I need to find a way to convince my papà you and I can be together without it ruining his business or skewing my judgment. I'm going to talk with him soon. You just have to trust me."

"Maybe that's the problem. I'm not sure I do trust you."

"Ouch." Maybe she did need someone like Nico. I left her alone in the bedroom to finish dressing. I took my coffee to the far corner of the kitchen, peering out the window. I did miss this apartment, especially this view, where I could watch the city waking up and feel like a king presiding over it all.

I startled when I felt a hand on my back.

"I didn't mean that. I know how much you value trust, and it's not like I think you're cheating on me. I'm just not sure I believe you're trying as hard as you could to fix things with your father. I'm worried maybe you're okay with this arrangement."

"I'm doing what I said I would do. It takes time."

"Are you sure you want to fix this?" she asked. Her voice remained strong, but the tears brimming in her eyes told me she was struggling. "You keep saying I'd be better off with someone else. Maybe the real problem is that you don't see any future where you and I are a real, normal couple."

"I don't."

Her shoulders drooped. Before she could launch into sobs, I gripped her biceps and pulled her close.

"Not being able to envision it doesn't mean I don't want it," I said.

"Luca, there is always going to be some obstacle for us. Wanting to be with me means wanting me more than you want anything else."

"I do."

"More than you want your father's approval? More than you want money and power and security, or whatever it is you think this life promises you?"

"It doesn't work like that, Giada. You know that. I can't just quit my job and find a new one. And don't feed me that line about us just running away together. That isn't the life you want, and you'd get bored of me in days with nothing else to distract you."

"Maybe let me worry about myself."

"If you want me to do that, then you have to let me do what I said I'm doing." I paused and waited until her eyes met mine. "I will fix things with my papà, and we can be a real couple again, just how you want. But I need a little longer."

"I think we've tried your way for long enough."

I turned to face her, concerned by her new, confident tone.

"What's that mean?"

She shrugged defiantly. "It means I'm sick of waiting for you to figure out how we can live like a normal couple. It's time for me to try it my way."

I considered what she was saying and tried to think of what all "her way" might encompass. "Giada, your dad won't have any pull in this. My papà hasn't felt loyal to him since I took the bullets for you, and your dad's not so keen on my family since we let him believe I was dead."

"It's not *my* father I plan to chat with," she said.

My hand shot out and clutched her wrist before I registered the thought. "Giada, no. You will not go anywhere near my papà. He is a dangerous man, and he is not your biggest fan right now."

She cranked her arm free. "I'm not a dog. You can't just bark orders at me and expect me to obey."

"I'm not…" I squeezed my hands into fists so tight that I felt my nails piercing into my palms. Never before had I met a woman as infuriating as Giada Conti, and yet I was well aware that the more I tried to control her, the less she'd comply.

She hoisted her purse onto her shoulder and kissed me on the cheek.

Shit. "Giada, I'm serious. You can't do anything. This is not the way to get what you want."

"You know what? I have absolutely nothing to lose right now, so I think it's worth a shot."

She reached for the door, but I leaned into it, pressing my hand into it right as she opened it, causing it to slam shut. She turned and glared, so I widened my stance, placing my other hand on the other side of her head and pinning her to the door with my thighs.

"Is that your plan? You'll just trap me here forever?" she taunted. "That's not so bad. I'm not sure I care if your father finds out about us."

I wanted to scream and shake her nearly as much as I wanted to kiss her right now. Gah!

"Tick tock, Luca. Don't you need to cover a meeting for Daddy soon?"

A chuckle escaped my lips, surprising us both. "You know why my papà said you weren't right for me? Because you don't listen. He said, that at the end of the day, the most important thing I need is a woman who doesn't ask questions and just does what I tell her to."

"Well, that will never be me. Not again, anyway," she said.

I raised an eyebrow, trying to decide if it ever truly had been her. "Don't I know it," I finally said, pressing the length of my body against her and kissing her like it was our last chance.

For all I knew, maybe it was.

CHAPTER 7

Giada

Uncertainty hit me the moment I was apart from Luca. I'd somehow spent the entire holiday with him without deciding whether or not to tell him what I'd learned from Nico. In a way, by not telling him, I had made my decision. But now, I was left with regret. If I took the information directly to his father, and it backfired, well, I could forfeit everything. Telling Luca I had nothing to lose was a bald-faced lie. I'd take any amount of him that I could get, and losing those small encounters now would kill me.

Certain I'd overthink it the longer I waited, I grabbed a ride to Oro the moment it opened. The club hadn't yet begun to fill up, and since I'd dressed to accentuate my assets, the bouncer motioned me to the head of the line. Once inside, I ordered a vodka with cranberry while I gathered my bearings.

I finished my drink, ordered a shot for liquid courage, then asked for directions to the bathroom. I started in the direction the bartender had pointed and quickly veered to the right, towards the offices. The hallway was long, and poorly lit, with several doors lining the side. I couldn't recall which rooms I'd been in before, when I'd come here to see Luca, but I assumed my destination today was the doorway at the end of the hall, currently blocked by two stereotypical goons.

My pulse skyrocketed as I approached the door. The two bored-looking guys turned to me, seemingly amused with my presence. The taller one made an obvious move of checking me out, his eyes lingering on my breasts much longer than appropriate.

The other one shook his head, gestured to the hallway, and quickly told me it was a private area, "Questo è privato."

"Ho bisogno di parlare con Salvatore Marino." *I need to speak with Salvatore Marino*, I said, my accent sounding even worse out loud than when I'd practiced in the shower earlier.

The guys glanced at each other then burst out laughing.

"No," the pervy one said. "There's no one here by that name."

"He owns the club, and if he weren't here at the moment, you guys wouldn't be stationed outside his office."

"Look, honey, you seem like a nice girl, and I'm not sure who put you up to this, but you should walk away. This isn't a game."

The other guy said something in Italian, and they discussed and laughed amongst themselves for a moment before turning back to me.

"If you stick around, I promise to show you a good time in a couple hours, but you can't wait here," the pervy one offered. Then they both laughed.

I sighed. "Tell Mr. Marino that Giada Conti is here to see him," I said, my voice finally sounding assertive.

Thankfully, my surname meant something to them. They curtailed their laughter, exchanged more serious glances, then discussed quietly for a moment. Finally, the non-creepy one started down the hall, hopefully to pass along my message.

His friend returned his gaze to my breasts. "The offer still stands about later…"

"Not a chance," I snapped.

Luckily we were only alone a moment before his friend returned to walk me down to the office. At the doorway, the man suddenly reached out to grope me. He moved his hands quickly, so I figured it was a lame attempt at a pat-down, probably a routine before anyone speaks with the boss. But when he lingered on my lower back and then reached for my ass, I slapped his hand away. Hard.

The door opened right then, and my first glimpse of Luca's father in over a year was of him chuckling to see me hit his worker. *Great.* The guy released me quickly, although, between my short, skin-tight skirt and low-cut, sleeveless top, it wasn't like I had any plausible hiding places for weapons anyway.

I stepped inside the office, not surprised to see that another burly man stood across from Salvatore. He was a well-guarded man, after all.

Mr. Marino smiled warmly. "Buonasera, Giada. How are you?" He stood and politely kissed each of my cheeks. "How's your father?"

"Fine," I said.

"I heard you traveled to Italy with your brother. I thought you were staying in Sicily."

I shrugged. "He had some business in Rome, so I tagged along."

He nodded skeptically, then motioned for me to sit. "What brings you to my club?"

"I wanted to see you. I had a matter I'd like to discuss with you, in private," I said, glancing at the bodyguard off to the side.

Salvatore chuckled then said something to the other man in Italian. A moment later, we were alone.

"So, what can I do for you?" he asked.

"I have some information I thought you'd like."

"Okay." He didn't look the slightest bit intrigued yet, and I began to panic that my information wouldn't be helpful enough to him to guarantee me what I wanted.

"Is this from your father?"

"No. Although he might find it interesting as well." I paused and took a breath, wiping my sweaty palms on my too-short skirt. "I've been seeing Nicolo Cotroni for a couple weeks now. I've overheard some things."

Salvatore leaned forward.

I shook my head. "I'm not just telling you to be nice. I want something in exchange for my information."

Now he laughed. "Mia cara, Giada, that isn't how I operate. People give me information not because they get something good in return but because they want to avoid something bad if they don't talk."

"Well, I'm not those people. I'm Giada Conti, and I'm not afraid of you."

Salvatore smiled again, and for the briefest of moments, I saw a hint of Luca in him.

"I assume this pertains to Luca?"

I nodded.

"What do you want my son to do?"

"Whatever he wants."

His eyebrow shot up, and he leaned back in his seat. He reached into his desk drawer and retrieved a cigarette. "Luca sent you?"

"God no. He'd kill me for coming here to talk to you," I said, cringing at my casual use of a term that probably had very literal meaning for Salvatore most of the time. "He doesn't know I'm here, and if you don't agree to my deal, I guess he never will, unless you tell him."

"My son works for me, you see. So it's impossible for him to do whatever he wants. He's still learning the business..."

"I want your blessing for us to date again." I clarified.

"But you just said you're seeing Mr. Controni."

"That was merely for convenience, and it's done now. Luca is the only one I want to be with."

He nodded slowly. "And you think my son would want this as well?"

I didn't answer. I was pretty sure he knew how Luca felt about me, but if not, and if my plan failed, I didn't want to get Luca in even more trouble.

"My son is very important to me. You're not only a distraction to him, but you tend to jeopardize his safety. How do I know your information is worth risking my son?"

"Decide after you hear it. I trust you to be fair." That wasn't completely true, but I had no other choice.

He tipped his head once, prompting me to begin.

"My brother has been diverting shipments of heroin to the docks without telling my father. He's transporting it to the church and repackaging it to sell domestically."

Mr. Marino's eyes widened, telling me my information was not what he expected.

"Angelo?" he asked after a minute.

"Of course Angelo." The thought of Matteo masterminding something that devious or illicit was laughable.

"And your father doesn't know this?

"As far as I can tell, he's clueless."

"He would've appreciated you going to him with this rather than me."

"That's what makes this information so valuable to you," I pointed out. "Besides, my father doesn't have anything I want." I assumed Mr. Marino would rat out my brother to my father, thereby garnering himself some extra points with my father and shutting down Angelo's operation before it became competition for him."

Mr. Marino tapped his fingers on the desk pensively.

"Obviously, I'd appreciate you keeping my name and Nicolo Controni out of this. I'd rather not get on my brother's bad side."

Now the man chuckled. "My son has told me you're already on that side. And as for Nicolo, he's an imbecile."

I didn't disagree, but I still didn't want him hurt. "He's harmless. And I may have led him to believe I already knew everything he told me, so he never meant to betray Angelo's trust."

Salvatore asked me a few more details about the whole operation but didn't jot down a thing. Crime bosses apparently all had impeccable memories.

Finally, he seemed to be satisfied that he knew all pertinent information.

Salvatore stood slowly and walked around his desk. "It has been a pleasure, as always, Giada. Please give your father my best regards." He kissed my cheeks again, then opened his office door.

"About my son—"

"Have him call me after you verify my information and talk with him," I said, praying he deemed my information worthy of my request.

Fortunately, he nodded in response. Then, his expression changed. "You should know he's seeing someone else now."

I wondered if he was only telling me that so I'd assume it was Luca's choice to blow me off if Sal never gave him the message. Regardless, it didn't change my reply. "I'm not worried about Chiara," I said.

Salvatore's eyes widened, and I beamed with pride at having impressed the man with my knowledge.

Then, he motioned to the less creepy of his two hall guards. "Giorgio will drive you wherever you are staying."

"I can get myself home, thanks," I said.

"Nonsense. You're a pretty young lady in a foreign country. Your safety is important."

He whispered something to Giorgio then patted his back and turned.

Shit, shit, shit.

I tried to think if there was anything in Salvatore's words that had hinted that he might be about to kill me. I considered making a run for it out of the club, like a fool. But what if I made a scene that jeopardized everything I'd requested in return?

I reassured myself. He couldn't hurt me. I was Giada Conti.

~

Adrian

*B*ack home, it was easy to relax. I visited an indoor golf place with my family, then passed the next day spending the cash and gift cards I'd received for Christmas. That night, I met up with some old high school buddies at a bar. My sister Annie joined us for a while, but when an old crush from high school, Claudia, showed up, Annie mysteriously developed a debilitating headache and left to head home.

Claudia and I stayed at the bar for another round, talking and laughing as we reminisced. She'd followed her dream of becoming a journalist, which surprised me, and she was equally stunned that I still intended to become a lawyer. I also learned she'd had a crush on me the same year I'd liked her, but neither of us had the balls to act on it then. Luckily for both parties involved, my confidence had skyrocketed since high school, and she had, if anything, gotten even hotter.

When she suggested we head back to her place, I didn't hesitate.

The next morning, I planned to sneak out before she woke, but I couldn't find one of my shoes.

Claudia groggily rubbed at her eye and pointed across the room where my shoe was mostly covered by her lace bra. I thanked her, then hesitated.

"You're welcome to stick around for coffee," she offered.

I focused on my shoe.

"I'm not trying to make this awkward. I don't want a relationship, especially with someone who lives out east, but as long as you're in town for the rest of winter break..." her sultry voice trailed off, and I slowly gazed up to her. She had tugged the sheets up over her breasts but let them drop as our eyes met.

I licked my lips, suddenly parched. "I could stay for a cup of coffee," I agreed, kicking off my shoes and returning to bed.

An hour later, still without coffee in my system, I was on my way back home. When my phone rang. I expected it to be Annie, or maybe one of my old friends, but instead, it was Matteo.

That couldn't be good.

"Matteo?" I said, answering as fast as I could.

"Hi. How are you?" he asked.

I groaned silently but moved through the preliminaries with him. Finally, he got to the point.

"I just wanted to let you know that something weird is going on with Giada. Well, with her and Angelo. They've had fights before, but this is different...somehow. Has she said anything to you?"

"About Angelo or Luca?"

He cleared his throat awkwardly. "Well, now that you mention it, Luca is in Rome now, and I'm pretty sure Giada thinks she and Luca are getting back together. Angelo might be mad about that."

I sighed. "I don't know anything about it. I haven't spoken to your sister since she left the country. But I agree with Angelo. Luca is bad news."

We spoke for a few more minutes, and then my phone pinged with a text from Claudia. It was a picture of the two of us from high school, standing side by side at a football game and smiling. We would've made a great couple back then. I wondered why we never gave it a shot.

"Adrian?" Matteo's prompt interrupted my thoughts.

"Sorry," I mumbled. But then, the text gave me an idea. If I had old flames, or old would-be flames, surely Luca did too. And just like I was back home, so was he. Maybe Luca would run into an old friend just like I did. And if not, at least I could plant that seed of doubt in Giada's mind.

"Hey Matteo, do you know of any of Luca's old girlfriends back in Italy?" I began.

The question clearly caught him off guard, so I continued.

"Some things Angelo said earlier made me wonder if maybe Luca was just using Giada to get between him and your dad. And I got the feeling that he was still involved with an old girlfriend in Italy," I added. "But like I said, I'm back in the U.S. I don't know details. I'm sure it's nothing."

Matteo's unconvincing tone as he wished me a belated happy Christmas brought a smile to my freezing face.

~

Giada

*M*atteo wasn't home when I returned from Oro, and for that I was grateful. My nerves overpowered me, and I barely made it into the apartment before vomiting. I didn't know how Luca handled this level of stress every day. I was giddy from the success of my meeting with Salvatore, and truly appreciative of the fact that I was still alive, but still, I couldn't stop shaking.

I stepped into the bathroom, certain a shower would relax me as much as anything. I slipped my shirt over my head, but as soon as I went to lower my skirt, a small plastic baggie filled with white powder plopped onto the ground. I frowned, reaching down to inspect it. Obviously, it wasn't mine, and I was equally certain it wasn't cornstarch. I honestly didn't know exactly what it was, but the longer I stared at it, the dizzier I became.

Certain I was about to die, I pulled out my phone and texted Luca. "I love you and I'm so sorry. I think I fucked up," I wrote, barely clicking "send" before the room began to swirl and everything went black.

CHAPTER 8

Luca

Everything about Giada's ominous message unsettled me. I was in the middle of negotiating a new fee agreement with a local business that enjoyed our protection services when I saw the text. I'd been playing hardball, and it was working. But the moment I saw the text, my mind went blank.

"Quaranta," he repeated, his expression indicating that forty was his final offer.

I'd planned to insist on fifty but I didn't have time now. Forty-five would suffice. "Quarantacinque," I countered. I hoped the look I gave him made it clear that I was not negotiating further.

After a pause, he relented. We shook hands, and I sped to the door, already lifting my phone to my ear. Of course, Giada didn't answer. That would've been too fucking easy. And I was nowhere near her apartment now. I dialed Matteo.

"Are you with Giada?" I barked the second he answered.

"Who is this?" he asked, sounding completely discombobulated.

"It's Luca, and your sister just left me a cryptic text message. I need you to check on her and confirm she's okay."

"I'm not home yet."

Fuck.

"I'll be there in five minutes."

"Fine. Text me if she's okay. If not, call."

"Do you want me to have her call you?"

"No. We aren't together anymore."

"Okay, but—"

"Hurry!" I ordered, disconnecting the call.

Alessio eyed me warily, but before I could explain anything, my phone rang. I panicked, thinking it was Matteo calling with bad news about Giada, but it was my papà. I cursed several times before answering.

"I had an interesting visitor earlier this evening," he began.

"I'm actually in the middle of something," I began. "I can come by Oro on my way into Argento if you want."

"Giada Conti came to see me," my papà continued, ignoring everything I said.

I stopped dead in my tracks. "She…what?"

His frightening off-kilt laugh boomed through the phone. "You didn't know she was coming."

It wasn't a question, but I answered anyway. "I had no idea. Why did she see you? When did she even—"

"She brought me some information. She wanted to exchange the information for something else."

I tried unsuccessfully to swallow the lump in the back of my throat. "*What* else?"

"You," he said.

My phone buzzed with a text. I glanced down and heaved a sigh of relief when I saw it was Matteo, confirming Giada was fine. She apparently had drank too much and felt woozy but was safely in her bed.

"Grazie Dio," I murmured, *thank God.*

"Eh?"

"Nothing. What did she want with me?"

Now my papà's laugh was downright salacious. "She didn't give details, but I suspect you'd enjoy whatever she has planned."

My stomach churned at the thought of my papà even briefly considering Giada in that way.

"I don't understand any of this. What information would she possibly have, and what gave her the idea to trade information for me?"

"Are you no longer interested in her?"

"I don't know. I've tried not to think about that since you made me break up with her."

"Well, if you aren't interested, then that may void my part of the deal…"

"I need to see her," I said, waiting for permission.

"Be my guest, just as soon as I've verified the information she gave me. I have some guys checking on it now, so hope to have answers sometime tomorrow. By the way, she knows about your little sidepiece," he said.

He hung up, leaving me with so many remaining questions.

I stared at my phone, still in disbelief.

"Did the boss figure out your secret?" Alessio asked, startling me.

I turned to him. Of course, Alessio knew that I'd been seeing Giada, but he would sooner die than tell my secrets. I caught him up on what my papà had said, and his expression of disbelief rivaled my own.

"Che palle!" Alessio exclaimed, essentially stating that the love of my life had big balls. As crude as it was, he wasn't wrong.

"I would've loved to be there to see that talk," he added.

I rolled my eyes, but honestly, I would've too. Few people would ever stand up to my papà, and they tended to be well-armed men and not delicate twenty-something girls.

"So, what's your plan?" he asked.

I wasn't sure yet. Just because Giada secured his permission for us to date again didn't mean we'd truly have his blessing. And the sheer fact that she approached my papà behind my back clearly demonstrated she was not the type of docile woman who would quietly sit at home and follow my bidding.

There was no denying Giada was a force to be reckoned with. Now I just needed to show my papà she was a force we needed on our side.

~

Giada

The next afternoon, Luca came over while my brother was out. He was pissed, as I'd expected, but he was there, with his papà's knowledge.

He lectured me on my recklessness for the better part of an hour, drifting back and forth between English and Italian so frequently that I couldn't have followed along had I tried. As it were, I hadn't actually tried. I was too focused on how sexy Luca was when he paced, and when he lectured, and when he spoke Italian, or English… And I couldn't stop smiling at the fact that this beautifully handsome, sexy, disgruntled man was all mine.

Finally, he paused for a breath then scowled. He dropped to his knees at my feet and plunked his head onto my lap. "You scared me half to death, Giada."

"I'm sorry about my text. I had a little panic attack after I met with your father."

He opened his mouth to speak again, but I shushed him and then ran my fingers through his short hair.

"I know you don't approve of my methods, Luca. Going forward, I completely agree we should make decisions like this as a team. In the future, we should do everything as a team."

"I'm so pissed at you right now," he said.

I nodded my head. "I know, babe. And I am prepared to truly work for your forgiveness." I leaned in to kiss him, so happy to have him back in my arms for real this time.

Luca let me make it up to him the best way I knew how, and after, we cuddled silently on my bed for the better part of an hour.

When he finally had to leave to go run some errand, I remembered the other thing…the part I hadn't told him earlier because it wouldn't make him happy.

"There's something else," I said lamely. I hated my awareness that what I was about to show Luca might stress him out, but we needed to start fresh, with no secrets. He followed me into the bathroom and watched curiously as I uncapped my conditioner, stuck my tweezers in, and retrieved the ziplock. I set the larger baggie in the sink, opened it, and retrieved the small bag.

"This was tucked into the back of my skirt after I spoke with your father. I figured I should keep it, but since I wasn't sure what it was…"

Luca snatched the baggie out of my hand and opened it.

"Stop! It could be anthrax or something!"

"It's not anthrax," Luca said. He licked his finger, dipped it into the baggie, then rubbed the white powder on his gums. He made a face.

"How do you know?"

"Because my papà doesn't distribute anthrax."

I winced at his implication that his father did sell whatever was in this bag. "So, what is it?"

"Cocaine." He resealed the bag, then stuck it in his pocket.

"Shouldn't you flush it?"

"That's like… four or five grams. It is expensive shit. I don't want to waste it."

"You do cocaine?"

"Jesus, Giada, no."

"You deal it?"

His expression softened. "Can we not do this right now? I need to go talk to my papà."

"What if it wasn't him? I don't even think he touched me."

"He doesn't do anything himself. Did someone give you a pat-down before you saw him?"

I nodded.

"Well, that was probably when they planted it."

"Why would your father think I do cocaine?"

"He doesn't. It wasn't a gift, Giada. It was an insurance policy. If he didn't like what you were saying and wanted to call the cops on you later, he could."

What Luca said made sense, but acknowledging that would require admitting that I had been in over my head in meeting alone with Salvatore Marino. So instead, I pretended it was no big deal.

"I'd feel better with you at my old apartment while I'm gone," he said.

"I'll feel better here," I replied.

Luca gripped my jaw in his hand. "Baby, you know I wouldn't leave you at all if I didn't think you were safe. But you just betrayed your entire family. I won't be able to concentrate unless you're on my turf."

I rolled my eyes but relented. At least Luca's way promised me nearly an extra half hour with him as we drove to his apartment.

~

Luca

I'd tried to downplay the seriousness of the situation when talking with Giada, telling her everything would be okay, but as I drove off, I couldn't convince myself that what I told her was true. The moment my papà told me what she had done, I realized the precarious and dangerous position she'd put herself in with her own family.

To Giada, it may have seemed no different than when they were children, and she tattled on Angelo or even pitted her brothers against each other to get what she wanted. But now they were adults, and whether she realized it or not, the stakes were higher. Life or death. So that was a problem, yes. But I didn't doubt I'd find a solution.

What I hadn't grasped until she told me about the drugs my papà planted on her was that her family wouldn't be our only problem. With Giada at my side, I'd be fighting a war on two fronts, with my papà an even bigger wildcard than Angelo.

I blew past the guys at the entrance without even asking if my papà was alone. Luckily, as I barged into the office, I quickly gathered that he was, aside from his usual bodyguard, Maximo.

Salvatore Marino slowly raised his gaze to me, his eyes void of any of the warmth one would expect from a father greeting his only son.

"It's impolite not to knock, Luca," he said coldly.

I gestured for Maximo to leave us. He waited until my papà nodded his permission before leaving.

"You planted drugs on Giada," I said the second we were alone in the office.

"I most certainly did not, and I advise you to watch your tone with me, Luca."

"What were you thinking? She's Giada Conti. Do you know the implications if she got caught?"

"Yes. Dozens of people who would flock to her rescue."

"You can't pull shit like that with her ever again."

"She came to see me without an appointment. It would serve her brother right if their family had some consequence for failing to keep a tighter leash on her. That girl is trouble, and if they can't control her—"

"Well, she's my problem now. You are not to do a damn thing

to her, for her, or even loosely relating to her. Do you understand me?"

"If you keep her in line, we have no issues."

"I'm serious, Papà. If you let anyone hurt her, my response will make Angelo look like the most loyal son ever."

"Is that why you came here, to threaten me?"

I searched for an appropriate response but came up empty.

"You know, Luca, whenever something happens and you handle it well, I'm tempted to think you're ready, that you can handle the family business. But then a mess like this crops up, and I'm reminded that you're still not the man I need you to be."

I shook my head. "You can't possibly blame me for any of this. Your business—*our* business—is benefitting because of me. Giada gave you that information solely because of me."

"Yes, and that was brave of her. Admirable, really. That woman is a force to be reckoned with. You, on the other hand…" He pursed his lips and gave me a disappointed once over. "You let your emotions rule you. You're upset that I took savvy precautions—before I even knew what Giada was here to tell us, mind you—which could have resulted in a minor hassle for your girlfriend. Instead of thinking through any of this or recognizing that I did what was smart for our business, you rush in here with empty threats."

"There is nothing empty about my threats, Papà," I said, practically spitting the last word at him. "I know you're disappointed in me. Jesus, the whole fucking continent knows that, but you're the one not thinking about the future of our business here."

Now I had his attention. He cocked an eyebrow and sipped the pale, fizzy liquid in his glass.

"Giada chose me over her own family. Angelo betrayed his father with the drugs. And Matteo, he's a teddy bear," I said. We both laughed at my characterization of Matteo, but it was the truth. He was a smart and kind-hearted man, and he wasn't cut out for any of this. He had all of Giada's naivety but none of her determination to fight for what she wanted.

I paused, knowing I was about to draw a line in the sand that couldn't be erased. But there was no other way. I was not willing to lose Giada again, and I couldn't fight off both our families at once. "You've always said the Conti family isn't a threat, that they aren't our competition. But this partnership can't go on forever, and now is the time to strike. With Marco Conti's access to the docks, his manpower, his resources, the Marino family will be unstoppable."

"What are you suggesting?"

"Don't tell Marco what Giada shared about Angelo's plans. We'll confiscate his shipment, and Angelo will be forced to lie to his father to explain where the money went. I'll marry Giada and make sure Marco sees she's fully invested in our family, not his. We'll help him out of the mess his son got him into, and when we tell him of Angelo's betrayal, he'll have no one to pass his legacy onto but me."

"You're proposing you marry Giada to take over her father's business?"

"Yes," I said, certain he'd entertained the same thought at some point in his life.

My papà nodded his understanding but clearly still didn't agree with my choice. "I understand why you like her. She's stunning, for sure. But she's not the sort of woman you need by your side in this lifetime.

I shook my head. "Giada is the only person I need in this lifetime," I said, standing to see myself out of the office before he could protest.

"Wait!" he called as I reached the door.

I paused with my hand on the doorknob but didn't turn to face him. I couldn't let him see the terror in my eyes.

"Do you think Giada will go along with this whole plan?"

I considered his question, certain without a doubt there

wasn't a chance in hell Giada would help me take over her own father's business. But that wasn't the answer my father needed to hear, not if I wanted him on my side.

"She'll marry me. And the rest she doesn't need to know about," I said, swallowing the lump quickly forming in the back of my throat. "Besides, you already saw—she will risk anything for me."

I heard the rustle of fabric as my father stood from his chair and approached me, smelled the lime he'd drowned in his tonic, and felt his warm breath in my ear as he leaned in, offering me a half hug and a pat on the back.

"I'm proud of you, son. I underestimated you." He retreated, so I tugged open the door.

"Let me know when to schedule the engagement party," he called as I left.

~

Giada

I hadn't expected Luca to be gone for so long, but I was determined to show him I had matured and was no longer the type of girlfriend to nag or check in on him every hour. Besides, I trusted him to call me as soon as he had a chance. Well, unless he couldn't.

I clenched my hands together, trying to convince myself that Luca was fine. The way he'd flown out of the apartment, it was obvious he wasn't going to hug it out with his father, but surely Mr. Marino wouldn't hurt his only son…

I had just decided to call Luca when there was a key in the door. I rushed to the door as it opened, falling into Luca's arms.

He stumbled backwards, clearly not having expected me to greet him so eagerly, but after a minute, he walked us both further into the apartment, shutting and locking the door behind him.

"Are you okay?"

I nodded eagerly. "I just was worried."

Luca's expression grew serious. He pressed his lips against my forehead and pulled me close for a hug.

Just as I was about to complain that I couldn't breathe, he released me.

"You should be worried, Giada. This is serious. I wish you'd talked with me before going to my papà."

"You would've told me not to."

"Yes! And for good reason. You don't want to be on Angelo's bad side."

"I'm used to it," I said with a shrug.

Luca shook his head. "This is different, Giada. This is... I don't know exactly what my papà plans to do with the information you gave him. It could be bad for your family or bad for you."

"It was the only way we could be together," I reminded him. "And Angelo deserves whatever is coming to him."

"I would've found a way for us, Giada. I just needed more time. And it's not just Angelo... my papà could use this against your entire family. Or he could turn your family against you."

"We'll get through it, Luca. We've faced bigger obstacles before. As long as we're together..."

"This isn't the same. I can't protect you when I don't even know who all is fighting us. I need to keep you safe."

"And you will," I said. I'd never before seen Luca so uncertain. Obviously, whatever had gone down with his father wasn't good. "I trust you."

His eyebrows twitched. "Do you? Completely?"

I nodded.

Luca immediately relaxed. "I have a plan. I know it'll work, and I promise I can keep you safe, but you have to do something for me. Otherwise, it won't work."

"Anything," I said.

Luca reached for my hands and stared so deeply into my eyes that I worried he could see right through me.

And then, he said the absolute last thing I'd been expecting.

"Marry me, Giada."

CHAPTER 9

Luca

"Marry me," I said again, squeezing Giada's hands.

Her eyes grew wide as saucers as she tugged free of my gentle grasp. Her palm splayed quickly across my cheek. I had only just registered the slight sting from the slap when she flew to her feet.

"What is wrong with you, Luca?"

I was speechless.

Giada continued to glare at me as though I'd just asked her to drink poison.

"Wrong with *me*? I just proposed, and you hit me."

She snorted like I was the crazy one. "That was not a proposal. You don't get to drone on about how we're both in so much danger because I'm to impulsive and blah blah blah and then expect me to marry you. You didn't even ask, Luca. You just commanded it!"

Giada's normally loud voice had surpassed its usual tenor, and I cringed at the realization that Alessio was hearing every word of her rant from his station outside my apartment door.

"So is that a no?" I asked calmly, hoping my gentle tone would rub off on her.

"Of course, it's a no!" she shouted back. "Do you even have a ring? Jesus Christ, Luca."

Stupidly, I'd assumed she'd say yes without a ring. Nowadays, lots of couples selected a ring together anyway. "I gave you a ring last time, and—"

"Exactly! Last time. Remember how that turned out? God. You can't propose to someone for the second time unless you've seriously upped your game. Where is the romance? Why on earth would I agree to marry you like…this?"

"Because you love me?"

She laughed hysterically.

Okay, *ouch*.

She shook her head at me. "The worst part here is that you truly don't understand what you did wrong, do you?"

I paused, then slowly shook my head.

Giada flung her hands in the air and then grabbed her purse. "Why don't I give you some time alone to think about it then?"

She started for the door, but I was faster.

"Giada, you can't go anywhere. I wasn't kidding about you being in danger. You have literally pissed off some of the most dangerous people on two separate continents. Your family might be after you. My family might be after you. Nicolo Controni might be after you."

"Nico is not after me," she said with an unconvincing eye roll.

"It isn't safe," I repeated.

"Move," she said, her eyes narrowing.

Concerned that she'd drive a knee through my groin, I complied, scooting to the side of the door. Giada quickly opened it and slammed directly into Alessio.

My relief that he hadn't left his assigned post was brief since the smug mixture of embarrassment and amusement on his face confirmed my suspicion that he had heard everything.

He placed his hands on her shoulders, holding her in place, presumably awaiting my command.

"Take your hands off me," Giada said, her words so firm and clearly enunciated that I could barely blame my friend for immediately obeying.

"You aren't going anywhere alone, Giada. It's him or me." I said. Knowing how much Alessio annoyed her, I stepped back to let her return to the apartment.

Instead, she turned to face me, stuck up her middle finger, then started off down the hall.

I swore under my breath. Alessio turned to me for instructions.

"Do not let her out of your sight. If anyone asks, tell them I didn't propose yet. And I swear to God Alessio that if she doesn't get back here in one piece..."

"She'll be fine," he said, his expression serious. Then the corners of his mouth turned upwards. "And I can't wait to hear this whole story later."

I cursed again as he dashed down the hall to catch up to her. I watched until they turned the corner and then retreated into the apartment. I needed a drink.

~

Giada

My Valentino slippers weren't made for athletic endeavors, so I'd have no chance of outrunning Alessio. That left me with eluding him or somehow convincing him to leave me alone. Not super familiar with the area, I figured I was more likely to annoy Alessio rather than outmaneuver him, at least not without also ending up lost somewhere in Rome. Besides, I was starving. I'd planned to let Luca take me out to dinner before he came home and lectured me for saving our relationship.

I was so annoyed I could spit. I mean, I singlehandedly orchestrated a plan to get us back together—something Luca had failed to do. I'd succeeded without hurting anyone. But instead of praising me as an ingenious mastermind, Luca freaked out.

Sure, there had been some risks in approaching the terrifying Salvatore Marino on my own, but Luca couldn't possibly think his own father would hurt me. It was even more ridiculous for him to suggest my family would ever harm me. Clearly, he was just envious that I'd been the one to come up with the plan and not him.

I started off in the direction of a café I'd found on my phone, but as I passed a lingerie shop, I decided my growling stomach could wait. I ducked into the boutique, casting a quick smirk in Alessio's direction. I anticipated he'd wait out front, so when he scampered in right behind me, it took me a moment to regain my cool.

Turning to hide my scowl, I stroked the silky fabric of a few different slips. I pretended not to notice when Alessio plopped down on a chaise in the middle of the room. I lingered by a fluorescent pink bustier that would drive Luca wild, and for the briefest of moments, I forgot how angry I was and started to picture his reaction if I wore that.

"See something you like, Principessa?" Alessio asked, his face eerily close to my ear.

I dropped the lace garment and walked to another rack just as the saleslady approached. Judging from her tone, I assumed she had offered to help me find something, but my Italian was rusty. Or, well, nonexistent.

Alessio rested his hand gently on my shoulder and smiled at the woman before jabbering away in Italian. I recognized a handful of words, but not enough to even guess what he was saying. The saleslady tossed her head back and laughed, then motioned for me to follow. I did, only to come face to face with the sluttiest collection of crotchless panties I'd ever seen.

I turned to glare at Alessio, who merely winked. With a huff, I stomped out of the shop.

Not surprisingly, he followed.

"What did you say to her?" I asked.

He grinned smugly. "I merely explained that you had…unique tastes."

I flipped him the finger.

"Hey, you were clearly trying to embarrass me. Two can play at that game. And unless you pick up on the local language real fast, I think you're at a disadvantage."

I kept walking until I reached a café. I sat down and browsed the menu. Food, at least, was something I understood in Italian. The place had a salad that sounded amazing, but as I glared at my uninvited dining partner, a better idea popped into my mind. I ordered veal medallions and bacon-wrapped asparagus. I wasn't in the mood for either of those dishes, but they seemed guaranteed to piss off a vegetarian like Alessio.

He made a face when I ordered but didn't leave.

"Veal…that's baby cow, right?" I asked.

Alessio rolled his eyes. "Have you ever had your cholesterol checked? If you keep eating like that, you'll have a heart attack before all the men you've pissed off get a chance to kill you."

I pulled out my phone and dialed my friend Gabriella. It was nearly lunchtime in New York, where she was, and luckily, she answered.

We chatted until my food arrived. I carefully avoided any discussion of Luca, the mafia, or my current predicament. Alessio was eavesdropping, though he was doing a decent job of pretending to be focused on his own phone. A few times a minute, he'd glance up and quickly scan the area, but otherwise, he seemed casual.

When the food arrived, I took a few bites, but the veal felt heavy in my stomach. The asparagus was delicious, although I wasn't a huge bacon fan. I unwrapped the thin spears and left the bacon on a pile on the side of my plate. Alessio continued playing with his phone but perked up considerably when a young blonde woman sat at a table nearby.

"This is ridiculous. I don't need a babysitter," I said after an eternity of silence.

"Luca says you do," he replied quickly, still checking out the girl behind me out of the corner of his eye.

"And you just do whatever he says?"

"Yep."

I rolled my eyes and poked at the platter of meat for another minute before scooting it away. No matter how much I wanted to annoy him, I couldn't force myself to eat when I had no appetite.

"You're just going to waste all that?"

"You're welcome to it," I said.

He made a face like he was going to be sick. I held out my credit card for the waiter.

"You know he's right, though," Alessio said. "And it doesn't help that we don't even know what guys your brother might have here. Think about it. You're in a foreign country, and you don't even speak the language or know your way around. You could go missing or end up dead, and we wouldn't even know which of your new enemies to blame."

"I could go to Matteo. He would never hurt me."

Alessio shrugged. "No, but would he disobey a direct order from your father or Angelo? If they tell him to hand you over, he's not going to refuse. He'd never believe that your brother might let someone else hurt you."

I chewed the inside of my lip. "Angelo wouldn't hurt me either."

"You sure about that?"

I couldn't let myself dwell on the answer to that question. Besides, it didn't matter. I wasn't a child, and I wasn't an idiot. I didn't need a bodyguard. "I'm not some helpless damsel in distress. I can take care of myself. I'm sick of being passed around from one overprotective, egotistical man to another."

I thanked the waiter as he returned with my credit card. I was starting to feel defeated. All I wanted was to be alone to mope, but Alessio would never let me return home, and I absolutely couldn't deal with Luca now.

I strolled out of the cafe, then spotted a familiar uniform in the crowd across the plaza. A brilliant idea came to me. I felt my cheeks widen into a smile as I turned back to Alessio.

"Are you armed?"

"Always," he replied, cocky as ever.

"Perfect," I said. I wasn't familiar with Roman laws but suspected they wouldn't take kindly to whatever collection of illegal weapons adorned Alessio at the moment. I stood and walked towards the pair of police officers about twenty yards away.

Alessio followed but quickly ascertained my plan. "Giada, stop. You're just going to piss off Luca even more. You don't know what—"

I swiveled to face him. "What I know is that I don't care about anything except being alone right now. So if you want to avoid pissing off Luca by getting yourself arrested, I suggest you walk away before I reach those police."

"You don't even speak Italian, Giada. What do you think you're going to tell them?" he asked.

I walked faster, but just as I was about to turn to see if he'd wisened up and left me alone, he grabbed my arm and tugged me close.

"Help!" I screamed, much louder than necessary.

Alessio dropped my arm instantly, but I kept screaming. I scurried towards the police, then pointed to Alessio and mumbled something about how he kept following me.

Not speaking their language, I was struggling to explain that this creepy dude was following me, but after a moment, they seemed to catch my point. I was shocked that Alessio didn't make a run for it, but once they stepped in front of him, I disappeared into the crowd and scampered off. I was a tad concerned that he hadn't tried to escape before the police reached him, but whatever. I had warned him. Whatever happened next wasn't my problem.

CHAPTER 10

Luca

When Alessio called to tell me he'd lost Giada, my initial response was concern, followed quickly by anger. I'd given him one job for the day, and he'd failed miserably. And Giada—why did she insist on fighting me when I was trying to keep her safe? For that matter, why couldn't she just accept that she'd made our situation even more complicated than before? If she'd just been patient for a few more days, I would've worked everything out.

I switched Alessio to speakerphone while I tied my shoes and fastened my gun into my holster. He rarely let me down, so I owed him the chance to explain at least. When I heard that Giada had attempted to get him arrested, I clenched my jaw so hard that my gums ached.

"I'm headed to the apartment where she and Matteo have been staying. If she's not there, I may need your help finding her," I said. I realized I owed him an apology for Giada, but that would have to wait.

When I reached the apartment, Matteo answered the door. Before I could even speak, he shook his head.

"She doesn't want to see you," he said.

I exhaled as relief filled me.

I texted Alessio that I'd found her before turning back to Matteo. "That's fine. I don't want to see her now, either. Did she tell you she tried to get Alessio arrested?" I paused, certain Matteo, though not as intricately involved in the family business as his brother Angelo, would still appreciate the problems it could've caused for Alessio and me if he'd been arrested.

Matteo squirmed uncomfortably. "She didn't tell me anything," he said apologetically.

I sighed, impatient with her games. "Please tell your sister I'm headed to the airport in the morning. I have some matters to handle back in Connecticut. It's probably best that she stay here anyway," I said. "I'll see her when I see her."

"You're leaving?" Giada said, poking her head around the corner.

I nodded. There was nothing else I could say to explain the purpose of my trip with her brother standing there.

She chewed on her lip and fidgeted, offering me a chance to look more closely. She had changed into sweatpants and a tank top and pulled her hair into a knot on top of her head. I could tell from the smudges around her eyes that she'd been crying and that she hadn't yet removed her makeup.

Suddenly, my anger dissolved. Why was everything always so complicated with Giada?

"Alessio made it home safely?" she asked.

"No thanks to you, yes. Luckily he's a persuasive guy."

"I didn't want to get him in trouble. I just needed to be alone," she said, casting a sideways glance at her brother. She walked around him and onto the front steps of the apartment, closing the door behind her. Up close, she looked even more fragile and sad.

"Do you really have to leave in the morning?"

"Yes, I do. Now that you got involved, the plan has changed. I need to find out exactly what your brother is up to before I decide how to proceed. If I hesitate, my papà will step in, and his solution won't be good for anyone."

"If you're looking into what he's doing at the church, I should go with you. I know that church better than anyone."

"It's safer for you here, away from Angelo," I said. Although, the idea of leaving her alone in Italy left a bad taste in my mouth, too. "Besides, you want nothing to do with me anyway. This way, you can have your space."

She dropped her gaze to her feet. "I don't want an entire ocean of space. I just needed a couple of hours to think. I've spent the last two months wanting to be back with you again, and now that it happened…"

"You realized you don't want me at all?" I supplied.

"No!' she lifted her eyes to meet mine. "That's not it at all. I do want you. I just… I thought we would talk. I thought we would finally be a team. I thought you might be grateful. Instead, you came home treating me like a wayward child and demanded I marry you. It wasn't at all what I expected."

I blew out a sigh. "We can't talk here, Giada. If you want to come back to the apartment with me for the night, you can."

"How long will you be back in Connecticut?"

"I don't know. A couple weeks maybe."

"Come in," she said. "I need to pack some things."

I followed her inside, but stopped in the doorway. Matteo had retreated to give us space, and once Giada went to her room to pack, I was alone. Giada's purse was on a table, so the moment she stepped out of sight, I reached in and grabbed her phone. My stomach churned to see that she'd added Niccolo Controni to her contacts, but I ignored the nausea and texted him asking if he could meet later that night. I hoped he'd respond promptly, since

I'd rather not have to explain to Giada how her actions had jeopardized his safety, as well.

While I waited for Nico's reply, I scrolled back through their texts. It was snooping, and I had no justifiable reason for doing it except that I was jealous. I didn't see anything too damning, which boded well for Mr. Controni. I believed Giada when she said she never viewed him as anything but a friend at best, but it was nice to have reassurance.

Just as I finished nosing through the messages, Nico replied and agreed to meet. I sent him the address of the warehouse, then deleted the last few messages before texting Alessio from my phone and asking him to detain Nico at nine p.m. at the warehouse.

"Why do you have my phone?" Giada asked, lugging way more bags than she'd need for one night.

My face flushed. "I was reading your texts with Nico," I said, sticking as close to the truth as possible. "And now I'm deleting him from your contacts." I scrolled back to the start of her texts with him then angled the phone to her, my finger poised over the delete key.

She rolled her eyes, then pressed the button herself to delete the entire string of text messages.

"You don't need that much stuff for tonight," I said, gazing back at her luggage.

"I'm flying back with you tomorrow."

I sighed, then said goodbye to Matteo. I said nothing as I carefully wedged her excessive amount of bags into the Maserati.

Giada

*L*uca was quiet on the drive home, but as we idled at an intersection, his hand gently caressed my thigh before returning to the shift. That had to be a good sign. I watched his face closely for any other hints, but he kept his expression blank and his eyes focused on the road.

I didn't understand what had happened. I supposed I'd known he wouldn't approve of me going behind his back to his father, but I'd assumed the ends justified the means and that he'd get over my sneakiness quickly. When he'd demanded I marry him, though, it was obvious he hadn't forgiven me. Luca was the most charming, romantic guy ever—when he wanted to be. His angry, rushed proposal felt like a punishment.

We rolled to a stop in the parking garage beneath his building. Luca stared at me, his chocolatey eyes searching for something. Finally, he squeezed my hand and then climbed out. He let me carry the purse and smaller duffel bag I'd kept on my lap in the car, but he lugged the rest of my crap up to the apartment. I hoped he planned to have someone else drive us to the airport, since there wouldn't be room for even one of his suitcases in the Maserati once my things were all reloaded.

"I have a lot of stuff," I mumbled apologetically as he struggled through the entrance to his apartment with everything.

Luca breathed a laugh as he deposited said stuff on the floor and kitchen table. "Yeah, you do." He reached for my hand and slowly pulled me closer. I expected him to kiss me, but instead, he simply hugged me.

When he released me, he checked his watch then sat on the arm of couch. "I'm sorry about the way I asked you to marry me," he said.

"You didn't ask so much as…" I began. Then I stopped myself. He was apologizing, so I should let him. "Nevermind."

"It didn't occur to me that you were expecting more. I was— am—mad about the way you handled things with my papà. He told me you're a weakness for me. What you did, approaching him without telling me…I understand why you did it, but it proved to him that you are exactly the woman he thought you were."

"And what kind of woman is that?"

"Independent, capable, stubborn. Strong," he added after a lengthy pause.

I frowned. Those were not the adjectives I was expecting to hear. "And that's a bad thing?"

"To him? Yes. He thinks I need a woman who won't ask questions, someone who's oblivious to what I do."

"What do you think?"

He shrugged and stood, walking to the kitchen. "I think I'm starving. Do you want a sandwich?"

I shook my head. "I meant about what your father said. Do you think he's right?"

Luca rummaged through his fridge then began assembling a turkey and swiss sandwich. "Of course, he's right," he said finally, not making eye contact. "I don't know how to do what I do every day if I have to come home and explain myself to you."

I clenched my fists. I'd given him the perfect opportunity to redeem himself, and instead, he opted to make everything worse.

He carried his plate to the table. "Oh, come on, Giada. Look at today. You didn't like my shitty proposal, and so you took off. I wasted an entire afternoon having my best man follow you around."

"That isn't my fault. You chose to assign me a babysitter."

"Yes. And I'd do it again in a heartbeat. That's the problem. I'm terrified of letting something bad happen to you. That makes you a distraction for me, a weakness."

"Then why propose at all?"

"I wanted to show my papà he was wrong, that I could control you."

How ironic, I thought.

"And I told my papà that I could turn your father against Angelo by telling him about this side business, marry you, and stand to inherit your family's business as well as my own."

I suspected that confession should've bothered me, but I had no compassion for Angelo these days. If I had to choose between Luca and Angelo, Luca would win every day, shitty proposal and all.

Luca crammed the last bite of the sandwich into his mouth and checked his watch again. "Say something," he urged.

"So you didn't want to marry me at all? It was just a tactic to get your father off your back."

He pushed away from the table and joined me on the sofa. "Of course, I want to marry you." He shook his head while gently stroking the back of my hand. "You are going to be the worst possible wife for me, but I will never stop wanting you."

I had no response for that. I supposed it should be reassuring that he said it all like it was going to happen no matter what, as opposed to it being hypothetical, but there was nothing flattering about being called the worst wife ever.

Luca glanced at his phone again, his forehead creasing.

"Do you have to be someplace?" I asked.

He flipped his phone over and turned back to me. "I'm expecting a message from Alessio."

"You should marry him if you want an obedient spouse."

"Yeah," he agreed, lifting a section of my hair and twirling it around his finger. "Alessio and I make a perfect team. You and I… we are a mess."

He wasn't wrong, but the way he was looking at me distracted me from the remaining points I needed to make.

"I was worried about you today." he continued. "I don't want a life that you aren't a part of. But when I'm concerned something might happen to you, I can't focus on anything else."

I opened my mouth to tell him that I could take care of myself, but before I could speak, his lips were on mine. His kiss was equally needy and uncertain, demanding reassurance and claiming ownership all at once.

Kissing Luca had the power to distract me from everything. He was right—we were a mess together, and we'd resolved nothing. But once his tongue stroked mine, I didn't care. I parted my lips wider, tilting my head to invite him further into my mouth. His cool fingers pressed into my cheeks, contrasting with the heat of his breath.

His tongue prodded further, seeking, demanding answers I didn't have. So, I responded in kind, claiming his mouth while shifting to move closer. Luca gripped my thigh, lifting me onto his lap, inching his hips forward to make room for me to straddle him. I felt his full length harden beneath me, spurring a similar tightness deep in my own groin.

My nerve endings were on high alert, eagerly awaiting his touch. As Luca's tongue stroked the side of my neck, his breath tickling me behind my ear, I moaned and reached for the buttons of his shirt. His palms caressed my breasts through the thin material of my top, doubling my need to feel his skin against my own. I lifted my shirt up over my head, feeling my cheeks flush in response to his heated stare.

No matter how frustrated I was with Luca, I'd never tire of the way he looked at me. No one could make me feel quite as beautiful, loved, or cherished as he did.

As Luca leaned closer, my lips tingled in anticipation of his kiss. He reached for the clasp on my bra as our mouths crashed together, and I tilted my hips, grinding against him.

A loud buzzing startled us apart.

"Cazzo!" Luca swore, reaching for his phone.

I didn't need a translator to figure out what that meant.

He glanced at his phone, pressed a feathery kiss against my forehead, then nudged me off his lap.

"You have to go," I surmised.

Luca nodded. He tossed my shirt to me before adjusting his

pants and reaching for his suit jacket. I watched as he retrieved a folding knife and a handgun from a drawer by the fridge. And just like that, our moment had passed.

"I won't be long. Can you promise me you won't leave the apartment?" he asked, his car keys jingling in his hand.

"Is Alessio coming to babysit?"

The corner of his lips curved up. "No. Do you need a babysitter?"

I shook my head. "Where are you going?"

"All the questions," Luca murmured, leaning in to kiss me again. "I'll be at the warehouse. Call if you need me, don't wait up, and I'll hurry back."

"We still have a lot to talk about," I reminded him.

"I know, amore, I know."

CHAPTER 11

Luca

As I approached the warehouse, Alessio was perched on a raised ramp just outside. A small white stick protruded from his lips, and his dangling legs swung back and forth like he didn't have a care in the world. I envied my friend's attitude, his casual demeanor, and his laid-back approach towards everything in life. He probably had phenomenal blood pressure.

Alessio nodded his head in acknowledgment of my arrival, and he casually tugged the stick between his lips, revealing a small purple lollipop.

"Taking a snack break?" I teased. "Or does kidnapping just pique your appetite?"

Alessio shrugged and climbed to his feet.

"You do have him, right?"

He nodded then gestured to my chest. "You missed a few buttons," he said, his expression telling me he realized exactly what I'd been doing when he texted.

I fixed my shirt while Alessio led me into the building. We

were in the smaller building of the warehouse, where basic supplies were stored along metal shelves lining the walls. The crates of items ready for export or arriving as imports remained in the other, larger, portion of the warehouse. My office adjoined to this smaller room, too, so it lent itself well to holding individuals I needed to chat with.

The room was dark, but I could easily discern the shape of a man on a chair. His arms were behind his back, pinned at the wrists with an excess of duct tape, and a cloth bag was loosely secured around his head. I didn't know Niccolo Controni well enough to be certain this was even him without seeing his face, but I trusted Alessio to have detained the right guy.

"Why isn't he moving?" I asked Alessio. Giada would never forgive me if we inadvertently suffocated her boy toy, and I thought I'd made it clear to Alessio that I needed him alive.

"I gave him a decent knock on the head earlier. He might still be sleeping it off. He'll be fine," Alessio assured me.

I blew out a sigh and approached the man. I tugged the cloth bag up over his head, relieved to see his eyes instantly pop open and widen. I eyed him warily, noting the gash on the side of his head.

"He's bleeding on the floor," I said to Alessio. Cleanliness wasn't his strong suit. I turned my attention back to Niccolo while Alessio retrieved a bottle of bleach and a mop.

"Mr. Controni," I greeted him. "I assume you know who I am?"

He nodded.

I started to sit in the chair adjacent to him, then paused and yanked the piece of duct tape covering his mouth. "Sorry about that," I said. "So, you do know me?"

"Yes," he said, clearing his throat.

"Any idea why I wanted to chat with you this evening?"

He hesitated. "No."

"Had any interesting dates lately?"

Nico's expression morphed into a grand mixture of regret and panic. "Nothing happened with Giada, I swear. I didn't touch her. And she told me you guys were done for good."

Alessio uncapped the bleach, but I motioned for him to wait. The smell made me nauseous.

"You would be well-advised not to pursue another man's woman, even if you think the relationship is over. In Giada's case, well, she may have thought we were done, but alas, we aren't." I leaned closer as though sharing a secret. "I'm working on a proposal, but the timing is less than ideal."

Nico didn't answer, but he was breathing so hard that it was distracting. Clearly, I'd made my point. He was frightened enough, and I just wanted to get home to Giada.

"I don't share well. I don't like when other men touch my toys. Heck, I don't even like it when Alessio here drives my car. And I certainly don't appreciate other men interfering with my women. Do you understand?"

Nicolo nodded eagerly.

"You will never again speak to her, look at her, or even think about her. Understood?"

"Yes."

I reached into my pocket and unfolded my switchblade, ready to cut the tape fastening his wrists. I stood, then I remembered the other issue we needed to discuss.

"One other topic we need to discuss. Angelo."

"Angelo?" he repeated lamely.

"Yeah, you know, Giada's brother? Your boss?"

He winced.

"I can't let you work for him anymore. I don't like you having any ties to that family."

"I…I can't just quit."

I chuckled. "Well, there's another way out, but I don't recommend it."

"He'll kill me if I tell him you told me to quit."

"Then don't tell him that, obviously. But anyway, it seems to me like a smart man would be less concerned about Angelo killing him and more concerned about what I might do. Is Angelo here right now?" I turned to Alessio.

"Nope," he said.

I turned back to Nico, who shook his head.

"Right. So maybe Angelo isn't the immediate threat?"

"Okay. I'll do it. If you let me go. I'll figure it out. I promise," he stammered.

I rolled my eyes. This moron couldn't figure out his own name if it hadn't been drilled into him. I certainly wasn't going to leave his own early retirement up to him.

"Tell him your mother is sick, and you need to move to Naples to care for her," I said.

He frowned, visibly confused. "My mom is in Naples, and she is sick."

I bit the inside of my cheek to avoid stabbing him out of exasperation. "Yeah, I know that. So move there and take care of her."

Nico nodded quickly. "Okay. I can do that."

"You are done for good with Angelo, do you understand?"

He nodded.

"I'm going to need a verbal response."

"Yes?" he supplied.

"You will never again work for him in any capacity, okay?"

"Okay."

"You are done with this line of work entirely. For good. Understood?"

"Yes."

"And you and I never had this conversation, did we?"

He shook his head. "No."

I glanced to Alessio, trying to confirm that was all. He nodded, so I walked around Nico and sliced through the tape securing his wrists. Nico gazed warily at me while rubbing his wrists.

I reached into my jacket pocket and retrieved a stack of bills. Nico accepted the offering but looked even more confused now, though I hadn't thought that possible.

"It's dirty," I cautioned him, "So be careful how and where you spend it. But it should help you get back on your feet in Naples."

"Oh, okay," he stammered, standing slowly. "Thanks?"

"If you ever tell Angelo or anyone else about this, I will kill your mother and your sister. Understood?"

He nodded. "Yes. Thank you."

I gestured towards the door. "Leave so we can clean this mess and lock up. I have a woman waiting at my apartment."

Nico nodded again then scampered out of the warehouse.

Alessio watched him go, then relocked the door. I poured the bleach into a mop bucket then scrubbed at the bloodstains. Alessio scooted the chairs back to my office then helped himself to a soda, offering me one as well.

I shook my head. "I should get home. I don't know what the fuck to do with Giada, but I can't keep avoiding her."

I caught him up on the basic situation, ending with how my initially tenuous plan was already failing because of Giada's stubbornness.

"Are you still going to tell Marco what Angelo is doing?"

"I don't see any other way. But I had hoped that an engagement to Giada would appease my papà long enough for me to figure out what exactly Angelo was up to."

Alessio laughed. "I got the impression she didn't like your proposal."

"I panicked."

My friend smiled as we walked out. "I see why you like her," he said. "She challenges you. I think you need that sometimes. But you're going to have to up your proposal game if you want her to agree."

I shook my head, then climbed into my car.

~

Giada

I awoke to the sound of a crash then a loud grunt.

For a brief moment, I panicked, but then the familiar stream of swears in Italian reminded me where I was. I crawled out of bed, wrapping a thin silk robe around my body in case Luca wasn't alone.

"Were you trying to kill me?" he asked when he saw me. He had removed his shoes and was grumpily clearing the path to the door.

I shrugged, gazing at the collection of books I'd stacked in front of the door as a rudimentary alarm system. "I wanted to make sure I woke up when you returned so we could talk."

"You could've left me a note."

He folded his suit jacket over the back of the sofa before moving on to the buttons of his shirt. He started near his collar, and I watched as he unfastened one, then another. Then something on his wrist caught my eye. I stepped closer, ignoring the breeze as my robe fell open.

"What is it?" he asked, pausing.

I reached for his wrist, then froze. That wasn't pasta sauce on his shirt sleeve. I dropped my hand to my side and swallowed the lump in my throat.

"Where were you tonight, Luca?"

He gazed at his wrist and swore again in his native language. He yanked the shirt off and wadded it in a ball before stomping into the kitchen and running water over the stain. He didn't answer my question, but then again, I supposed his silence, especially when combined with blood on his sleeve, told me everything I needed to know.

I trudged into the bathroom and began cramming my stuff back into my suitcase. Since I hadn't unpacked any nonessential items, there wasn't much to do.

I heard the faucet stop, then felt Luca behind me.

"Giada, don't go. Please," he said. His voice was uncharacteristically calm.

I shivered as his fingers stroked my bare forearms. "You're begging now?"

He breathed a laugh. "Ordering you to stay didn't help. Maybe asking nicely is the trick."

"There's no trick. I need to trust you."

Luca sunk onto the bed and shook his head. "I honestly don't understand. You said you wanted me back. At the cabin, everything was good. And then when you followed me here today, I thought it was because you wanted to be with me. I thought the whole point of everything you did, with my papà, with Nico…I thought it was so that you and I could be together again."

"It was." I sat beside him.

"But now you don't want to be with me anymore."

"I never said that."

"I asked you to marry me, and you said no."

"You told me to marry you, and it was the least romantic proposal ever. And we haven't even been back together for a full day. You can't just boss me around and expect me to listen."

Luca chuckled. "I've noticed."

"And you can't keep secrets from me."

"I can't tell you everything. I will never be able to tell you everything. Some secrets aren't mine to share, Giada."

"What happened with your father? What made you rush home and demand I marry you?"

He shook his head. "I told him not to worry about you. I said you would marry me, and I would make sure you stayed out of trouble."

I started to speak, but he shushed me.

"My papà views you as a threat, a wildcard. I don't want to worry about him ever hurting you. If he knows you're mine, you are off limits. He will respect that, and so will everyone who works for him. But if he doesn't think I can control you, he isn't going to bless our union."

"Where were you tonight?" I asked. "Who did you hurt?"

"No one. I was…I was with Alessio, at the warehouse, like I told you. I didn't hurt anyone."

I could tell from his squirming that he wasn't telling me the whole story. "Whose blood was that? You don't look hurt."

"It's not mine. I just…I took care of one of the problems."

"Took care of?" I flew to my feet. "What does that even mean? Did you kill someone tonight?"

He stood in turn, gripping my shoulders. "No! Jesus, Giada. No."

"Whose blood is it?" I repeated.

"Alessio and I had a talk with Niccolo Controni."

"What?" I jerked free from his grip.

"I took care of him. It's fine. He's not a threat anymore."

I backed up slowly, not even sort of understanding how Luca could think any part of that was okay.

"Giada," he began.

"Don't touch me, and don't come any closer."

He flung his hands in the air. "None of this would've happened if you hadn't given his name to my papà. Do you know what Angelo would've done to him if he found out Nico blabbed his secrets to us?"

"Don't put this on me. You make your own choices. I didn't force you to kill anyone."

"I didn't kill Nico!"

Something in his tone gave me pause. I'd never before heard Luca sound so desperate for me to believe him. "Then tell me what happened."

"We talked, that's all. I didn't tell him you hadn't already known about Angelo and the drugs. I also didn't tell him that, thanks to his big mouth, my papà now knows about Angelo's side business. All I said was that I didn't like him dating you and that you and I were getting back together. I made him promise not to see you anymore, and I told him to tell Angelo that he was moving to Naples to take care of his mom."

I considered everything Luca was saying. It seemed plausible enough.

"If Angelo ever found out Nicolo betrayed him, even unintentionally, he'd kill him. Angelo doesn't solve problems the same way I do. Nico's only hope is to be far away. I can't imagine he was one of Angelo's good recruits, so hopefully, Angelo will have no problem parting with him." Luca paused. "I gave him money to start over in Naples, so he won't be tempted to go back to Angelo."

From that side of the story, Luca sounded like a saint. Except saints didn't come home with bloodstains.

"Whose blood was that?"

"Nico's," he said apologetically. "He's fine. It was nothing. He just…got a little bump on the head before I arrived." Luca tentatively walked closer again. "Giada, I know you hate what I do and the way I do it, but I'm doing the best I can. If people think I've gone soft, I've got no leverage. I don't have enough money to pay off everyone who gets in my way. People need to fear me."

I didn't know what to say.

He brushed past me and poured himself a drink. "I haven't booked flights yet, so if you don't want to come, you don't have to."

"I want to go home. I want to spend Epiphany with you."

"Okay. You should get some sleep then."

"We need to talk."

"There's nothing to say, Giada. You claim you want to be with me, but you treat me like a monster."

"I'm sorry," I said. I stroked his back lightly. "I don't mean to. I think you're a good man. I don't like the choices you have to make, but I trust you to do the best you can."

He swiveled to face me.

"No, you don't. You see a tiny speck of blood on my shirt and assume I killed someone. That isn't trust. Even when I told you I didn't hurt him, you still didn't believe me. Trusting me would've been giving me the benefit of the doubt, not jumping to the worst possible scenario when I'm just trying to make sure the man you used to make me jealous doesn't get killed by your brother."

I opened my mouth to protest, but there was nothing to say. He was right. I reached for his hand, but he jerked away.

"I want to be with you, Giada, but this is my life. I can't change what I do, and I don't think I can handle constantly disappointing you."

"I'm not disappointed."

Luca simply stared at me. Suddenly, I could see his exhaustion. His eyelids drooped, he had hazy purple bags under his eyes, and his stubble was starting to remind me of our days in the secret cabin.

"You were really worried about me today, weren't you?" I asked.

"Yeah."

"I didn't mean to make more work for you. I honestly just didn't think I could survive another week without you."

"I know."

I reached for his hand again, and this time, he didn't pull away. The proximity gave me a moment to figure out how to explain my thoughts.

"Everyone in my life treats me like I'm helpless. I hate that. I think I wanted to show you all that I'm not, and I guess I didn't think through all the consequences. I didn't consider it from your perspective earlier today," I said. "I'm sorry."

"Anch'io,' he said, quickly translating. "Me too."

I rose to my toes and kissed him softly. When we pulled apart, he chuckled.

"You're no more likely to stop being stubborn than you are to learn Italian," he said. "We're doomed."

"We don't have to be."

Luca quirked an eyebrow.

"How about I promise never to assume you're out murdering people, and you promise not to murder people?"

He frowned.

"Seriously? That's too hard?"

"No, but the fact that you think I'm out killing people haphazardly…"

I smiled shyly. "It's possible I'm teasing you."

"Can we make a real deal?" he asked.

I nodded.

"Don't go behind my back. If you have a plan, tell me. I've lived in this world my whole life. I know how guys like my papà, your brother, and your father operate. If you could just trust my experience, that would go a long way."

I considered that. "I can do that. But can you make the same promise?"

"No."

"What?"

He shrugged. "I can't tell you everything I'm up to, and trust me, you don't want to know. I've got too many secrets that aren't mine to tell." Luca paused, and his expression softened. "If it's something about you or your family, though, I'll share as much as I can. And if I don't have to worry about you scampering off and doing something stupid without running it by me first, I'll tell you a lot more."

I nodded. I could live with that. I tried to focus on the issues we were currently facing, certain he wouldn't fall asleep with everything weighing down on him still. "So you took care of Nico, but you still have to figure out what my brother is up to and how to use that information to get your father off your back without turning my entire family against me?"

Luca stared blankly for a moment, then nodded, apparently approving of my recap. "Yeah."

"I'd like to talk to Father Ryan when we're back in town. He can help us."

Luca lifted my hand to his lips, kissed it softly, then tugged me back to the bedroom.

CHAPTER 12

Luca

The flight back to JFK was the most relaxing ten hours I'd experienced in over a month. We left in the afternoon, Rome time, and arrived home early evening, East Coast time, so neither of us slept during the flight. Instead, Giada and I talked. We didn't discuss my papà or hers, whatever mischief Angelo was up to, or anything pertaining to my work. We didn't even discuss our future.

Rather, we caught up on everything in each other's lives over the past several weeks. We played cards, I Spy, and twenty questions. We shared headphones and watched a movie, we laughed, and we fed each other crappy airplane snacks. It reminded me of high school, when we started out as friends. Back then, life was easy. Those days, being with Giada was easy.

"Promise me that from now on, we'll spend all the major holidays together," Giada said, roping her arm around mine and staring up at me with those big brown eyes of hers.

"I'd love that," I said, "But we might have different definitions of what constitutes a major holiday." I was mostly teasing her since she tended to put a lot of emphasis on the random commercial holidays and her birthday, but technically there were also several cultural differences, too, especially this time of year.

She made an adorable scowling face and shimmied even closer. Normally by this point in a flight, my legs were aching to move, but I'd missed having Giada in my arms so much that I was still enjoying the cramped quarters.

Suddenly, I remembered something I'd meant to discuss with her. I pulled out my phone and navigated to the listing I'd saved. I angled the phone towards her. "What do you think of this apartment?"

I watched her face as she clicked through the pictures. It was nothing impressive—a newer, two-bedroom unit in a modern, industrial-style building in Stamford, but the location was great, and the views were the best available outside of the City. Her expression was unreadable, which I suspected was intentional. She gazed up as she finished with the last picture.

"Why do you ask?"

"I thought maybe you'd want to live there," I said, proceeding cautiously, adding. "With me." I paused, resisting the urge to tell her I didn't feel safe with her returning to her childhood home where Angelo had unfettered access.

A shy smile broke out on Giada's face then widened. "Are you finally asking me to move in with you?"

I nodded. "Yes, as long as that doesn't conflict with your moral code, you know, since we aren't even engaged."

She stuck out her tongue then snatched back the phone to look at the photos again. "Have you already rented it?"

I cringed, hoping she wasn't disappointed by my answer. "Yes. I signed the papers a couple weeks ago. Thomas and Giovanni moved my stuff from storage in this week, but it's still pretty bare bones. So if you know any good interior designers…"

Giada squealed excitedly then hugged me.

When we finally reached the apartment, we broke in the new bedroom, ate takeout dinner on the living room floor, then Giada promptly passed out for the night. I touched base with my guys before trying to get some rest myself. Alessio was flying in the next day, and the plan was for the three of us—Giada, Alessio, and I—to attend the regular mass that weekend. Giada would stay after the service to chat with Father Ryan, leaving Alessio and me free to explore the church without raising too many eyebrows.

On Saturday, I didn't anticipate any hiccups with the plan and felt uncharacteristically calm as we rolled into the parking lot shortly before the service was to start. Giada's smile widened as the sprawling church campus came into view, and I couldn't help but envy that she had a place that brought her so much comfort. My family had attended church regularly when I was growing up, but I couldn't recall ever paying attention to the mass. I certainly never extrapolated anything out of it to apply to my own life.

For Giada, though, the familiarity of mass was soothing, serving as a constant reminder that God's presence in her life was unchanging. For the most part, she truly believed in the teachings of the church, just as she believed in good and evil and the possibility of redemption.

As Alessio parked the car, Giada hopped out without waiting for me to open her door. I followed, flashing Alessio a stern look to remind him to be on his best behavior during the mass. He, too, had been raised Catholic, but his split with the church was more formal and resulted from his early realization that the Church didn't support his lifestyle. I didn't blame him, but I did expect him to play the role of the good Catholic today.

I reached for Giada's hand, concerned she'd dash into the church ahead of us if I didn't remind her of our presence. She blushed and slowed her pace. "I'm excited to be back," she said.

"Clearly," Alessio mumbled.

Then, Giada stopped so abruptly that Alessio slammed into her back. I steadied her as Alessio apologized. Then we both followed her gaze across the breezeway to where Angelo stood, shaking hands with one of the priests.

"Shit," Giada said. She turned to me. "I'm so sorry. He's never here. I mean, literally, I've never seen him come on a Saturday. Rarely on a Sunday, but—"

"Shh, it's okay," I said, squeezing her hand for emphasis. So much for the plan going smoothly. I tugged Giada in her brother's direction, pausing to let other parishioners enter.

Angelo gazed up right as we reached him, his eyes bouncing from his sister, to me, to Alessio, then back to me.

"I didn't expect to see you here on a Saturday," Giada said, her voice filled with unease.

I squeezed her hand, wishing she'd stay quiet.

"I didn't expect to see you here at all, especially not with your ex-boyfriend."

"We're back together," she said, holding up our clasped hands.

"Since when?"

"Earlier this week," she supplied, clearly determined to ignore that I was now clenching her hand so tightly that it had to be painful.

Angelo's frown deepened. "I heard you were seeing someone else. What happened to him?"

Alessio cleared his throat loudly. "Maybe we should discuss all this later. Or someplace else. Some of us have a lot of shit to repent for and need to get moving in there."

We all glared at him, painfully aware that dozens of people pouring into the church probably heard him swear.

"You're welcome to go," Angelo said.

"We broke up. I mean, we weren't really dating, though. We only went out like two or three times, and only because I missed

Luca and had nothing else to do in Italy." Giada said, smiling at me and batting her thick eyelashes. "He said something about moving back to take care of his mom. He wasn't my type anyway."

I dropped Giada's hand altogether. My fingers were starting to go numb, and clearly, she wasn't going to shut up any time soon anyway.

"Where's Julia? Is she not Catholic?" she continued.

"Working. Saturday is a busy day for the salon."

Giada shrugged then peered past her brother. "Hi, Eddie, Rico," she said, greeting Angelo's henchmen. I was pretty sure one of them was her cousin, but honestly her family tree was too complicated for me most days, especially since the Contis didn't fully distinguish between blood relatives and blood oaths.

"When did you get back in town?" Angelo said. If his eye contact was any indication, the question was directed at me, but Giada answered anyway.

"Thursday. I figured Matteo would've told you." She paused. "I hope he comes home soon."

Alessio cleared his throat again. "We should get inside. I don't want to miss the call to worship."

He sounded so sincere that I actually snickered aloud. Angelo's glare only intensified.

"You should come speak with Dad," he said finally, turning to his sister. "He'd appreciate knowing you're back in town. Both of you. And it seems curious that you're attending mass while apparently shacking up together, so maybe you should revisit your living arrangements while you still have some hope of keeping the illusion of your virtue intact."

I felt Alessio's hand on my shoulder blade and guessed he worried I was about to hit Angelo. He underestimated my self-restraint.

"We got in late. She was tired. And I bet you have bigger

things to worry about than your grown sister's virtue," I replied. "Enjoy the service."

With that, I tugged Giada into the church. Since the service was moments away from beginning, we were able to sit towards the back without raising any suspicions. Angelo and his henchmen sat on the opposite side of the sanctuary. Shortly into the mass, Rico quietly scooted out of the pew, disappearing into the hall behind the sanctuary.

Alessio turned to me and tilted his head, silently asking if I wanted him to follow. I shook my head, dismissing the idea. There was no chance of Alessio leaving without Angelo noticing, and while I now fully intended to let Angelo know I was the one who stole his precious drugs, I didn't want him to realize I knew they were his at the time.

~

Giada

I hadn't realized how much I'd missed my church until I was back at home, seated in the pew, absorbing all the familiar sights, sounds, and smell. It was nice having Luca by my side, too, even if he was there with ulterior motives. I liked to think that in the future, we would attend church regularly. I wasn't naïve enough to hope the faith would ever become as integral a part of Luca's life as it was mine, but I'd be happy even if he'd learn to appreciate the other benefits the church offered— the break from the chaos, the chance to reflect, and the bite-sized life lessons.

I walked over to my brother after mass, Luca and Alessio trailing behind, each bearing a mixture of annoyance and boredom on their faces.

"Wow, you survived the whole service without getting struck by lightning. I'm impressed," I teased.

Angelo rolled his eyes.

"Tell Dad I'll come by the house later," I said.

His eyebrow shot up. "You can come with me. I'm headed there now."

I shook my head. "I wanted to chat with Father Ryan. I haven't seen him in weeks. He's headed out on a mission trip soon, so I've got to check when they want the ladies group to start gathering the supplies." I paused when he looked sufficiently bored, then turned to Luca.

"You could go with Angelo," I said.

Luca's eyes widened. Angelo grimaced.

I shrugged. "Or not. I just thought then you wouldn't have to wait for me, and you guys could catch up."

"I'm good here," Luca said. Then he turned to Alessio, "Maybe I should go talk with this Ryan and see what makes him so fascinating."

Angelo blew out a sigh and turned. "I'll see you at the house later." He motioned to his guys, and they all went to the car.

"I need to make a call," Alessio said. "Can I just wait for you in the car?"

Luca nodded then walked me towards Ryan's office. Of course, the priest wasn't there yet, since the service was still letting out. Saturdays were less chaotic than Sundays, but there were always people eager to talk after mass.

"Next time, stick to the script," he said softly.

"I made it more believable. Now he isn't suspicious." I glanced at the door. "Who is Alessio calling?"

"No one. He's making sure Edoardo and Federico both leave with your brother."

I stretched my neck to the side. Luca shuffled his feet from side to side, his tension mounting visibly. We were alone in the hallway directly outside the clergy offices, though someone could've been within earshot. I reached my hand towards the back of his neck, pressing until he angled his head downward. I kissed him gently on his lips, lingering long enough to calm him.

"What was that for?"

I shrugged. "You seem nervous."

He glanced at his phone for the billionth time, then jammed it back into his pocket. "So that was Father John, the one leading the prayers?"

I nodded.

"Do you know him well?"

"Not really. I mean, he knows who I am, and we're friendly, and he gives the best homilies, but—"

"Is he a good man?" Luca interrupted, his jaw ticking to the side.

"Why?"

"Giada…"

"He's a priest, Luca. He's dedicated his entire life to serving God and helping other people. What do you think?"

"I think he's helping your brother smuggle drugs, and I'm curious why," Luca replied, his voice a mere whisper.

Well, there was that. I honestly hadn't been able to reconcile the Father John I knew with the one who, apparently, had fallen in with my brother. My only explanation was that he didn't have a choice. "Angelo may have threatened him. Or blackmailed him."

Luca gripped both of my hands and turned to me, tilting his face to rest his chin on my head. A small group of people passed by while his back was to them, leading me to wonder whether he was merely avoiding recognition or actually wanted to be closer to me. Once they were gone, he brushed his thumb along my cheek, then kissed me.

"If you think he's a good man, that he's truly not involved with Angelo by choice, you need to get rid of him, and soon. I don't know how Angelo will react, but if there's a chance Father John is innocent, I'd like to keep him out of the crossfire," Luca said, his voice even quieter now that his lips were an inch from my ear.

"Get rid of him how?"

"He needs to leave town, permanently. The further the better. I don't know how this church stuff works, but you do. Just don't give anyone else a heads up."

He kissed me again, then a loud throat clearing behind us caused me to jump. I turned to see Father Ryan sheepishly waiting.

"Father Ryan!" I greeted him cheerfully. "How are you?" I rushed forward and gave him a quick hug. He seemed incredibly uncomfortable, which I assumed was thanks to Luca's presence.

"You remember Luca, right?" I asked.

The priest nodded and smiled politely, offering his hand.

"I'm going to go find Alessio," Luca said. "You two catch up or whatever."

Father Ryan motioned for me to head into his office. I sat on the couch across from his desk, and he started to take the chair adjacent to me.

"Actually, can you close the door?" I asked.

He hesitated, but complied, this time moving to his desk. Suddenly, I remembered a not-so-distant time when a more jealous Luca had maybe accused my favorite priest of untoward behavior. Apparently, that incident was fresh on Father Ryan's mind too.

"How have you been?" he asked.

I gave him the generic low-down, then asked about a few things at the church. It was obvious that he was very excited about the mission trip, and the more he rattled on about that, the more apparent it was that the solution was for a different priest to go.

"Could we speak confidentially for a moment?" I asked, glancing to the door to make sure no one was waiting.

He paused. "Is everything okay? Are you…concerned for your safety?"

I supposed he would never truly trust Luca, and to some extent, I understood. No matter how firmly I believed Luca was good for me, even if he wasn't good in the traditional Catholic meaning of the word, others wouldn't understand.

"No, I'm fine. Do you…well, you know my brother Angelo?"

"Yes. He was here this afternoon."

"Yeah. Well, is he with Father John a lot?"

Father Ryan considered that, then shrugged. "I've seen them together a couple times. Your brother has been attending church more regularly the past couple of weeks, though."

I chewed over my words, trying to decide how to make my point without throwing my brother under the bus. Finally, I gave up. This wasn't a time to be vague. "I think Angelo is mixed up in something bad, and I'm pretty sure he's gotten Father John involved too."

Father Ryan immediately broke eye contact, turning to the wall and taking several breaths.

"Look, I won't pretend to know everything about the situation, but I have reason to believe it's serious. You should talk with Father John. He needs to go on the mission trip instead of you. It might not be safe for him to stay here."

"Are you telling me you're worried your boyfriend might hurt Father John?"

"No!" I shook my head vehemently. "Luca is not the bad guy here. I know you don't want to believe that, but he is trying to protect Father John. He told me if there was any way I could get him to leave town soon, I should do it."

The priest sighed and shook his head. "I don't even know what to say, Giada. If you have concerns, we need to call the police. And I think you should have this discussion directly with Father John."

I gritted my teeth. I wasn't sure how long we had left to talk, but as soon as Luca and Alessio found whatever they were looking for, they'd want to leave quickly. There was no time left for beating around the bush. "What I told you before is true. My brother is smuggling heroin and storing it here at the church. I'm pretty sure Father John not only knows about it but is helping him. Luca is trying to get rid of the drugs and make sure Angelo never tries something like this at the church again, but he can't protect Father John."

He started to interrupt, but I kept talking.

"The police can't help you, or any of us. And if they get involved, we're all in danger. Angelo deals with some…not nice people."

"I don't understand what you want me to do."

"I want you to go to Father John. Don't tell him how you know or anything that I've said, just that you know he's involved with Angelo and that he's done some bad things. Tell him to go on the mission trip instead of you, and ask him to stay far away. Tell him his life is in danger if he doesn't go or if he talks with anyone about any of this ever."

I glanced at the door just as Luca peered in.

"You have to trust me, please. Pray on it, then talk to Father John. Please."

His frown deepened, but he didn't say anything as I stood and walked to the door. I paused, wondering if Luca would want to say anything to Father Ryan, but he simply slipped his arm around my waist and walked me away from the office without ever looking back.

When we stepped outside, Alessio was already in the car, engine running.

"Is everything okay?" I asked, suddenly feeling like we were jumping into a getaway vehicle.

Luca's nod was relaxed. "Do you want to ride in the front? I have some calls to make."

"I want to sit by you."

Alessio shrugged as if to say he wasn't offended, and I climbed into the back, scooting over so Luca could sit beside me. I was still exhausted, so him ignoring me during the drive was fine by me.

I leaned against his arm, and he shifted, wrapping his left arm around me and scrolling through his phone with his right hand. I wasn't surprised when he reverted to his native language for the conversation. I wouldn't have felt quite so excluded, except that Alessio kept chiming in with comments every few minutes, even though he, too, could only hear Luca's portion of the conversation.

When Alessio pulled in front of the apartment, I started to climb out, but Luca tugged my hand and motioned for me to wait. I rolled my eyes, spurring Alessio to laugh out loud. Adding insult to injury, Luca ended the call in English, saying, "Sounds good, talk later," and confirming that the sole reason for speaking in Italian was to keep me from following along.

"Someday, I'm going to learn Italian," I said.

Luca and Alessio both laughed. "No, you're not," Luca said. He lifted my hand to his lips and kissed it gently. Then, he climbed out and waited by the open door for me.

"Un minuto," he said to Alessio.

I groaned out loud, not needing a dictionary to translate that. Luca was dumping me off in the apartment then heading out again with Alessio. "I can walk myself in," I said.

"Of course, you can," he replied, his tone more patronizing than usual. "I wanted to talk with you, though. How did it go with Father Ryan?"

"I'm not sure. You haven't exactly made a great impression on him, and I wasn't able to give him enough details to convince him."

"Well, you did what you can."

Luca didn't seem too concerned about Father John's welfare.

"What is that supposed to mean?"

He shrugged. "Either he'll leave town, or he won't."

I swiveled to face him. "What if he doesn't? Do you think Angelo will hurt him?"

"Maybe. I don't know what the parameters of their arrangement are, and I don't know how Angelo responds when he feels cheated."

I frowned. "But aren't you the one cheating him?"

"He won't know that."

"What if he does?"

"Tesoro, don't worry. Alessio and I know what we're doing."

I wrinkled my nose. Luca reached for my biceps and stepped closer until our lower bodies touched. Oddly enough, the feeling of him pressed against me distracted me enough to lower my heart rate just a tad. He increased the soothing effect by kissing me then, slowly.

Just as I was about to lose myself in his expert touch, he pulled back.

"Trust me, Giada. In two days, this will all be behind us."

He scampered into the bedroom and returned a moment later.

"Wait, two days?" There was no way Father John would leave by then. The mission trip wasn't for another month.

Luca nodded. "Can you promise me to stay here until I get back?"

"When will that be?"

"Late," he said. "Don't wait up."

I sighed. At least he was being honest. "It's Saturday night," I reminded him. "I might as well go back home if you're going to ignore me."

"This is your home now," he reminded me. "You just need to figure out when to get your stuff here. Plus, if you leave now, I can't have you moaning my name within five minutes of my return tonight." He winked. "Besides, it isn't safe for you at home until this is resolved."

"I need to at least call my dad."

"That's fine. Just don't go anywhere with anyone from your family except your mom or dad."

"Enzo?"

Luca's eye twitched. Still a sensitive subject, apparently.

"Call if you need me. I love you." He kissed me again then left.

I went into the bedroom to change then flopped on the bed. I only had the clothes with me that I'd brought to Italy, which luckily was a fair chunk of my closet, but I was sick of all that. I wanted my full selection. I needed to go home.

I rolled onto my back and peered around the room. I adored the apartment. It wasn't exactly spacious compared to what I was used to, but given its proximity to the city, the two-bedroom, two-bath unit was luxuriously sized. The entire building was newer, so the unit featured modern, high-end appliances and finishes. Luca's traditional furniture gave the entire space a clean, yet homey feel, but he'd made it clear I had free reign when it came to furnishing and decorating the space.

I was eager to start with the design, but I figured I needed to tell my family I was moving out first. With as often as Luca proposed, they must have suspected this was coming, but they'd probably hoped for an official engagement before the cohabitation. Not that such antiquated traditions had stopped Angelo from moving in with Julia, but my family always employed different rules when it came to me versus my brothers.

I slid off the bed and changed into comfier clothes, then made my way to the kitchen. Opening the fridge, I groaned. Of course, there was no food. We'd just returned from Italy, and neither of us had gone to the store.

"There's no food in the apartment," I texted Luca, pressing the letters on my phone screen harder than necessary, as though my annoyance would be magically conveyed with the message.

My phone rang almost instantaneously. I didn't have to check the caller ID to know it was Luca.

"Order whatever sounds good. There's cash in the freezer. And inside my tennis shoes."

I rolled my eyes. Of course, there was. "I have money." Although, technically, *I* didn't. I had credit cards, but the bills went to my father. Since I'd been splitting my time between two continents, I hadn't exactly had opportunities to earn my own keep just yet.

"Why don't you call Gabriella and see if she can come over? You guys could have a sleepover or whatever," he suggested. "But, um, it might be best if you don't distract me for a while. Maybe only text if there's an actual emergency. Okay? Love you."

He hung up before I could protest. I groaned at his mention of an emergency. Like, people could die of starvation. The lack of food in the apartment did constitute an emergency. Luca clearly could've been a tad more concerned for my wellbeing.

I'd already told Gabby I was back in town early, but I'd assumed Luca and I would be busy tonight. Well, or that I'd be with my family. It was a longshot to see if she was still free, but I let her know my plans changed and invited her over. By some miracle, she said she'd head right over and that she'd bring the wine. We agreed on Thai, so I ordered the food.

I had at least forty minutes till either she or the food would arrive, but instead of doing something productive, like finishing unpacking, I started stewing about Father John again. I told myself my brother would never hurt a priest, and while I was pretty sure that was the truth, I was positive I'd never forgive myself if I was wrong. I paced from one end of the apartment to the other, thinking over my options. Then I went into the closet to stare at the clothes waiting to be unpacked.

This was stupid. I just needed to do something.

Before I changed my mind, I called Father Ryan. It was his personal cell phone that he probably gave to lots of parishioners, but I suspected no one else was so inappropriate as to ever use the number. I expected him to let the call go to voice mail, but he answered.

"Father Ryan?"

"Yes."

"It's Giada." I barely paused, certain he'd assume I was in danger if I was calling him on a Saturday night. "Did you talk to Father John yet?"

There was a long silence. "I did, but I didn't say everything you'd mentioned. I only reminded him that I was there for him if he needed to talk."

I groaned. "Look, I was wrong on the timetable. He needs to leave tonight. Tomorrow at the latest. You have to tell him."

"I don't know what to tell him. I'm not..." he sighed. "Why don't you speak with him directly?"

"Father John will assume it is some kind of trap if I talk with him. Can't you just tell him that someone told you he's been working with Angelo and that you don't need to know the details and aren't judging him or anything, but that he is in danger if he doesn't leave right away?"

He took his time answering. "Are you sure about this, Giada?"

"No. I'd like to think Angelo wouldn't hurt a fly, but I'll never forgive myself if something happens to Father John because he doesn't listen."

"Have you spoken with Adrian about this?" the priest asked.

I frowned at the non sequitur. "No. Why?"

He hesitated. "He approached me before the holiday and was worried about these same issues, but he seemed to think Luca was responsible."

"Adrian is wrong," I said, rolling my eyes. I glanced down and spotted Luca's running shoes. I bent to pick them up and felt my eyes widen as I retrieved the aforementioned cash. Yes, I could've used it to buy Thai food. I also could've used it to buy a Thai restaurant, though, judging from the amount.

"Jesus," I mumbled, interrupting whatever Father Ryan was

saying. Then I cringed, realizing what I'd said and to whom. "I have plenty of cash. If he needs it for travel, let me know. I…um, someone can come get it. I can't leave."

He sighed audibly. "He's not taking your money. I'll talk with him. But I promise you, the police can help."

"They can't, and if you call them…"

"I won't. Take care of yourself."

"Thanks." I hung up right before the doorbell rang.

CHAPTER 13

Luca

I met with my guys for about an hour, hammering in every detail of the plan. Finally, I was confident they understood it well enough to proceed without me. As much as I wanted to oversee everything, I couldn't risk being seen. The effectiveness of the scheme hinged on my plausible deniability.

To bolster said plausible deniability, I also secured the best possible alibi—Marco Conti himself. I'd texted him and requested a meeting, leaving the time open to him. Once he replied, that was our cue to launch the plan.

Alessio stayed behind to supervise everything at the church, so I went alone to the Conti house. They buzzed me right through the gate, and when I reached the front steps, Giada's mom was already swinging the door open. Her expression dampened the moment she saw it was just me. When I'd said this was a personal, not business, visit, she assumed I'd bring their daughter.

Martina recovered quickly and smiled warmly. "It's nice to see you again, Luca. How have you been?"

"Good. Busy," I said, leaning in for a hug. "You were expecting Giada, too," I said. She didn't deny it. "I'm sorry. I should've been clearer on the phone. She's with Gabriella. She's been exhausted since we flew back, but I know she plans to come by real soon."

Tina smiled. "Well, at least she's back in the country. I can't get a straight answer from Matteo about when he'll return." She shook her head. "You kids just jet back and forth like it's nothing."

She started into the house and motioned for me to follow. "Marco's in his study. Can I get you a drink?"

"I'm good, thanks." I considered asking her to stay for the discussion since, really, her opinion mattered just as much as Marco's, but I didn't. Giada's father was a traditional man, and I needed him to assume my only reason for coming to him was to honor those conventions.

I tapped on the door to Marco's study, leaning forward so I could hear if he called for me to come in. For reasons I completely understood, his study was fairly soundproof. If he wanted to speak to someone outside the door, he practically had to shout, which he did.

I cracked the door open to make sure he knew who he'd just invited in, waiting until he acknowledged me with a tight smile and a comfortable nod before walking in and closing the door behind me.

Marco asked how I was doing, how business was doing, and how my trip to Italy had been. I gave polite but vague answers to everything. Then he wanted to know if Giada had come with me and if we'd be staying for dinner.

"No, but I wanted to talk with you about Giada," I said.

His eyebrow shot up.

"I know my relationship with her has had its ups and downs, but we're in a good place now. I love Giada. She's the one I see a future with." I paused, clearing my throat awkwardly. "So I wanted your blessing to marry her."

Marco frowned. "Did you already ask her?"

I winced at the loaded question. Marco knew we'd been engaged before. That time, he'd practically begged me to propose, thinking his daughter would be safer with me in her corner. "Well, I mean, not...since the last time," I mumbled, hoping it sounded more coherent out loud than in my head. "I wanted to get your permission first. I want to do things right this time."

Marco stared at me, still silent.

Crap.

The man intimidated people for a living, but having grown up with a similar father, I'd never fallen for Marco's antics...until now. "We've talked about it, Giada and I," I continued. "She wants a big, traditional wedding, probably a long engagement, too. So I assume she'll say yes when I ask, but..." I made a sour face as I realized how naïve I was to ever assume anything about Giada's reactions.

Marco nodded. "What does your father have to say about all of this?"

I hesitated.

"The last time I spoke with him, he seemed to think my daughter was a distraction for you. He sent you all the way to Italy to ensure you stayed away from her."

Cazzo. "Uh, yeah. Well, my papà does think she's a distraction for me, but he is aware that I want to marry her, and he supports that. We talked before I left Italy. He likes Giada, of course, and he really likes that she's your daughter. I wouldn't go so far as to say he wants me to be happy, but now he at least realizes I'm more distracted without her in my life."

I couldn't believe how awkward I sounded. I wished Marco would say something. Or that I could just shut up in the meantime.

"Look, the bottom line is that I need Giada in my life. She's... everything to me, and I'm pretty sure she feels the same way about me. Since we were kids, you and my papà have always joked about the two of us ending up together, and there've been all these suggestions over the years that it'd be good for business if we stayed together, but that's not why I want to be with her. I really do love her. I think I can make her happy, and I promise I'll take good care of her."

Marco cocked his head to the side, a wry, bemused grin on his face.

He didn't say anything, but at that point, I was done. I had nothing left to say, not that I could possibly humiliate myself any further if I tried.

"Okay," he said finally. "I give you my blessing. And I wish you good luck," he added with a wink.

I thanked him just as my phone buzzed. It was Alessio. I'd told Alessio not to call unless it was urgent.

"I'm sorry, I might need to take this," I said.

Marco motioned for me to go ahead. I stood and excused myself to the hall, painfully aware that any number of the people I was currently robbing could be listening to my call.

"It's done," Alessio said.

I glanced at my watch, shocked they'd already finished. That was impressive. "Alright, thanks."

"Should we head on to the shipyard or…"

"Yep."

"You still with the father-in-law?"

"Yes."

Alessio laughed until I disconnected.

I thanked Marco again, bid goodbye to Martina, then left.

Giada

*A*ll my tension over Father John and my brother's crazy schemes began to melt away the moment my best friend rushed through the door. She embraced me like it had been years, rather than weeks, since we'd seen each other. I supposed that since we'd grown so accustomed to seeing each other multiple times a day during college, multiple weeks was essentially an eternity.

"God, I am starving," she groaned, twisting the top off the bottle of white wine she'd brought.

I quit searching for the corkscrew and instead handed her two glasses. "Fancy," I teased, eying the cap warily.

"Convenient," she corrected, pouring a healthy portion into both of our glasses. She poised her glass in the air for a toast. "To long lost friends," she said, clinking her glass against mine.

"Salute," I said, mostly out of habit from Luca. "Although I wasn't exactly lost. I was in Italy."

"With no specific timeline for your return," she reminded me. "Where is Luca tonight?"

"Working."

"That sucks. It's a Saturday night. He should be out partying with his hot girlfriend."

It took me a moment to realize she meant me and wasn't implying that he was out with another woman.

Gabby tugged on the refrigerator door and peered in. "Wow. You weren't kidding. There's literally nothing edible in here."

I peered over her shoulder. There were some condiments, plenty of beverages, and a jar of olives. I wondered what Thomas had done with all the other foods in Luca's old fridge when he moved this stuff over. I reached for the olives, checked the expiration date, and opened the jar while she moved on to the freezer.

"Ooh, fancy vodka," she said, retrieving the bottle. "That'll teach him to ditch you on date night."

I giggled, but Luca wouldn't care if we drank his vodka. I checked my phone to see how long we had until the food would be delivered.

"Umm…" Gabriella turned to face me, a wad of cash in her hand. "Don't tell me he doesn't trust banks either."

I cringed. Probably shouldn't have let my bestie rummage through the freezer. "Oh my God, Gabby. Put that back. The food will be here any second."

She complied, and as if on cue, the doorbell rang. "Who keeps money in the freezer anyway?" she asked while I went to the door.

I didn't answer. Luckily, the enticing aromas of the food distracted both of us. We opened all the containers and sprawled them on the bar, then tucked into pad Thai, chicken curry, coconut shrimp, and chicken satay. We ate until we were both stuffed, but it barely looked like we made a dent in the food.

"Hmm, guess I wasn't that hungry after all," Gabby mused.

I stood and stretched. "I'll stick it all in the fridge. Luca might be hungry when he gets home."

"And when will that be?"

"I don't know. Late?" I crammed everything into the fridge then spread it out so the shelf didn't look so pathetically empty. "He suggested you sleep over, so if you do dip into the vodka…"

Gabby giggled. I brought the bottle of wine to the couch and divided the rest of the pale yellow liquid into our glasses before snuggling against a pillow.

"So tell me about Italy? What was the highlight?"

Instantly, each of the times we'd made love in secret some-where inside Luca's club flashed through my mind, playing like a deliciously erotic highlight reel. I felt my cheeks blushing. "I stayed with my brother. There wasn't anything too thrilling."

She eyed me skeptically.

"Well, Luca proposed," I said slowly.

Gabriella nearly tackled me reaching for my hand. When she did, she held it up then quickly dropped it, eyebrow raised.

"I said no."

Her jaw dropped. It looked as though she started to say something multiple times, but stopped herself. Finally, she just shook her head. "But you're still together? Living in his apartment?"

"I haven't officially moved all my stuff in here yet, just..." I stopped talking before I said too much. "We're still together, though. It's going well, actually. I mean, for the most part. We went to church together earlier, and—"

"Why did you say no if it's going so well?" she interrupted.

"I didn't like his proposal."

She stared blankly at me for a moment and then burst into laughter. "Really?"

I nodded.

"And he was okay with that? Luca doesn't strike me as the type of guy whose ego could survive that kind of rejection."

I shrugged. "It caused a little fight. But we made up. Twice."

She rolled her eyes. "Of course you did. But you can't just stay with the guy because he's good in bed. You need to be with someone who makes you happy outside of the bedroom, too."

"He does," I assured her. "The timing just wasn't right. Things have been so crazy with us lately."

"It's always been crazy with you two," she said, shaking her head. "Honestly, when you first came back to school that fall and said you guys were together, I wasn't surprised at all. But then, not too long after, it almost seemed like you were scared of him. The way you used to borrow my phone to call Adrian...that never sat right with me."

I didn't reply because, well, what could I say? She was right. I'd learned Luca was a ruthless mafioso and decided he was using me to appease his father, so of course, I was scared. But then I realized he wasn't as cruel as he seemed and that he did love me.

"I was shocked when you left him for Adrian, though. But

then, I mean, when you went back to Luca…I was even more shocked. You seemed so relieved to have gotten away from him once, so why go back?"

I suspected it was a rhetorical question, but I answered anyway. "Because I loved him. And I wasn't ever relieved to be away from Luca. I didn't need to get away from Luca. I just…well, it's always been so intense between us, like it gets so hot that we might burn up if we aren't careful."

She eyed me skeptically. "He convinced you he died at one point. That isn't normal. You cried yourself to sleep for weeks."

I chewed the inside of my lip. That one was harder to explain. "That was his father's doing, and it was complicated. But Luca didn't do that to hurt me. We weren't even together at the time. I was with Adrian. And if none of that had happened, I might not have realized that Luca is the one I can't live without."

"So you'll say yes the next time he proposes?"

"If there is a next time. Like you said, I don't think his ego can take more rejection."

She laughed. We talked late into the night, starting on a second bottle of wine, and reminiscing about all sorts of trouble we'd caused freshman year of college. When Gabby finally left, I was relaxed, happy, and exhausted.

I fell asleep quickly, but awoke suddenly, some time later. The bedroom was dark, and the bed beside me was empty. I was about to go back to sleep when I heard a noise.

I froze, terrified, then decided it wasn't the sort of sounds a burglar would make. Rubbing my eyes, I crept out of the bedroom, exhaling with relief when I saw Luca. He was in the kitchen, shoving bites of the leftovers into his mouth with a fork. His back was to me, but he'd always had an acute sense when someone was nearby. He turned abruptly and smiled.

"Hey, baby. Did I wake you? Sorry. There was a half-empty bottle of wine on the shelf on the fridge door. It clanked when I opened the fridge." He cast a glance at the second bottle, which was empty on the counter.

"Gabby came over," I said.

Luca crammed another bite into his mouth and then walked closer, rubbing my arms to warm me while he chewed. "Did you have fun?"

I nodded, then glanced at the clock. It was four am. Yikes. "How was your night?"

He hesitated. "Fine."

"Anything I should know about?"

"No."

"Is Father John…"

"Everything went well. Go back to bed, Giada. I'll be there in a few. I just need to shower."

Still sleepy, I obeyed.

~

Luca

$\mathcal{E}$verything had gone so smoothly at the church Saturday evening that I was nervous. Nothing ever went off without a hitch. It had to be a bad omen. And yet, as I soaked up the praise from my papà and divvied up amongst my guys the fifteen percent of the total stash that we weren't returning to Marco, I didn't see any potential problems.

Alessio and the guys had covered the security cameras and snuck into the church undetected. They'd cleaned out the entire load of heroine, and they'd gotten out of there without anyone seeing anything. Everything had been done, and perfectly.

Except, of course, I still had to talk with Marco. And after how awkward I'd been the day before, I wasn't looking forward to the discussion. Besides, a lot more was riding on my ability to stay cool today. Not that Giada wasn't an important topic, but I could've married her regardless of what her dad said. If I fucked up today, there would be serious consequences.

Marco was at his office at the shipyard, which seemed odd since it was Sunday, but I preferred to meet him there, anyway. I'd specified on the phone that I wanted to meet alone but did confess it was a business matter. Thomas rode with me to the shipyard, then stayed in the car.

Marco was waiting when I arrived. Stefano, Marco's cousin and one of his closest partners, was with him.

"Drink?" Marco held up a bottle of bourbon.

When I didn't answer immediately, he continued. "I feel like we should have a drink if you're about to ask me for a favor the day after you claimed your love for my daughter was wholly independent of business matters."

I nodded in acceptance of the drink, my best sheepish look on my face. "I agree my timing…isn't ideal. I don't need a favor, though."

Marco handed me a glass, kept one for himself, then raised his. "Salute," he mumbled. Then he turned to Stefano. "You can go."

"I think I screwed up," I blurted out the moment we were alone in the office.

Marco lowered himself to his chair, eyebrow raised.

"I, uh, well, my guys took something, and um, I think it might belong to you," I began. "I wasn't there, so I didn't realize till after, or obviously, we would've backed off."

"What makes you think it was mine?"

"One of my guys overheard some of Angelo's guys, um, Georgio and Federico, talking. That's how they initially learned about it. My guys didn't know who they were right away, but when I went to church with Giada, Federico was with Angelo, and my friend Alessio mentioned he thought it might be the same guy." I paused. "I told them to wait, but that message got lost, and they decided to go ahead with it anyway."

I sighed. "Had I been involved, this never would've happened. I've talked to my guys already, and—"

"You're blaming your guys for the mistake?" he asked.

"No. I should've personally been there. I should've looked into it more before giving them the go ahead to take the drugs. It's just, well, we heard that someone new was bringing drugs into town, and I knew my papà wouldn't approve of just letting that go on—"

"Drugs," Marco interrupted. "What drugs?"

I frowned, feigning confusion at his question. "The heroin," I said, as though I was certain he already knew about it. "The big stash you'd been storing in the basement of the church."

Marco's eye contact was impeccable. Every fiber of my being desperately yearned to look away, but that was the wrong move. Instead, I just stared back at him, no longer even having to feign the sheepish expression.

After an eternity, he leaned back in his chair. "I don't have anything to do with heroin."

My lips parted slowly. "Uh, well, that was what I'd always thought too. But I figured you must have started, since—"

He shook his head. "I appreciate you coming to me, but your intel is mistaken. Those aren't my drugs."

I was tempted to look relieved at this point, but I had to make sure he understood. So, I furrowed my eyebrows and leaned forward. "I don't mean to overstep, but I… I looked into it more after my guys mentioned seeing Georgio and Federico. One of my other men—a newer guy, obviously, he said he overheard Angelo's name. It was clear they were reporting to Angelo, so if he wasn't doing it for you…"

"You're telling me my son is orchestrating some big heroin trade behind my back?"

I shrugged. "I'm just telling you what I heard. I'm not trying to get anybody in trouble, I just figured I should come clean and get the stuff back to you if it's yours. I don't want to step on any toes, not with family. Not when you and me and Angelo might be sharing Thanksgiving dinners for the rest of our lives."

"I don't know what your game is here, Marino, but you and I won't be sitting around any holiday tables together if you're trying to pull me into some elaborate scheme."

"I'm not trying to do anything like that." I raised my hands defensively. "I'm sorry. Just look into it all, okay? If it's not yours, forget I ever said anything. If it is, let me know when and where, and I'll return it."

Marco continued glaring. I stood and let myself out, dodging the stares of the various Conti associates filling the entry to the warehouse.

CHAPTER 14

Adrian

The day before I was to fly back to campus, my phone began buzzing seconds after I rolled off of Claudia. I wasn't going to check the message immediately, being too much of a gentleman for that, but Claudia grabbed it and handed it to me, casually glancing at it long enough to read the message.

"Who's Giada?" she asked, right as a second message came through.

Both texts were from Angelo. "FYI Giada back in town," was the first message. "Luca too," was all he'd written in the next. I dropped my phone on the nightstand and turned back to Claudia.

"Ex-girlfriend," I said.

She quirked a brow. "Is she hot?"

I hesitated, acutely aware of the impropriety of discussing one woman's assets moments after being inside another. But Claudia and I weren't even in a relationship, and she had the kind of confidence I'd never before seen in a woman.

"Yeah," I said, scowling.

"Do you have a picture?"

I hated to admit that I did, but I quickly located one on my phone. "Why so curious?" I asked, reaching for the glass of water on the nightstand after handing her my phone.

"Just seeing if I'd like to invite her to join us sometime," Claudia replied.

I choked on the water, spewing it halfway across the room. "What?"

"You're right. She is super hot. Think she'd be down for a threesome?" Claudia's mischievous grin told me she realized she'd caught me off guard.

"No. Nor would I be interested. Besides, she lives in Connecticut."

Claudia smiled and pinched my cheek like a grandma. "So that's a maybe then?"

I smacked her ass, then rolled over to get dressed. I was going to miss casual sex when I returned to campus. And now that Giada was back in town, I was going to need a distraction, too.

On my way back to my parents' place, I called Father Ryan at the church. I planned to simply pretend the purpose of my call was to thank him again for meeting with me before Christmas, but of course, I hoped he'd inadvertently share some intel on Giada. I had a feeling I was running out of time to turn her against Luca.

When I called, though, the receptionist answered and asked if it was an emergency. I cringed to think of what might constitute a church emergency.

"No, it's not an emergency," I replied. "Is everything was okay on your end?"

"Uhh, it's just a little...chaotic here. Father John went missing, so if it isn't an urgent matter, it would probably be better if—"

"Missing? Oh my God." I cringed at my terminology, but the frazzled woman didn't comment. "I'm so sorry. I'll um, pray for him." I hung up and immediately dialed Angelo. There was no way it was a coincidence that a priest went missing right as Luca returned.

~

Giada

When my father called to say he was in the neighborhood and wanted to stop by, I was surprised. It was completely unexpected. The entire time I'd been away at college, my father never dropped by. Come to think of it, I didn't recall whether he ever even saw my apartment senior year. It struck me as even stranger when he confirmed that Luca wasn't home.

Of course, I said he was welcome. Then I began to worry about the reasons behind his visit. My father would never hurt me, but the unexplained visit did make me think of Luca's warnings about my family.

The doorbell rang before I could panic much, though. I opened the door, surprised to see he was alone.

"That was fast," I said.

"I was in the neighborhood," he claimed.

Liar.

"You can come in," I said, realizing he hadn't stepped out of the hallway.

"Luca won't mind me dropping by?"

"He's not here," I reminded him. "Do you want a drink or something?"

"I can't stay long," he said, pacing awkwardly. He appeared to be looking for something, or perhaps just snooping. Luckily, there wasn't anything out. We hadn't been back in town long enough to trash the place, and Luca wasn't one to leave incriminating evidence in the living room.

"Let's sit," I said, motioning to the couch. Reluctantly, he followed.

"Did Luca tell you he came to see me?" he asked.

"When?"

"Saturday. He said you were with that friend of yours."

"Gabriella," I supplied, even though he'd met her no fewer than twenty times.

He nodded.

"What did Luca want?"

"He wanted my blessing to propose to you."

I didn't have to fake my surprise at that. It made no sense. Had he asked my dad every time he'd proposed? If not, why now? I didn't know what to say.

"You didn't know about that?"

I shook my head. "What did you say?"

He frowned.

I felt the color drain from my face. "You gave him your blessing, right?"

"Do you want to marry him?"

"Yes."

"You think he'll make you happy?"

"Yes." I sighed. "What is all this about anyway? You've always loved Luca. You should be thrilled that I actually want to marry the man you've forced on me since birth."

He scowled as if to suggest I were exaggerating. "How well do you know him?"

Now I scowled. "I've known him since we were kids. I'd say pretty well."

"And you trust him?"

This was exasperating. "Of course I do. Why would I want to marry him if I didn't trust him?"

My dad shrugged. Then there was silence.

"Did something happen? I don't understand why you have all these questions all of a sudden."

He shook his head dismissively but then leaned closer. "How much does he share with you about his work?"

My stomach tightened, but I was determined to stay casual. "I don't know. He talks about it some. His family does a lot of exporting, or importing," I began, uncertain which was correct anyway. "I guess I've never been super interested in business stuff. It's not like he's hiding anything, though. And he's definitely making enough money to support me if that's what you're worried about."

My dad's expression was completely unreadable. As I always did when faced with an awkward silence, I kept talking.

"Are you talking about the clubs?" I supposed how I could see a father being concerned that his potential son-in-law owned and operated not one but three gentlemen's clubs across various continents. "He told me about those, and it's fine. It's just business."

My dad stared at me for another minute, then nodded. "Okay then."

I frowned. *Okay then?* That was it?

"Why don't you come home with me? Your mom would love to see you, and it seems…improper for you to be sleeping here before you're even engaged."

"It sounds like I might be engaged soon," I replied in lieu of reminding him that he'd practically forced me to live with Luca in the not-so-distant past.

My father didn't budge.

"I have an interview tomorrow. I need to stay close to the city tonight."

"An interview? For what?"

"A job. Well, an internship technically. At a design firm."

"Design?"

"Yes, you do know that was what I studied in school, right?"

"Yes," he spoke slowly, which made me suspect he actually hadn't known my major. "But you just finished telling me Luca could support you fine. Why do you need a job? Does Luca know about this interview?"

"He doesn't, in fact. I didn't want to jinx it by getting excited too soon." That was true, but also, I'd sort of forgotten about the interview. Between all of the drama with Angelo and my concern about Fathers Ryan and John, I hadn't thought much about it.

My dad shook his head. "I should let you get back to your evening. Good luck on your interview."

"Thanks." I was still scratching my head as he left.

~

Luca

$\mathcal{I}$ had just settled in at my desk at the club late Monday afternoon when Giovanni informed me that Marco Conti was at the bar waiting to speak to me.

"Send him back," I said, my tone conveying my annoyance at the fact that they'd even delayed.

"He might be armed," Giovanni said. "Do you want me to search him?"

"No! Of course, he's armed. He's Marco Conti. He's also about to be my father-in-law. I'd rather not make him wait."

A moment later, Marco reached my office.

"Mr. Conti, so good to see you again," I began, extending my hand.

He brushed it away and sat. "I'm on a tight schedule today, so let's skip the preliminaries."

I nodded and sat.

"I looked into what you said, and you were right. Angelo was involved with that shipment," he said.

I feigned shock.

"In light of the situation, I'd appreciate your discretion."

"Several of my guys already know," I paused for believability.

"I wasn't happy when I learned they might have taken something of yours, and I let them know."

"That's fine. I meant that I'd rather they not know Angelo was acting outside of my direct knowledge." He paused. "I'm dealing with him separately."

I searched my desk for a scrap of paper and quickly jotted down the location of the heroin. "We can deliver it somewhere for you if you prefer, or you can send someone to get it here." I paused, another idea coming to me. "Or I can have my guys distribute it and give the proceeds to you. But they'd need a cut for doing the work."

He shook his head. "Angelo got himself into this. He can figure out how to offload it." He blew out a sigh then leaned forward. "I asked Giada if she trusted you. She said yes, so I'm going to as well. But if this is some game…"

"It's not, Mr. Conti. I'm busy enough without added…dealings in my day."

Marco seemed to accept this as the truth. It felt as though our business was concluded, the conversation done, but he didn't move. The knowledge that he must have something else to say was unsettling.

"A man can only serve one boss," he said finally. "Are you familiar with that expression?"

"I am, and I agree. But with respect to my papà, he won't always be the boss, and I don't anticipate doing business the exact way he has. And in the meantime, I can obey his commands and still respect yours. There's no conflict here." I licked my lips, which had run dry now that I was actually spouting the truth. "Giada means everything to me. I will do everything in my power to preserve her family name without breaking loyalty to my own."

Marco appeared to consider this, then slowly stood. "I'm headed out of town for the weekend. Angelo will be in touch. I'm sure he'll want to pick up the goods himself," he said, waving the scrap of paper in his hands.

Then he surprised me by leaning forward and offering me a small, half hug.

~

Giada

I spent two hours choosing an outfit for my interview, only to realize on the way there that I had no idea what to expect. I'd never interviewed for anything before. I'd never worked before. I'd bolstered my resume with details of design projects I'd completed for class, but the hard truth was that I was completely inexperienced and not even the star student. I was average, or a little better. When I'd initially sent over my resume and cover letter, they hadn't responded, so I called. I kept calling until they agreed to meet with me. If anything would get me the job, it would be my persistence.

I now regretted not telling Luca about the interview. He may not have approved of me working, but he could've shared brilliant tips with me. Luca could talk anyone into anything, and that was the exact skill I needed today.

I reminded myself that I had nothing to lose and, therefore, no reason to be nervous. I didn't need them; I was offering them a wonderful service. And they'd be lucky to have me.

I took a deep breath, then marched into the office, my biggest smile plastered to my face. As expected, the lobby was stunning. Light poured in through massive windows, and the crisp, cream-colored modern furnishings appeared to glow. An oversized rug that resembled the fur of a ginormous polar bear sprawled across the middle of the room. It didn't feel right to tromp across his back, so I walked around it to reach the desk.

"Hi, I'm Giada Conti," I began, smiling sweetly at the receptionist. She had long blonde hair, gorgeous earrings, and a funky pattern on her nails that made me suspect we'd become fast friends…if I even got the job.

"Ms. Conti?" a voice behind me called. "I'm Audra."

We met in the middle of the room, squarely atop the dead bear, to shake hands. She motioned for me to join her in the conference room—an all-glass room in the middle of the office with a table fit for twelve.

"It's a pleasure to meet you, Ms. Conti, but as I said on the phone, we aren't hiring right now. I'm happy to hold on to your resume."

"Please, call me Giada," I began, channeling my inner charm. "And I'm not looking for a job. I only sent the resume so you'd know I'm not completely insane. What I'm looking for is an opportunity to continue my education in interior design. The university offered me excellent professors and several opportunities to work on real-life projects, but if I ever want to reach my full potential as a designer, I'll need experience working with the absolute best design firm."

Audra nodded, seeming somewhat receptive to my idea, so I continued, feeling empowered.

"What I'm offering your firm isn't just dedicated intern services for free, but also a unique design perspective. You see, my family is Italian. My boyfriend is *really* Italian. We travel there frequently. When we are abroad, he works, and I shop. Not for accessories and jewelry, though Italian handbags absolutely can't be beat. I like window shopping for home furnishings. Italy has dozens of mom-and-pop style shops with amazing handcrafted home furnishings and accent pieces. These stores don't have websites, and they don't offer the sort of items you could find anyplace else. I'm offering you the risk-free opportunity to provide your customers with authentic, custom pieces that no other design firm can obtain."

Audra took her time answering. "You're proposing you just shop for us?"

I nodded. "If you shared details about ongoing projects with me—confidentially, of course, I could look for items that might suit that client. If I find something, I'll send you photos and pricing details. If you want it, I'll buy it. You'll pay the cost of the item and any shipping or duties, but my services are free."

She still looked skeptical.

"You have nothing to lose by giving me a chance. If you don't like what I'm finding, we can part ways, no hard feelings. If you do, I'd love to someday expand my duties. I adore design. It's my passion. And I'd be so grateful for the opportunity to learn from the best."

Audra sipped her coffee, then asked me a few design questions. She didn't give any indication of her decision, claiming she'd have to talk it over with her partners, but she did offer me a tour of the office. Obviously, that was a great sign.

I practically skipped all the way back to the apartment.

~

Luca

At eight o'clock, I made my way to the bar to tell Alessio I was heading out. He was staring at some spreadsheets, which amused me to no end.

"Is this where you concentrate best?" I teased. The club wasn't busy yet, but the music was loud and there was a bustle of activity around him.

He shrugged. "Just checking the numbers." He handed the stack of papers to the bartender then frowned, something behind me catching his eye. I followed his gaze and immediately spotted Angelo.

"Well, that was fast," I said to Alessio. I quickly made my way over to Angelo.

"Two Conti men in one day grace the halls of my club. I am honored," I said, offering my hand.

He glared. "Can we talk in private?"

"You look angry. Are you going to shoot me?"

"I should," he mumbled.

Alessio followed as I led Angelo to my office, closing the door once the three of us were inside.

"He can go," Angelo said.

"He won't be any trouble," I replied.

"No habla ingles," Alessio added.

Angelo's glare deepened, and he flipped his middle finger at Alessio. Apparently, he didn't appreciate being mocked. Although, in Alessio's defense, it was easy to assume Angelo's understanding of Italian was as weak as his sister's, even though that wasn't the case. She probably wouldn't know the difference between Spanish and Italian.

"I'll wait," Angelo said.

I nodded for Alessio to leave us.

Once he did, I turned to Angelo. "I assume you're here to make arrangements for... transporting?"

Angelo leaned forward. "My father seems content to believe you're dumb enough to not realize what you're doing, but I'm not. You knew exactly whose shit you were stealing, and you did it anyway."

I stared, unwavering. "Okay. That's a lot of work, just to give it all back. Or most of it, anyway."

Angelo's eyes darkened, his brows dipping even lower. When Angelo was that angry, I couldn't see the resemblance to Giada at all. That was probably a good thing.

"What's your game plan here, Marino? Are you just trying to make yourself look like a hero so my dad will sell my sister to you?"

"Some of us don't have to try to look good. This isn't a

competition, Angelo. I've got my own papà to satisfy, so I'm content to let you focus on yours."

Angelo shook his head slowly. "He wants us to get along. He told me to invite you to a dinner at his house. Bring your paisano, and my sister."

"Isn't your father out of town?"

"Yes, so is my mom. He wants to see if we can survive a casual family dinner without any violence. Friday night free?"

It probably wasn't, but for the Contis, I could rearrange everything else. "I'll clear my schedule." I paused then stood. "I'm busy, so if that's all…you can talk with Alessio about when you want to pick up your stuff."

"I'm not leaving until you told me who tipped you off. Was it that big-mouthed priest?"

"No. I don't even know which priest is which, and no one tipped me off to anything."

"Convenient that he went missing right when you returned to the country. Does Giada know you're out murdering priests?"

My stomach clenched. I supposed Father John was safer if Angelo thought he was dead, but I hadn't intended that to be his assumption. I tried to play it cool. "I don't know what you're talking about Angelo. Like I said, I didn't know you were involved. I assumed you shared your father's stance on the drug industry."

"So it was Giada who blabbed," he concluded.

"You're getting paranoid, Angelo. As I told your father, I would never intentionally steal from Marco Conti. You and I are on the same team here, amico."

"That's fine. You don't have to talk. She will." He stood as if I'd let him leave on that note.

"Angelo!" I stopped him before he reached the door. "I assume you're kidding, that you won't ever get your sister involved in any of this. But if you ever touch Giada, guiro su Dio—I swear to

God—I will make you regret ever being born. Do you understand me?"

Angelo smiled, his grin creepier than a Cheshire cat. "Sure. La Principessa is off limits."

It took all of my self-control not to hit him. How this pretentious asshole was related to sweet creatures like Giada and Matteo blew my mind.

"I'll send some guys to pick up my stuff in two hours. Does that work for you?" he asked, opening the door.

I glanced past him to Alessio, who was standing guard at the door. He nodded.

"Yeah. Have a good night. I'll see you Friday."

"Angelo?" I paused and walked around my desk to make sure he was listening before continuing. "Right now, you and I are just fine. We have the resources, and if we team up, we'll be unstoppable. But if you want to be my enemy, if you want to fuck with me, take your best shot. I'll fight fair."

Angelo tipped his head in acknowledgment, then strolled out of my office. He paused by one of the dancers and glanced back at me.

"Sporco maiale," I mumbled. *Dirty pig.* Still, I needed to make an effort, and Brittany, the girl he was eying, could certainly handle herself just fine with him.

"Brittany, could you take care of my soon-to-be brother-in-law here?" I asked, handing her a rolled-up bill so she understood I'd be paying.

She raised an eyebrow but nodded, leading him down the hallway.

CHAPTER 15

Giada

The entire week was nuts. Luca met with my brother and my father multiple times. He told me everything was resolved, and that he'd agreed to meet my brothers for a casual family dinner that weekend. Apparently, he and Angelo were trying to make amends, though I didn't see why the rest of us needed to suffer through an awkward meal just so those two could learn to play nice. Luca suggested I bring Gabriella, and he invited Alessio, so I supposed the extra people might help soften the tension of the meal.

Father John had left the church. And, he wasn't headed to Uganda for the mission trip, but rather to Ohio, which seemed an odd choice. Still, I was relieved he was safe, even if I had to lie about it all. The official story was that he went missing. Luca assured me Father John was safest under that lie, but it seemed that no one but Luca, me, and Father Ryan knew the truth. My heart ached for the rest of the church family who still worried about Father John.

Amidst all of that chaos, I barely had time to talk with Luca that week. I'd received some amazing news, but decided to wait until the dinner to share my job news with Luca. Hopefully, having something to discuss that was unrelated to either the Conti or Marino family business would help everyone get along.

Although Gabby had to head out right after dinner, we all rode to my house together. She and I relaxed in the back seat of the SUV, while Luca and Alessio were in the front, chatting amicably in Italian as we drove.

"Can you understand what they're saying?" I asked her quietly. Though we'd met in first year Italian, Gabriella had gone on to minor in the language while I'd nearly flunked out a semester later.

She made a face. "No. Something about a head I think."

Laughter arose from the front seat. "Testa di cazzo," Alessio repeated, then translated, "dick head."

"I didn't realize you spoke Italian," Luca said, his tone almost accusatory.

"Clearly, I don't anymore," Gabby replied.

Alessio swiveled around to face us. "If you ever want a private lesson, I'm free," he said, winking at my friend.

"Hard pass," she said, prompting another chuckle from Luca and Alessio. I cringed at the thought of my friend with Alessio, although I supposed if she dated him, they wouldn't worry so much about keeping secrets from her.

When we arrived at the house, it felt…weird. It was my home. I'd lived here since birth, and technically, it was still my address. But now, I felt like a guest. I marched up to the front of the house and turned the knob, but the door was locked. Luckily, we didn't have to wait long.

"Matteo!" I exclaimed. "I didn't know you were back!"

He smiled warmly and hugged me tightly. He greeted Gabriella with the same warmth, confirming my suspicions that he still had a crush on her. Then he shook hands with both Alessio and Luca. Heading inside, I introduced Gabby to Angelo's stupid girlfriend Julia, then we both met her friend, Shanna. I couldn't wait to be alone with Gabby long enough to mock those two later.

Luca realized I wasn't a fan of Julia's, but somehow he'd forgotten his obligation as my boyfriend to share my sentiments about people my brother dated. While I caught up with Matteo, Luca cozied up to Julia. I was starting to get distracted by my annoyance when I realized he was getting me a drink. Apparently, he was not completely inattentive after all.

Except then, he brought the drink to Julia.

I clenched my teeth together so hard that my jaw hurt. Gabby apparently noticed and jumped in to rescue me.

"Let's get some drinks," she said.

"Actually, the food is ready," Julia announced.

I rolled my eyes and dragged Gabby off to the kitchen. I wasn't about to let that tramp tell me when dinner was served in *my* house. Who did she think she was?

As we rounded the corner into the butler's pantry, I smacked into a man.

"Enzo!" I pounced, hugging him much longer than necessary. His presence was always comforting, plus maybe I wanted to make Luca jealous.

"Hey Giada, how are you?"

"Good. Are you joining us?"

"I thought I would. Is that okay?"

"Yes!"

He eyed Gabby and me warily. "Did you guys need something?"

"Shots," I said.

We brushed past him to the bar. He stood watch behind us as we downed two shots apiece before pouring ourselves a glass of wine. As I started to follow Gabby back to the dining room, Enzo stopped me.

"Everything okay?" he asked.

"Yep."

He blinked. Clearly, I wasn't so convincing.

"Luca's been flirting with Julia since we got here."

Enzo gazed past me to where I assumed my boyfriend was still with the witch. "He's probably only using her to annoy Angelo," he said.

I turned around. Angelo was now happily chatting up Gabby.

"She would be quite the step down from you, Princess," he assured me.

"Don't call me that," I said. Suddenly, for no logical reason, I felt like I was about to cry. I missed Enzo, missed this house, missed the time when I believed Father John was just as perfect as every other priest. I even missed the days before my eldest brother and I hated each other. Life was so much simpler then.

Now it felt like the only thing I could count on was Luca showering me with affection nonstop. Except today, well, that wasn't happening.

"Giada," Enzo said quietly now, his expression softening as he reached to smooth my hair down. "Please don't cry."

"I just don't know what's wrong with me," I said, leaning against him.

He wrapped his arms around me as I relaxed against his chest. I wished—not for the first time—that Enzo was my big brother. He was good for me in all the ways Angelo wasn't. I was about to pull away to head to the table when Enzo tensed suddenly.

I let go and turned, coming face to face with Luca. He was glaring at Enzo.

"Am I interrupting? Just wanted to tell you dinner was served," he said, without glancing away from Enzo.

"Yes," I said. "We'll join you all in a minute."

Luca's nostrils flared at my audacity. I turned back to Enzo in time to see his eyes widen. I supposed it was nice to see I could still surprise the men in my life.

"It's rude to keep our host waiting," Luca said, grabbing my hand and jerking me away.

I lunged for my wine, nearly spilling it as I tried to keep pace with him.

Luca and I were seated beside each other at the table, and Gabby was across from me. That annoyed me, but since Enzo was also across the table, I decided I could just look at him and further piss off Luca. Julia was off to Luca's other side, with Angelo at the head of the table by her and Matteo at the other head. I wondered if it was Angelo or Julia who decided to stick Alessio on my other side rather than Gabby. Either way, I'd be sure to get my revenge somehow.

A rush of warm breath fell against my cheek, startling me from my thoughts. "Are you alright?" Luca whispered. To his credit, he truly looked concerned. He dropped his right hand beneath the table, squeezing my hand then resting his hand on my thigh. I nodded. Maybe I could give him the benefit of the doubt tonight. He was already stressing about this meal going smoothly.

His hand inched slowly up my thigh, darting under the hem of my skirt. I looked up from my wine, questioning how far he was going to take this game. Then I saw that Luca was no longer looking at me, but at Enzo. *Great.*

I swatted his hand off of me. "I think you made your point, Luca," I said loudly. As if Enzo could ever forget that I belonged to Luca.

Angelo raised an eyebrow.

We were all distracted for a few minutes as we passed the food, and once the table fell silent again, I decided it was time.

"I have some news," I said, pausing for emphasis and waiting until everyone was looking. Gabby looked excited, and I assumed she probably had guessed the news. Enzo looked pallid, so I suspected he probably feared I was pregnant. I didn't dare look at Luca to see whatever disapproval he held.

"I am the newest intern for Sash and Lowens Interior Design Firm!" Just to clarify, I added, "I got the job."

I grinned, assuming everyone would take the hint and congratulate me, but when I dared turn to Luca, I wouldn't describe his expression as excited.

"You did what?" he asked.

"They offered me the job, and I accepted," I said, staring pointedly. It wasn't exactly a hard concept to grasp.

"Congratulations," Matteo said. Everyone else—except Luca and Angelo—chimed in with similar sentiments.

"Thank you guys. I'm really excited, so it feels good to share my happy news with you all," I turned to Luca again, hoping he would take the hint and at least pretend to be happy for me.

"You didn't think we should at least talk about this first?" he said. "You just got a job without even mentioning it to me?"

So many responses floated through my head. I mean, I'd barely seen him that week. I assumed he'd be happy for me and support me. I was an adult, and it was my decision. Besides, he was already stressed enough about the crap with my family. But instead of saying any of that, I simply reached for my wine and drained it in one single sip.

Gabriella caught my eye and offered a sympathetic smile, then refilled my glass.

"I think we should have a toast to Giada," she said, raising her glass. "May you find happiness and satisfaction in your new employment adventure. The design firm is lucky to have you on their team."

I blew her a kiss, touched by the sweet toast, then we all clinked glasses.

Luca was staring at me when I turned to him. He actually had the nerve to look disappointed. Well, too bad. *I* was disappointed in *him*, too.

Luckily, the conversation moved on. I supposed everyone was

getting along well, but I was still too annoyed with Luca to fully participate in the discussion.

~

Luca

$\mathcal{I}$ rubbed my forehead and prayed we could just get through dessert without anyone stabbing anyone else. Nothing had gone according to plan, and I couldn't even pinpoint where we'd gone wrong. The evening had started off well, with me casually chatting with Julia while Alessio distracted Angelo. Going forward, I'd never glean any useful information from Angelo, so I was determined to be friendly with his girlfriend in hopes of learning more from her.

But before we'd even started the meal, Giada had gone off the rails. I wasn't sure if Angelo had said something to upset her, or if she just didn't understand why it was important for me to talk with Julia, but she seemed determined to make me jealous. And while I could handle a night of jealousy, what I didn't need was for her to make me look like a total patsy in front of her brother.

She'd started the meal by flirting with Lorenzo, then surprised us all with the news of her employment. I hadn't had to feign my shock, as she hadn't bothered to mention a damn thing about the job offer to me. It took me several minutes to regain my concentration after that revelation. Finally, we were almost done with the meal, and nothing too damaging had been done at least. Angelo and I could still tell Marco that we were perfectly capable of getting along for a few hours.

I couldn't wait to be alone with Giada so we could talk. She'd been pissed at me since we got here, and I didn't even know why. Then Enzo had clearly said something to upset her, and then with the job announcement…we just had a lot to catch up on.

"Did you all hear Father John went missing? I bet they fired him." Angelo said suddenly, wiggling his eyebrows like it was salacious news.

Julia's eyes widened.

"I'm sure he wasn't fired," Giada said. "If anything, he switched parishes. Priests do that all the time."

I slipped my hand under the table, searching for her hand. When I realized it wasn't there, I squeezed her thigh, gently, just to remind her not to overstep. Angelo didn't know she had any idea why Father John actually left. It was critical he continue to believe the man was missing.

"That's just what Father Ryan said because he has the hots for you," Angelo replied.

"Angelo!" Matteo was the one to scold him, which I appreciated.

Under the table, I tapped Giada's leg, silently praying she'd get the message and let it go.

She didn't.

"You're an asshole," Giada told him.

"Giada…" I began.

She ignored me. "He doesn't have the hots for me. Father Ryan is a good man. He would never betray his oath to God for me or any other woman."

"Or man?" Angelo added.

Giada's middle finger shot up.

"Anyway, I heard Father John was caught with an altar boy. Kind of a cliché, but—"

Giada leaned as if about to lunge out of her chair, but I pressed her legs down against her seat. "How dare you!" she yelled at her brother. "Why are you so disrespectful?"

Angelo laughed. "Me—disrespectful? You're the one swearing and flipping off your brother at the dinner table. You're the one ignoring your fiancé and running off and getting a job without even telling him. Talk about disrespect."

"He's not my fiancé," she quickly retorted. "And that's not

even the point. Father John dedicated his life to serving God. He doesn't deserve to have his name dragged through the mud by someone like you. You know exactly why he left, and it sure wasn't because of some altar boy."

I felt like the air had been punched out of me. I dug my nail into Giada's thigh, hoping she'd realize the significance of what she'd just said and finally shut up before she created any more problems. Thankfully, she did, and she kept talking before Angelo could interrupt again.

"He's given twenty years to that congregation. It's time for us to share his wisdom and passion for the lord with another parish, and it wouldn't hurt for them to bring some new perspective into our parish either," she said, shaking her head.

I exhaled with relief, and judging by Alessio's expression, he was doing the same. Quickly, I tried to come up with a new topic to discuss.

"Who do you even think you are? You can't just manipulate people like little pawns," she continued.

Okay, we'd definitely crossed a line. I clenched my hand around Giada's thigh under the table while straining to keep my facial expression calm.

"Giada, can I have a word with you down the hall?" I asked, my voice clipped.

She brushed my fingers off her leg. "Nope, I'm good." Her hand wrapped around the delicate stem of her wineglass, but before she raised it to her lips, I carefully pried it from her hand.

"It's important," I said, making eye contact with her.

Her posture made it clear she had no intention of moving. *Fuck.* Of course, she picked tonight to be stubborn.

I blew out a sigh and smiled politely at the rest of the table. "Pardon us," I said. Then I stood, reaching for Giada's hand. "Come on," I said, hoping she couldn't misinterpret my tone or the look in my eyes.

When she didn't initially budge, Alessio shifted in his seat, but

I stopped him in his tracks with a quick shake of my head. It definitely wouldn't help things for Angelo to see that it took two of us to keep his sister in line. I squeezed her hand—hard—and pulled her out of her seat, using my foot to nudge the chair out of the way. Once she was on her feet, I planted my hand on her back and guided her out of the room.

I led her up the stairs, not loosening my grip enough for her to part ways with me. At this point, I was confident she wouldn't be returning to the dinner party, so she might as well go straight to her room. When we reached the top of the stairs, she shook free of my grip and scowled at me.

"Fuck you," she spit.

I pushed her into her room and shut the door behind us. "What is wrong with you?"

She had the gull to look annoyed. "Wrong with me? You're the one who just dragged me out of my own dinner party like some testosterone-laden junkyard dog."

"I asked you politely to come with me. You're the one who decided to make a fucking scene."

Giada plopped onto her bed and crossed her arms over her chest like a petulant child.

"The whole point of that dinner was to keep things casual and friendly and to show your brother I could control you."

"Excuse me?"

I rolled my eyes. "Jesus, Giada. You know what I mean. He needs to know that you're not a wildcard as long as you're with me. And I was hoping this dinner would show him we could be on the same team."

"Well, I don't want to be on his team if it means sitting around and kissing his ass." She paused, then added. "For the record, I don't want to be on your team, either."

"Yeah, well, after that performance, it might not be an issue."

Her posture relaxed a little. "You can't just boss me around. I'm not one of your crew."

"That's for sure. If one of my guys behaved the way you do, they'd be lucky not to end up in a fucking ditch." I shook my head. "You're not even supposed to know half the shit you know. When you're around your brother, you need to remember that."

"I just mentioned Father John. I didn't say anything top secret. Besides, he started it."

"You crossed a line, and it's unacceptable. It can't happen again."

"Or what, you'll ground me? I'm not a child."

"Then stop acting like one!"

She flipped me the middle finger, so I started to the door. Obviously, the conversation was getting nowhere.

"Stay up here until everyone is gone. I'll tell them you had too much to drink and needed to lay down. Everyone should believe that, given your behavior."

"Gabby isn't going to just sit there and eat with you after the way you dragged me out of the room."

"I think she will," I said. "Now, stay here."

Giada's middle finger shot up again, but she settled back onto the bed.

I took a moment to straighten my suit jacket before returning downstairs. I was relieved to find conversation had resumed, but of course, every eye was on me as I sat.

"Where's Giada?" Gabriella asked, the anger pouring out of her eyes.

"Laying down," I said, placing my napkin back onto my lap. "She had a bit too much to drink."

"I'll go check on her," she said, scooting her chair back.

"She asked that we leave her alone."

"I won't bother her. I'll just bring her some water."

"She doesn't want you up there. I already gave her some water."

Gabby and I glared at each other for a full minute before Matteo changed the topic to the recent earthquake in Sicily.

~

Giada

I'd grown bored with the stack of fashion magazines I'd been leafing through and turned to my phone for entertainment when there was a soft knock at the door. If he was knocking rather than barging in, that meant Luca was here to apologize.

"Come in," I called, briefly regretting not having changed into something sexier. It would've been fun to tease him with more provocative views of the body he wouldn't be touching tonight, thanks to his jerky behavior.

When I saw who stepped through the door, I was relieved I'd kept my dinner clothes on.

"Hey," Gabby said, approaching slowly. "You ok? I don't want to disturb you, but I'm heading out in a few minutes."

"It's fine. Come in."

She came and sat on the edge of the bed, facing me. "Luca said you weren't feeling well."

I rolled my eyes. "I didn't drink that much."

Gabby nodded, seeming to agree with that statement. Then she eyed me suspiciously. "So you're okay?"

"I'm fine, just annoyed."

Her cheeks flushed, and she looked away briefly before speaking again. "Did Luca hurt you? You can tell me if he did."

I cursed in my head at my own failure to see this coming. "No, he's not like that. And it's Angelo I'm mad at. I just don't want to look at him again tonight."

"Luca practically dragged you away from the table. You said no, and…it didn't seem like he takes no for an answer."

"He doesn't," I agreed. Then I stopped, having forgotten what I was trying to prove. "I mean, he's pushy with everyone. Not just me. But he would never make me do anything I don't want to do, and he would never hurt me. Promise."

My friend nodded but looked completely unconvinced.

"He needs to tone down that whole dominant alpha male thing, I agree. And he was being a total dick tonight. He was just stressed about…stuff, and he thought I was about to stab Angelo," I said.

"Look, I know this might be overstepping, but I'm worried about you. I don't like the way he talks to you or how he controls."

"He's trying to cinch some business deal with Angelo, that's all."

Gabby hesitated before saying the next part. "You didn't act this way with Adrian. You're a completely different person with Luca…"

She stopped abruptly as the door swung open.

"I thought I asked you to let her rest," Luca said to my friend.

"I wasn't resting, and we were in the middle of a conversation," I said.

His expression softened as he turned to me. "Yeah, well, it's late. I wanted to talk with you."

I stared back until Luca sighed, clearly not wanting to discuss anything in front of Gabby. "Matteo said he'd take you home if you don't want to pay for a ride," he told her.

She caught my eye. I frowned.

"I'll go talk to him," she said. Then she left the room without another glance at Luca.

"You know she thinks you're beating me," I told him.

He shrugged like that wasn't the worst thing.

"Seriously? You don't care?"

"I don't have time to focus on what your friend thinks of me. I have real problems to solve. Like how to get you back into your family's good graces when you keep acting like a wild horse."

I wasn't sure I understood his analogy, but he continued anyway.

"Besides, Gabriella is getting to be a problem anyway. I don't think you should keep seeing her so often."

I felt my jaw drop. "You must be joking."

"No." He sat on the bed beside me. "She has questions, and now that you know the answers, you can't put yourself in the position where she'll start asking."

"That makes no sense."

"You can't tell her what I do for a living, what your family does, or half the things that go on during the day. She already knows too much." He paused and shook his head. "Giada, if the cops brought her in for questioning...I mean, the things she could tell them."

"Are you high?" I asked. "I mean, you don't have to pick a new fight with me. I'm already pissed at you for flirting with Julia, acting like a jealous monster when I was talking to Enzo, not—"

"Flirting with Julia? Eww. Why would I flirt with her? She's an idiot."

"Agreed, but you were all over her from the moment we came in. You completely ignored me."

"I need to be on good terms with Julia. She's our best chance of getting insider info about Angelo's whereabouts and goings on. Besides, you were talking with Matteo, and I didn't have a choice. She accosted me. I can't exactly blow her off when I'm trying to get in Angelo's good graces."

I supposed I could've let my hatred of Julia cloud my observations about what I had seen. But still, Luca wasn't entirely off the hook. "Well, I wasn't throwing myself at Enzo. We were talking."

"You were embracing like long lost-lovers reuniting."

I quirked an eyebrow. Luca sat beside me.

"Giada, I trust that you're not going to cheat on me, but you have a history with Lorenzo. And I see how he looks at you."

"Enzo thinks of me as a little sister."

Luca laughed. "Not even a little. Look, I'll admit I can't control my jealousy when it comes to you and him if you admit you are completely oblivious to what men think of you."

I shook my head. We weren't going to see eye to eye about Enzo, and besides, we had bigger issues to resolve.

"Why didn't you tell me about the job?" he asked, his eyes searching mine as if the answer were written on my face. He actually looked…hurt.

"I did. You didn't seem very excited."

"I mean earlier. You never even told me about the interview. I tell you so much that I'm not supposed to, and you don't even think to mention you're looking for jobs? I have to hear about it along with a roomful of people you don't even like?"

Perhaps I'd misunderstood his reaction to that, too.

"You're not mad that I got a job?"

He shook his head. "Of course not. I encouraged you to find something you'd love. Remember? I would've loved to celebrate your news with you, just the two of us. Stupidly, I assumed I was important enough to hear big news in your life before everyone else."

I wrinkled my nose, hating how badly I'd messed up. "You know, the next time your feelings are hurt, you could just tell me instead of acting like a controlling nineteen-fifties husband."

"Noted."

"I'm sorry I lost my temper with Angelo. He's just such a colossal jerk. And he knows exactly what buttons to push."

"You have to ignore him. Don't let him get the reaction he wants."

"That's hard."

Luca tilted forward until our foreheads pressed together.

"Tonight didn't go the way I imagined," I said.

Luca snorted, then pushed away from the bed.

"Hey, where are you going? You're not leaving without me?"

"You seemed like you could use a break from me. Besides, Alessio and I have work to do."

"You guys always have work to do. It could wait. What can't wait is the makeup sex."

"Alessio and I didn't fight though. We always get along," he said, grinning.

I let him distract me with a quick kiss.

"Wait, so Matteo is taking me and Gabby both home?"

"No, just Gabby. You are home."

I chewed my lip. If he considered this my home still, that meant he didn't want me living with him. *Ouch.*

"You're going to leave me alone with Angelo?"

"Angelo and Julia already left. But Matteo will be here all night. So will Enzo."

"Wow. You really plan to leave me."

He took his time answering. "I'm not leaving you. I just think it would be good for you to have a few days with your family."

"A few days?" My voice came out a tad more desperate than I'd intended.

Luca chuckled. "For someone who looked like she wanted to stab me an hour ago, you sure are being dramatic."

"I just don't like being apart from you for so long."

"Then why haven't you actually moved in with me? You're sleeping in the apartment but haven't arranged for any of your other stuff to be moved. Maybe you could work on that tomorrow, and then when you come back to the apartment, it'll truly be *our* home."

I smiled. "I'd love that."

Luca kissed me again, this time a long, languid kiss. He gently cupped my cheek in his hand as he pulled away. "I shouldn't keep your brother waiting. Can you please tell Gabby you're okay so she'll let Matteo drive her home?"

I nodded, then remembered the other thing I needed to tell him. "I start work Monday."

He winced. "Like full time?"

"No. I'm just going in to look at the client files and stuff. After that, I'll just work whenever I want."

"Sounds like a good gig."

"They're not paying me anything."

"Tesoro, I'm not sure you get how this whole job thing works," he teased.

I swatted at him. "Send my friend back in, please."

He nodded, kissed me again, then left.

Gabby took her time before returning. "Okay, what is going on?"

"I'm staying here tonight, but Luca asked me to pack so I can move in with him!"

She frowned. "Did you tell him to go fuck himself?"

"No. It was all a misunderstanding. Things are good now. Promise." I glanced down at my phone, where a GIF from Luca showing a closet bulging with clothes appeared on the screen. I giggled. "But he thinks I should stay here over the weekend and kind of catch up with my brothers or whatever."

She made a face like she'd just drank rotted milk. "Giada, I think he's cheating on you."

I shook my head at the preposterous notion. "He isn't."

"Look at the signs, Gia. He's out late at night, he's hot and cold with you, he gets these phone calls, and then all of a sudden his plans change. He dumps you at your parents' house for the weekend… There is no other explanation. Luca is having an affair."

"He's not," I repeated.

"You told me he was seeing his ex back in Italy."

I cringed, having forgotten I'd told her that. "He saw her; he didn't date her," I clarified. "Look Gabby, I get why you have concerns, but trust me. Luca isn't cheating on me."

She shook her head. "Call me tomorrow morning?"

I nodded.

CHAPTER 16

Giada

After Luca left, I locked my door, took a long bath, then went to bed. I was surprised at how well I slept without Luca by my side, but I supposed the familiarity of my old bed couldn't be beat. I was starving in the morning, and desperately needed coffee, so I trudged into my closet, threw a sweatshirt over my pajamas, and went downstairs.

As soon as I reached the bottom of the stairs, I remembered one of the downsides of living at home—I was never alone.

Sure, with Luca, there was always a chance Alessio would stop by, but other than that, we were pretty much left to ourselves. At my family home, there was always a crowd. I contemplated sneaking back up the stairs to put on real clothes and maybe some makeup, but the need for coffee was too strong.

I poked my head around the corner and saw my aunts Bianca and Jess. Matteo and my cousin Vinny were seated at the table. Past them, in the family room, my uncles Stefano and Vincenzo were watching television.

"Giada!" Aunt Jess exclaimed, pulling me to her for a hug.

Aunt Bianca grabbed me next, so I was already a little disoriented by the time I reached the table.

"I missed you, too," I said, blinking the sleep away.

Matteo chuckled. "Would you cry if I said we drank all the coffee?"

I stuck out my tongue and padded over to the coffee maker, which was actively brewing a fresh pot. "Thank you," I mumbled. I poured a cup quickly then stuck the pot back to finish percolating. I added flavored creamer, stirred, and already felt a bit perkier by the time I inhaled the vanilla aroma.

"So what's this I hear about a job?" Vinny asked.

I motioned for him to wait, needing to enjoy a full sip before addressing any kind of serious questions. Once the coffee hit my stomach, I topped off my cup then joined the guys at the table. I caught everyone up on all my gossip, focusing primarily on the new job and moving in with Luca, then grabbed a second cup of coffee and headed upstairs.

Having no actual plans for the day, I changed into workout clothes. I returned downstairs determined to talk Matteo into driving me to the gym. We had a decent gym at the house, but I felt like being social.

On my way downstairs, though, I literally bumped into Enzo.

"That's the second time in twenty-four hours that you've slammed into me," he said. "Way to make a guy feel invisible."

"Sorry. I was looking for Matteo."

"He went out."

"Out? Hmm. That's not vague or anything."

He made a face. "Did you need something?"

"A ride to the gym."

"Alright. You ready now?"

"I was going to grab a granola bar first. I need something to soak up all the coffee."

"I could use a workout. I'll change while you eat."

That worked for me. I texted Luca while I nibbled on some

dry cereal, then remembered my promise to call Gabby. I texted her promising to call after the gym.

When Enzo reappeared, I grabbed a bottle of water and went out to his car with him.

"So dinner last night sucked," I said as we fastened our belts.

He laughed.

"Why wasn't Sara there?" I asked, wondering if her absence meant they'd broken up.

"I try not to get her involved with work stuff."

"Work stuff," I repeated. He seemed so much like family, and he was apparently living at the house now, so it seemed odd to get a reminder that he was, in fact, an employee of my father. "But things are still going well with you guys?"

He took his time answering. "I don't know. Maybe?" He adjusted the rearview mirror before turning. "I like her. I just can't picture how it'll work out long term."

I supposed that made sense. "Luca asked me to move in with him," I said after a long pause.

"You said no?" Enzo seemed surprised.

"Of course not. I'll move next week."

"Hmm."

"Hmm?" I turned to face him. "What does that mean? Do you think it's a bad idea for me to move in with him?"

"I didn't say anything."

"Enzo, you know I'm not going to drop it until you tell me."

He breathed a laugh. "I just got the impression you two weren't getting along so well last night."

"Yeah, I could see that." I tried to think of how to explain it. "It was a bunch of misunderstandings. I thought he was mad that I got a job, but he was just hurt that I didn't tell him sooner. I thought he was flirting with Julia. He thought I was flirting with you."

"Were you?" Enzo grinned and cast a sideways glance.

"As if." I paused. "Anyway, he also thinks I should be more...I don't know, docile, I guess, around Angelo."

"You should."

"If Angelo wants me to treat him with respect, he's going to have to earn it."

"He's sort of exempt from that rule, Giada. People respect him because of who he is and what he can do if they don't."

I rolled my eyes. "Yeah, well, if he's exempt, then so am I."

Enzo shook his head, and we were quiet for a moment.

I was the one who broke the silence, blurting out, "Gabriella thinks Luca is cheating on me."

"He isn't," Enzo said dryly.

"You said that last time," I reminded him. I didn't have to say that he was wrong that time. Of course, the circumstances were different back then. Luca was different. Knowing what I did about the way the mafia operated now though, I also understood that Enzo wouldn't necessarily know if Luca was or not, and even if he did, he might not tell me.

"Do you think he is?" he asked.

"No."

"Well, your instincts were right before, so they're likely right now. Plus you're a lot wiser than you were then. I think you'd know, but honestly, I'd be shocked if he was."

"Me too. I can't explain why, but I do trust him now. But how do I convince Gabby?"

"You don't. What does it matter what she thinks he's doing?"

"She's my friend."

He shrugged.

I rolled my eyes. "Luca would prefer I not be friends with Gabriella much longer anyway," I said, eying him to see how he responded. I wasn't sure if he'd openly call Luca out for his behavior, but I assumed he'd agree with me. Apparently, I was wrong.

"That's understandable," he said calmly.

"Umm say what?"

He glanced at me then back to the road. "You and Gabriella have gotten close. You can't honestly think that'll work out long term. I'm sure you guys could stay friends, but…"

"Geez, I get that Luca doesn't need a bunch of strangers poking into his business and everything, but I'm allowed to have friends. I want a normal life."

"If you wanted a normal life, you should've picked Adrian."

I tried to picture whether Luca's mom had any close friends, but I didn't know her too well. My mom, on the other hand, did. "My mom has two super close friends."

"Who?" he asked.

"Alessa and Jess."

"Okay, and who are their husbands?"

I didn't answer the rhetorical question. They were both associates of my father. "So you think Luca's issue isn't with me having friends but having friends whose husbands aren't… working for him?"

"Yes. Or maybe working for your father. I mean, I think he'd feel comfortable if you and…Julia, for example, were to hit it off." He grinned proudly to show he was aware the concept was nauseating. "Hey, you could get Gabby to go out with Matteo, then you could stay friends."

He did have a crush on her. "Maybe she'd go out with Alessio," I mused.

"She's not his type."

I supposed his type was probably any bimbo with a low IQ and even lower self-esteem. "He's a good-looking guy. She might agree to give him a try." For all his faults, Alessio was attractive.

Enzo chuckled. "Yeah, I don't see that working out."

"Hmm, you're probably right." I gazed out my window, and then the idea came to me. "I know. I'll become best friends with Sara. If you like her, she must be normal." I paused and turned to him. "She's not like Julia, right?"

Enzo made a face. "No, nothing like her."

"Perfect! When are you guys free for a double date?"

"With you and Luca? Never."

"What? Why not?"

He steered into a parking spot, killed the ignition, then turned to grimace at me. "Can you think of anything more awkward? Luca and I don't exactly get along."

"Oh please, you could both behave for one night. Besides, you both like me, and obviously Sara will like me. I'm a likable person."

He shook his head, chuckling, as we climbed out of the car. "You are, but zero chance she's becoming your new best buddy. No offense, but I don't need her mixed up in Luca's shit."

I sighed.

~

Adrian

*B*ack on campus, life felt like business as usual. Classes, work, studying, and long romantic walks with…my dog. After the holiday fling with Claudia, I wasn't interested in dating for a while. She had satisfied the only legit needs I had in that department, and now I was ready to focus on school. Well, and my other mission— bringing down Luca.

I'd made zero progress finding anything out about the missing priest from Giada's hometown church. The church wasn't offering any explanation, but also no longer referred to him as missing. Now, they simply said that he was no longer with the parish and that the bishop would be selecting a new priest soon. There was nothing about him in the news, either. I even tried searching the internet and came up empty-handed. His old phone number had been disconnected, and his old home was owned by the church and now clearly vacant.

I was out of options, so I called Angelo.

He answered in an alarmingly chipper voice. "Well, hello there. To what do I owe the pleasure?"

I cleared my throat, assuming he thought someone else was calling. "It's Adrian," I said. "Adrian Patras."

Angelo's laugh reminded me of a barking dog. "Yeah, I know. What's up?"

"Look, I was just wondering if you'd heard anything about that priest that went missing, Father John?"

"What about him?"

"Well, that's the church your family attends. Giada brought me there a few times. Don't you think it's suspicious that a priest just disappeared?"

"I have a few theories," he said after a pause.

I doubted he'd share any of those theories with me. "Do any of them have to do with Luca?"

"I'm listening," he said, completely sidestepping my question.

"Giada had mentioned he was poking around the church some. And it seemed like he'd been going to mass with her more often lately. I just wonder if he has anything to do with the father going missing."

Angelo was quiet for long enough that I started to relax. Clearly, I was on to something. But then he continued.

"Luca has been spending more time at the church because he embezzles for a living. He just had a big heroin deal, and when that all went down, Father John disappeared. He could be running from the law or from Luca, could be dead, I don't know. Not my problem."

I shuddered at the casual tone with which he spoke about a member of the clergy. How could anyone have such callous disregard for a human being? But then I thought more about what he'd said. "Angelo, isn't Luca still involved with your sister?"

"Yep. They're moving in together. My father apparently gave

them his blessing to get married. Guess that ship has sailed for you."

"I don't want to be with your sister," I repeated, for what felt like the hundredth time. "But you can't seriously be okay with her marrying a murderer. Or a drug dealer!"

Angelo sighed loudly into the phone. "I'd prefer Luca be out of her life, but as long as my father thinks their relationship is good for business, my hands are tied. If it's any consolation, though, he won't hurt her. Just because someone doesn't like when a grown man stumbles into the middle of their drug deal doesn't mean he's a wife beater."

There was so much wrong with his sentence, but before I could point that out, he disconnected. *Whatever*. Still, I'd learned something new about Luca and the priest, and Angelo's statement made me realize something else. The Contis already knew about Luca's criminal undertakings and didn't care. If I wanted to show Giada—or any of the Contis—that Luca was a bad man, I needed to focus on his potential as a husband. And the best indicator of that was his past performance as a boyfriend.

Luca

By Saturday night, everything was calm in my world. Or rather, it was active, but in a good way. We'd gotten the rest of Angelo's drugs back to him without incident, we'd taken a cut, which my guys loved, and both Marco and my own papà were uncharacteristically pleased and indebted to me. Life was good.

My papà had brought in a couple of new guys back when I was presumed dead by the rest of the world, and Alessio and I had finally finished vetting them and officially pulling them into our own inner circle. It seemed like a good night to celebrate. We locked up the office, grabbed the best seats in the house, and enjoyed the club from the customer's point of view.

Normally, I tried not to waste much time watching the dancers. I only spent time on the floor if there was a problem. The entertainment aspect of the club was a distraction, and besides, it was uncomfortable to watch ladies undress when I had to sign their paychecks the next day. But tonight, I didn't care. I wanted the new guys to see me unwind, to know that there were, in fact, perks to this lifestyle. So I let myself pretend I was just another one of the guys, maybe even just another customer.

"Aw shit," Alessio said, shooting me a panicked stare.

Following his eyes, I gazed over my shoulder while nudging the girl off my lap. For a moment, I was relieved when I saw the cause of Alessio's curse, having thought someone was coming to hurt us. But then, I realized I was more terrified of the woman approaching me than any would-be attacker.

"Giada," I began, keeping my voice casual as I stood. From the look in her eyes, there was no chance she hadn't seen the nearly nude woman sprawled over me. Still, I hoped I could at least keep her calm.

Or not.

She lunged at me, the slap resounding through the air before I even registered the contact.

Shit.

If it were just Alessio and me, I'd let it go. Hell, even Thomas and Giovanni knew how Giada got and understood the way things were with us. But the new guys, the ones who weren't even captains yet, no. They couldn't see my girl hit me and get away with it.

"Fuck you!" she sputtered, swiveling away right as I grabbed her arm.

"Excuse me, gentlemen," I said calmly, guiding Giada out of the room.

"You need help?" Jordan, one of the new guys, offered.

I noticed Alessio biting back a laugh.

"No," I said. "I can handle my girlfriend just fine on my own."

I rolled my eyes as I loosened my grip on Giada, praying she didn't attack me again before we made it outside. I led her towards my car, then stopped at the passenger door.

"Get in."

"I'm not going anywhere with you."

"Giada," I began in a sharp tone, then stopped myself. What

was I doing? We didn't have an audience now, and she was right to be pissed.

I nudged her backwards then stepped closer so she was trapped between the car and my torso. I reached for her chin and tilted it upwards, catching a glimpse of the tears in her eyes before she swatted my hand away.

I blew out a sigh. "I'm sorry," I said, placing my hand on her arm, this time in a gentle, comforting way.

She didn't answer, but it was obvious from the tension in her muscles that she was still upset.

"Nothing happened," I continued. "The guys and I were just messing around. It never would've progressed beyond that, even if you hadn't shown up."

"Why should I even believe you? You're a narcissist, and you'd say anything to get me back on your good side."

I cringed, certain she was quoting Adrian. Although, as far as I understood the word, she was probably right.

"You shouldn't believe me," I said, adding, "But you do, because you know I'd never lie to you."

She frowned. "Why is that?"

Her question surprised me. There was a time when nearly everything I said to her was a lie, when my entire existence was a carefully crafted character from a play written solely to trick her into compliance with my ulterior motives. I'd wanted her in my life, and I followed the script to ensure she stayed by my side.

But somewhere along the way, I'd realized I *could* tell her the truth. For me, that revelation had changed everything. Now I didn't just want her in my life, I needed her there.

Giada was the only person I could be completely honest with. She'd seen the worst, and she hadn't left. And now, she was practically my savior. Anytime I was riddled with guilt, I had only to confess my misdeeds to her, and I felt better. I felt clean.

"Because you forgive me," I said, nearly having forgotten that she'd asked me a question. "Even when I don't deserve it, you forgive me. So there's no reason for me to lie to you."

I tried to make eye contact, but she gazed to her shoes. So I followed suit, pressing my forehead against hers. I breathed in the spicy scent of her jasmine lotion and exhaled with relief.

When she still didn't speak after a minute, I began explaining. "We were celebrating. Nothing big, just hanging out. There are some new guys, and they've passed their training, so to speak, so we wanted to show them a good time." I winced, remembering how Jordan's question insinuated I wasn't in control of my girl.

Giada looked up in time to catch my expression. "What?"

I sighed. "It's hard to maintain my authority with the new guys when you come storming in swearing at me and hit me."

"Then you shouldn't accept lap dances from hookers."

"I only did that because they were all watching me," I said, opting not to point out the nuanced distinction between a stripper and a prostitute.

Giada turned to the side. I quickly directed her chin back towards me.

"Hey, look at me," I said. "I mean it. I don't want her. I'm not even attracted to her."

Giada remained unconvinced.

"It's your hair I love," I said, kissing the top of her head. "It's your eyes I love," I continued, kissing her eyelids. "Your nose. And your lips." When I reached her lips, she kissed me back briefly, then pulled back.

"You smell like beer."

It was whiskey, but that wasn't the point. I had a pack of mints in my pocket and popped one into my mouth before continuing.

"I didn't enjoy watching her dance."

"You sure looked like you did," she said. "I saw you."

"I was having fun. Not because of the girl. I would've much rather had you on my lap. Although, not with all those people around." I shuddered, thinking back to the time in the cabin when Giada had offered me a brief striptease and lap dance.

"You're the one I want," I said, stepping closer so she could feel the evidence of my desire against her lower abdomen. I reached down and ran my hands up her legs, stopping at her hips and squeezing them. "It's your legs I want wrapped around me, your hips that belong by mine."

She giggled as my hand grazed higher along her ticklish side. I tilted my head and kissed her neck as she squirmed.

As Giada stiffened suddenly, I realized we had an audience. The whole crew was outside watching us, but only Alessio had walked close.

"We're heading out." He phrased it like a statement, but he paused at the end, eyebrow raised, waiting for permission.

I nodded, then tugged Giada's keys free from her pocket where I'd felt them during my exploration a moment before.

"She'll ride with me. Can you take her car back to the apartment?"

As soon as the words left my mouth, I cringed, half expecting her to protest and make me look even worse in front of the guys. But luckily, she didn't. Instead, she pressed her head against my shirt.

Alessio nodded and winked, then took off.

Giada was uncharacteristically quiet as we drove back to the apartment, but she reached her typical level of vocality as I worked my magic in the bedroom. After, though, she immediately stood and reached for her shirt and bra.

"You're still mad," I said, tugging her bra out of her hands while stating the obvious. "How many more times do I need to make you come before you forgive me?"

From the look she shot me, I almost thought she was considering my offer for a moment. But then she simply rolled her eyes and slipped into her shirt without the bra.

"You're not even sorry," she said, sitting on the edge of the bed to gather the rest of her clothes.

"I am. I said I was sorry."

"You're only sorry you got caught."

I hesitated, and she noticed. *Cazzo.* "No, that's not it. I'm sorry that it bothered you. Honestly, I don't see what the big deal is with me being at a strip club, but I didn't mean to upset you."

She rolled her eyes dramatically.

"It's just a way to bond with the guys," I continued. "It's not sexual. I told you, I don't want any of those girls. I just… I don't know. Tits are tits."

Her eyes widened with horror. Clearly I'd just dug myself into an even bigger hole. Distracted by my ever-worsening standing with my girl, I loosened my grip on her bra, and she stole it back.

"I can't even believe you just said that," she said, removing her shirt to put the bra on.

Seeing Giada's beautiful, perky breasts, their creamy slopes rounding to tips that pebbled before my eyes, I couldn't believe I'd just said that either. I lunged for her, wrapping my arms tightly around her and capturing one of those perfect tits in my mouth.

Giada swatted at me, her hits increasing in firmness until I regretfully released her. This time, she turned away to finish dressing.

"It's disrespectful," she said after a lengthy pause. "Even if I know you're not interested in those other girls, the fact that you have to go out to a club like that to get your kicks checking out other women, well how do you think that makes me look to all your friends?"

I tried to see what she was saying, but it didn't fully make sense. "My friends have all seen you. No one would choose ogling strippers over you."

She turned to face me now that she was dressed. "How would you feel if I was at a club and some guy was all over me?"

My stomach tensed even at the thought of it. "That's different."

"You know it's not." She sighed and scrolled down her phone. "If you're truly sorry, then don't do it again."

"Don't do what?" I knew from experience that I needed to understand exactly what I was agreeing to before making a commitment.

"Don't get lap dances from women who aren't me," she said.

I could agree to that, but then she continued.

"Don't watch other women strip when you're out with your friends."

"You want me to wear blinders when I'm in the club? Maybe I could walk with one of those canes to help me find my way around."

She lowered her eyes so her dark lashes nearly covered her rich brown irises. "Don't go to strip clubs then."

"That's not fair."

"How do you figure? You'd never let me go to see men strip."

"I own two clubs with dancers. I can't boycott my own businesses."

Giada appeared unswayed. I followed her into the living room as she searched for something.

"You *could* do a lot of things. You just choose not to," she said, right as she located her car keys.

I silently cursed Alessio for so promptly returning her car. "Where are you going? It's late."

"Home."

"This is home."

She shook her head.

"Giada, come on, you can't seriously be mad enough about this to leave. Just go to bed, and we can talk in the morning."

She paused and sighed. "You've always said how tiring it was, doing everything you could as a child and even now to try to earn your father's approval. And there's nothing you wouldn't do to guarantee your reputation with the guys. But you tell me I'm the most important person in the world to you, and yet you make it clear you don't care at all how I think of you."

"I do, too. I just don't see how—"

"Good night, Luca," she said curtly, seeing herself to the door.

I rolled my eyes, but followed her out, wearing only the thin pair of sweatpants I'd pulled on when she made it clear we weren't returning to bed. I watched as she climbed into her car, then pulled out of the parking space.

I missed the days when Giada didn't drive herself. Life was so much easier then. I texted Matteo that she was on her way to the house, then walked back inside, cringing at the thought of everything I might have stepped in with my bare feet.

~

Giada

My body was on the verge of convulsing with tears, but once I started, I'd never pull it together by the time I got home. I didn't need any more men in my life thinking I was emotional and immature. So instead of crying, I blasted music and sang along as I drove.

I shivered as I replayed the last hour in my mind. Why had I slept with him? The moment I'd let Luca touch me—with those same hands he'd slid all over that slut at the club—I'd basically convinced him he was forgiven. I couldn't blame him for being confused after, when I was still upset at his behavior. What kind of woman had sex with the man she's pissed at?

Me, apparently.

And I'd done it for the dumbest reason. After seeing him with that girl on his lap, I just had to know that he still wanted me. Hearing him say he did in the parking lot helped. It really did. But then by the time we'd gotten home, somehow I'd started to think it was a ruse. Maybe I was too boring for him, too classy, too conservative or something. Maybe what he wanted was a girl who'd do anything with her body for the right price. Maybe he wanted that Chiara girl back in Italy.

My reasoning was flawed, though. Even if that was what he wanted, of course he wouldn't have turned down the opportunity to have me also. The fact that Luca eagerly had sex with me meant nothing about his feelings for me, it only made me feel even more pathetic now as I realized I was no better than that stripper. Hell, I was worse, actually. At least she got paid for using her body that way.

I pressed harder onto the accelerator and cranked up the radio. Luca thought I was being ridiculous. I could see it on his face. He used to look at me like that often, like I was some immature, unreasonable child with no awareness of what the real world was like for him and every other male in my life. But I wasn't naïve, and I wasn't oblivious, at least not anymore. I saw what their world was, but I also saw options they didn't seem willing to acknowledge.

If Luca needed to own a strip club—or two—so be it. But that didn't mean he needed to celebrate with a lap dance. I felt fairly certain that his own father would've conducted himself at work the exact same way decades ago, and now he was a philandering jerk. I wasn't sure he even tried to hide his girlfriends from his wife anymore. That was not how my life would be. I was going to conduct myself with dignity, and I would demand respect from Luca.

As I rounded the corner, bright flashing lights blinded me, and sirens began to wail. I gazed at the speedometer then up to the rearview mirror.

"Shit!"

My hands were shaking as I slammed on the brakes and then steered to the shoulder. I'd never been pulled over before, but I'd seen enough movies to know the general procedure.

I bit my lip, certain my father or Angelo or maybe even Luca would halt my driving for good once they found out I'd been pulled over. Thinking about them made me remember the gun in my glove compartment box. My registration was probably in the same spot.

I gazed up again, confirming I still had time before the cop reached me. He was just now exiting his vehicle, so I leaned over and rummaged through the glove box, shoving the gun to the back and pulling out the envelope I suspected contained the registration. Just as I shut it, there was a knock on the window.

"Hands where I can see them," the officer said through the glass.

I opened the window, raising my other hand.

"Were you hiding something?" he asked, the suspicion apparent in his eyes.

I shook my head. "I was looking for my registration." I reached to the passenger seat and held up the envelope.

The officer shone a bright flashlight into the car, checking out the back seat and the floor behind me before settling it uncomfortably close to my face. It wasn't directly in my eyes, but it was close enough that I winced and struggled to see anything.

"Have you been drinking?"

I hesitated, trying to recall the truth. "No."

He lowered the light. "Do you know why I pulled you over?"

"If I was speeding, I'm really sorry. I just had a terrible fight with my boyfriend, and I wanted to get home."

"Do you know how fast you were going?"

I shook my head, although I had an idea.

"I clocked you at eighty in a fifty-five. That's serious stuff."

"I'm really sorry," I repeated. "I didn't mean to speed, and it was just for a minute. I was distracted by everything my boyfriend said, and I didn't..." I paused, and a new wave of panic washed over me. "Oh god he's going to be so pissed that I got pulled over."

"License and registration," he said calmly, clearly uncon-cerned with my romantic life. He shone his flashlight on my purse as I retrieved my wallet and then rummaged around for my license. I supposed he was trying to be helpful, but it felt like a huge invasion of privacy for this strange man to see inside my purse. Luckily, I located my license quickly and handed it to him. Then I pulled out the registration from the envelope. I glanced at it before handing it to the officer, not surprised that the car was registered to my father and not to me.

I watched the expression on his face change as he read the information I'd handed him. He looked up again, less certain now, then sighed.

"Is this your dad, Marco Conti?" he asked, pointing to my registration.

I nodded.

"And this is your current address?"

I squinted to see the tiny numbers then nodded. "Well, I mean that's my parents' house. I sort of live there, but sort of live with my boyfriend."

"His name is….?"

"Luca Marino," I said, uncertain of the relevance of that.

The officer frowned. "Don't move. I'll be right back," he said, walking back to his car with my license and registration.

I chewed my lip nervously while I waited. I toyed with texting someone for help, but who? Luca or my father would probably just forbid me from driving ever again. Enzo would surely help me out, but then he'd still have to tell my father, and I'd be screwed anyway.

The officer returned before I'd made a solid decision anyway. He handed my cards back to me through the window.

"I'm letting you go with a warning tonight, Ms. Conti. Please drive more carefully in the future."

I thanked him but remained parked on the side of the road until after he'd left. I glanced down at the additional paper he'd handed me when he returned my information to discover he'd issued a formal written warning. Oddly enough, though, it listed my speed as 65mph, not the 80 he'd claimed.

When I reached home, the house seemed quiet as I flipped on the light to the hall by the garage. I looked up, and jumped.

Enzo was waiting for me just inside the garage door.

"Shit. You scared me."

He shrugged apologetically. "Matteo told me you were headed home, and I should make sure you arrived safely."

"Matteo?"

"He's not home."

"How did he know I was…" I began, then I shook my head. "Luca," I answered my own question. Heaven forbid he just trust me, an adult, to safely drive myself home.

Enzo remained expressionless.

"Well, I'm home. So you can return to your previously scheduled activities."

He chuckled. "Too late for that. I'm staying the night here anyway."

I shucked off my shoes then went to the kitchen. "You are my favorite drinking buddy," I teased, checking which wines were open before selecting a sauvignon blanc. I offered Enzo a glass, which he accepted, but he reached for a bottle of pinot noir for himself.

"Just one glass, then I'm going to sleep," he said. "Long day tomorrow."

I raised an eyebrow but he shook his head. Apparently knowing what he had planned was above my clearance level. *Whatever.*

"You want to tell me what the fight was about?" he asked once we were settled in the living room.

"What makes you think we fought? Did he tell Matteo that too?"

"No, but you're here. So I figure he must have done something."

"He did, but I'd rather not get into it. You'd take his side anyway."

"Not necessarily."

I sipped my wine, swirling the cool, tart liquid in my mouth for a moment before swallowing. "I went to meet him at his club, and he was in the middle of a lap dance."

"Oh."

"Yes. All his friends were there, so it was completely mortifying having everyone know we're together, but that he still needs lap dances from some random girl."

"It's not like that," he said.

"See? I told you you'd take his side."

"I'm not taking sides. I'm trying to make you feel better. Everyone knows how Luca feels about you."

"Yeah, because he treats me like a possession. I am his. So why can't he be mine?"

"He is."

Enzo of all people didn't need to be reminded how Luca would've responded if the tables had been turned and it had been me with another man in that club. But the fact that he still thought it was different drove me crazy.

"I'm sure it meant nothing to him and that it never even occurred to him that it would bother you."

I rolled my eyes but changed the subject. "If I tell you something, can you keep it secret?"

"From Luca?"

"From everyone."

"Depends on the secret."

I sighed. At least he was honest. "I was pulled over for speeding tonight."

Enzo sat upright. "Jesus, Giada. Seriously? How fast were you going? Did you get a ticket?"

I pulled the warning out of my pocket and handed it to him. "I got this warning. The funny thing is that the officer said I was going eighty."

"Was that before he saw who you were?"

I nodded.

He shrugged and handed back the warning. "You're lucky you were close to home. If you'd been further away where the cops don't know your family, you'd have gotten a ticket."

That didn't make sense. From my understanding of the world, my father was a criminal. If the police couldn't catch him doing the big stuff, it seems like they'd at least want to stick it to him on the little things. Unless…

"Are the police afraid of my father?" I asked.

"You should get some sleep, Giada." Enzo kissed the top of my head then walked upstairs.

CHAPTER 18

Giada

The next morning, I woke to several missed calls from Luca, but I didn't bother returning them or even listening to the voicemails. Instead, I practiced yoga, showered, then dressed for church. Since my parents were still out of town, I planned to go alone, but Enzo insisted on driving me. He dropped me off at the door, saying he'd wait in the car. In case he changed his mind, I left enough room for one person between me and the end of the row when I selected a pew.

Merely sitting in the sanctuary calmed me, even though it was a crowded service, being a Sunday and all. I skimmed the program, and then just as the choir began the opening hymn, there was activity to my side. I cringed as Luca plopped down beside me in the seat I'd saved for Enzo. Alessio squeezed past and sat on the other side of me.

It was too late for me to move to a new seat without causing a scene, and besides, the way they'd sandwiched me in had me more or less trapped. Luca flashed me his most wicked grin then gripped my hand. I glared in return and scooted my hand to my lap, but he simply followed and grabbed it again.

I caught Father Ryan staring with concern. I shook my head dismissively and offered him a peaceful smile, determined not to distract the priest with my stupid relationship woes.

"Are you afraid I'll run?" I asked Luca.

He shrugged. "I figured some religion might be good for Alessio," he whispered back.

I glanced over at Luca's best friend and most loyal minion then back to Luca.

"Just don't let him touch the holy water. His lack of conscience might make it sizzle."

Alessio shot me a dirty, look but Luca chuckled.

They behaved the entire mass, and even gave me space to chat with Father Ryan in private after the service. The bishop still hadn't found a new priest to replace Father John, so he was too busy to chat as he normally would. It seemed the deacons were now fulfilling most of the counseling services at the church.

When I left the sanctuary, Luca was outside. He had draped his suit jacket over his forearm and was leaned back against the brick wall of the church. Dark sunglasses covered his eyes, lending him a mysterious look. I let my eyes drift down his body, then back up.

Damn. That was why I could never stay mad at him for very long. The man looked so good in Italian suits.

I blew out a breath, practically drooling, then noticed the side of his lip quirked up. One dimple appeared on his smoothly shaven cheek, then he pushed off the wall and sauntered towards me.

"When you look at me like that, I wish I were a mind-reader," he said. He lowered his head and offered me a polite, chaste kiss on each cheek before lightly gripping my hand.

"If you could read minds, you wouldn't have kissed me like that," I replied.

His chuckle rumbled deep in his chest. "Am I forgiven then?"

My body craved Luca in a way that made my lips begin forming the word "yes," but my brain shut that down. "Why should I forgive you? Your apology was hardly sincere. And it isn't just the crap at the strip club. You caused a scene at that dinner and made my best friend think you're cheating on me, too."

Luca abruptly swiveled to face me, dropping down to his knees. His new pose terrified me. Surely he wasn't about to propose.

"Amore, I beg for your forgiveness. I am nothing without your love. I implore you to accept my most humble apology."

I rolled my eyes, feeling my cheeks burn with embarrassment. "Get up, Luca," I whispered. There were barely any people left in the parking lot, but I didn't want anyone to see us and speculate. Fortunately, he rose to his feet on command.

"You should tell her about my newest acquisition," Alessio said, sneaking up behind me from God-knows-where.

I glanced from him to Luca until Luca nodded.

"Alessio is the new owner of 4th and Main. I don't want to own a business that made you sad or reminds me of any bad feelings between us."

"Wait, you sold your club? You're just out of the sex industry, just like that?"

Alessio chuckled at my terminology, but I ignored him, eager for Luca's confirmation.

"I still own L'Occhio. My office is there, and I need the business to help legitimize some other businesses. But I wanted you to see that I was listening, and I do care what you want. Someday, hopefully, I can unload them all."

"Or at least get rid of the naked girls," I suggested.

Alessio cringed.

I turned to him. "Could you wait in the car?"

He snickered. "I see my ride pulling up right now," he said, pointing to a black sedan approaching.

Luca watched his friend climb into the car before continuing. "I know it doesn't make up for everything, but I'm trying. I meant what I said— you are everything to me. I want you to be proud of me."

Gazing into those beautiful brown eyes, it was impossible to stay mad at him. I pressed my palms against his cheeks and pulled his face down to mine, kissing him on the lips.

"I am proud of you. And I love you, even when you're being an ass," I said finally. "And maybe I overreacted about the strip club. I just…Gabby said all these things after our fight at my house and it made me self-conscious. I want her to like you, and I need her to understand why I'm so invested in this relationship. I know that doesn't make sense to you, but it's part of why I was so upset when you did something that was exactly the sort of thing she thought you'd do."

Confusion was written all over his face, but he smiled. "If our positions had been reversed, and I saw you with another man, I would have lost my mind. You didn't overreact. Sono un fesso. I'm a fool. And I'm sorry."

"You're forgiven," I said.

He beamed like a little kid. "So does that mean you'll move the rest of your stuff into the apartment? It's lonely without you there."

I nodded. "I'll pack the rest of my stuff tonight and you can have whoever you want move it tomorrow. My parents are back tonight, so I'm having dinner with them, and then Lorenzo is driving me to work in the morning."

"Your first day," he said, smiling.

Another nod. "You're welcome to come to dinner tonight."

"I'll pass. But maybe I could see the outfit you're planning to wear to work tomorrow?"

I giggled. Luca surely just wanted a chance to see me naked, but as he was interested in fashion, it was a semi-plausible line.

"It's a deal. But no flirting with my brother's girlfriend if she's at the house."

Luca wrinkled his nose in disgust then led me to a Porsche Cayman.

"Umm, what's this?" I asked.

"New present for myself. It's been a rough year. I thought I deserved a treat. You like?"

It was a fire red, with tires that looked enormous compared to the slight size of the car. It reminded me of a race car. "It's gorgeous."

"Good. I look forward to making many memories with you in this car," he said. The mischievous look in his eyes told me exactly what type of memory he meant, but judging from the tiny interior of the sports car, I didn't see much potential for that.

"Would you let me drive it?" I asked. I spoke without thinking, but once the words were out there, I decided it was the perfect test. There was no way he'd agree to let me drive his baby. Luca barely tolerated me driving my own car, and never with him in it. And his cars were like children to him.

"You want to drive this? Like…now?" Luca's eyes widened further than I thought possible.

I shrugged, trying to act casual. "I mean, if you don't trust me, that's fine. She's new and all, so…"

Luca pressed his finger to my lip, shushing me. I smiled against the pressure, already dying to know what excuse he was going to offer for the refusal.

"If it makes you happy, of course you can drive. Just don't kill us."

My heart pitter pattered in a way that had only before happened for first kisses and proposals. I hadn't even really wanted to drive the car, but of course now that he said I could, I couldn't back down. He had passed the test with flying colors.

We climbed into the car, and I couldn't tell which of us was more nervous. I started the ignition, then spent a moment familiarizing myself with the fancy dials. Luca showed me how the car would automatically adjust the seat and mirrors, then he gripped the grab bar above his window.

I shifted into drive, then paused. "This reminds me of high school, when you taught me to drive." He'd been such a perfect boyfriend that day, just like he was today.

Luca smirked. "The fact that *I* taught you to drive is the only reason I trust you with this car now."

I pulled towards the exit of the parking lot. "Thank you, babe. This means a lot," I said, turning to smile at him.

Luca's eyes widened. "Eyes on the road, Giada!" he scolded.

I giggled but complied. And against the odds, we made it back home safely.

~

Luca

The next week flew by. Lorenzo drove Giada to her first day of work Monday, and Thomas brought all of her stuff to my apartment while she was out. Actually, judging from the quantity, it wasn't *all* of her belongings. It was all of her clothes, but I suspected she still had enough possessions in her childhood bedroom to fill another SUV.

Giada seemed to enjoy her first day as a working woman, and we celebrated that evening, dining at a fancy restaurant ten minutes from our apartment.

The meal had been perfect, but after I'd paid the bill, Giada pouted. When I'd asked what was wrong, she admitted it was the perfect sort of place to propose.

"You think I'd risk a rejection in public?" I'd teased.

Giada hadn't seemed too upset, and if she was, she got over it quickly when we got home and spent the next couple of hours tangled together in the sheets before actually going to bed.

She'd explained to me more how her new "job" would work, so I wasn't surprised when she stayed in bed Tuesday morning when I left to meet Alessio at the shipyard. I wasn't certain how she'd take the news that I brought home Tuesday evening, though.

Alessio dropped me off, coming into the apartment briefly to grab some papers before leaving.

As we entered the apartment, we nearly tripped over a multitude of paper sacks.

I eyed the bags, which all appeared to be filled with food. Lots of food.

"Giada?" I called.

She popped her head out from behind the refrigerator door. She smiled when she saw me.

"What's all this?"

"Groceries."

"I see that. Wait, you went to the grocery?"

"No. I ordered online. They deliver."

I was well aware of that fact, as I personally tried never to set foot in an actual grocery, on this continent anyway. Markets in Italy were pleasant. The Italian shops were clean and filled with colorful, fresh food. Those, I could handle.

"Are we feeding all of Stamford?"

She made an adorable fake angry face.

"Are you planning to learn how to cook?" I asked, noticing a pack of raw chicken resting on the counter. I reached over her, shoving that into the fridge.

Giada wrinkled her nose. "No, I figured you could handle the meat."

I nodded, still taking it all in. "So, you'll just lounge around at the apartment all day while I work, and then when I get home, you want me to cook for you?"

"Yep."

"Why do I keep you around again?" I teased.

She wiggled her eyebrows seductively. Alessio grabbed the papers he needed and waved as he left us.

I turned back to Giada. "Well, we might need to freeze some of this food," I began. "I spoke with my papà today, and he wants me back in Italy for a week or two."

"Already?"

I nodded. "And I know you just started your new internship, but in light of everything with your brother, I don't feel comfortable leaving you here while I'm overseas." I paused, waiting for her to protest.

Instead, she smiled. "Okay."

"Okay? You're not mad about missing work? Or Gabby? We just got back from Italy."

She shrugged. "Gabby's not as much fun in bed as you. And my job requires me to shop in Italy. That's why they hired me."

Having prepared myself for yelling or shrieking, I wasn't sure what to say.

"When do we leave?" she asked.

"I, um…I'll check for tickets. Is Thursday too soon?"

Her eyes passed over all the food. "Nope. I don't know what to do with most of this anyway."

I laughed and dragged her in for a kiss. Her lips curved into a smile as we joined together, and I remembered a moment too late that she had been wearing bold red lipstick. I pulled back, pressing my finger to her cherry lips, assuming she'd wipe off the color. Instead, she quirked an eyebrow and reached for my belt.

The moment her delicate fingers grazed my pants, my cock reacted, straining against the fly. Giada's seductive grin widened as she carefully worked the zipper, freeing me. She dropped to her knees, treating me to a breathtaking view of her cleavage.

"What are you doing?" I asked, even though her intent was obvious.

She peered up at me through long, dark lashes. "I've got to wipe off this lipstick somehow."

Her eyes locked on mine just long enough to send my pulse into overdrive, and then she wrapped her perfect lips around my length. As she worked her mouth up and down, the sensation was exquisitely intense, and I struggled to keep my eyes open. But the sight of Giada devouring me like a cone of her favorite ice cream was nearly as amazing as the feel of it. I gathered her hair in one hand, keeping my view of her unobscured.

She gazed up and smiled coyly before dragging her tongue in circles around the head of my cock. When her eyes dropped back to her work, her grin widened. Of course, her lipstick had now left smudges of red all over my dick. Not that I was complaining.

With a groan, I nudged her off of me, guiding her to her feet. I reached under her dress, not surprised when I found she wasn't wearing panties. I cast her a fake scolding gaze, to which she simply shrugged. Then I lifted her onto the kitchen counter. I tugged her dress below her breasts, taking the bra with it.

As always, I had to pause for a moment to admire the view. I'd never seen the Grand Canyon, but I doubted even it could compare with the sight of Giada's full, unencumbered breasts. I ducked my head, nipping at her chest before closing my lips around her left nipple for a moment, then her right. I used my fingers to tease one breast while my tongue laved attention on the other.

I could tell when she was ready for more as her breath fell fast and heavy against my forehead. I didn't dare withhold the main course from her any longer. I released her breasts and gripped her thighs, scooting her to the edge of the counter. I positioned myself at her entrance, then she wrapped her legs around my hips, tugging me closer. I dipped my head to kiss her, relishing the taste of her tongue. Giada moaned when I thrust into her, and the sound of it was so erotic that I knew I wouldn't last long.

Our sloppy kiss continued for a couple more minutes until I

pulled back, needing to focus all of my efforts on the movement of my lower body. I sensed she was close, felt her channel start to tighten around me, so I reached one hand to her breasts. The moment I pinched her pert nipple, Giada screamed my name, and her body shattered into the most erotic convulsions I'd ever witnessed. Her fingernails pierced into the flesh of my butt as I followed her lead, nearly blacking out as wave after wave of pure pleasure wracked my body.

We both caught our breath, and I pulled back slowly, handing her a tissue from the counter as I did. She smiled shyly, then reached behind her back. She bit her lip, trying unsuccessfully to hold back laughter. When she shifted her hand to show me that she'd apparently been leaning against a cucumber the entire time we made love, I started chuckling too.

"Luca?" she said after we'd both stopped giggling and I'd gathered her in my arms to carry her to the bedroom.

"Si?"

"I'm relieved we're returning to Italy so soon. I have no idea how to cook a cucumber," she said.

This time, my laughter came out like a whisper. "I know, tesoro, I know."

~

Giada

On our first day in Rome, Luca met with his father alone, leaving Alessio as my escort around town. Even though he was basically a babysitter, I didn't mind his presence. He spoke fluent Italian and understood the exchange rate, so he was helpful with my shopping mission. Plus, having an attractive man at my side kept the other men from constantly flirting and catcalling, a phenomenon which I rarely experienced in New England but was obnoxiously frequent in Rome.

As a thank you, I treated him to dinner. Well, on my dad's credit card.

"Luca said you still have family here?"

"My grandparents live in Napoli, but my mom is in Roma."

"How did you end up at high school in Rhode Island then? Isn't that where you met Luca?"

"When I was younger, my parents divorced, and my mom moved to the New England area with me and my sister. After I graduated, my mom moved back here to Rome."

"Oh, I wasn't aware your parents were divorced," I said. Suddenly, I realized how little I actually knew about him. Especially in light of how much he knew about me.

"Yep. My dad and I don't...speak, but my mom and I are close."

"Does your sister live here?"

"No. She's married and living in Massachusetts."

"Do you see her a lot?"

"Yeah. She has twins, so they're a lot of fun now."

He pulled out his phone and showed me a series of pictures. His sister was cute, and the twins were adorable. I paused on a picture of him holding both babies and beaming proudly.

"I would've never guessed you could hold one baby, let alone two. I honestly pegged you more for the type who eats little babies."

He raised an eyebrow.

"You come off as kind of intimidating," I explained.

"Is that why you don't like me?"

I cringed. "I like you just fine."

"You didn't for a while. In fact it wasn't too long ago that you tried to have me arrested."

"Sorry about that."

"It's alright. If we're being honest, I wasn't a fan of yours at the start either," he said. "From my perspective, it seemed like you made Luca jump through an awful lot of hoops and cared more about your next pair of new shoes than him. And you also nearly got him killed a lot. Mostly though you just struck me as shallow, materialistic, and manipulative."

Hmm. That was super honest. "You spied on me and told Luca when I was with Enzo. He ended up in the hospital because of you," I said. I wondered if Alessio would confirm my suspicions that he was the one who hurt Enzo, but either way, it was Alessio's fault. He sent the text to Luca that set everything off.

"I didn't make up anything. You were with Lorenzo. In fact, I didn't say a damn thing. I just took a picture. Lorenzo would have been just fine if he'd kept his hands to himself." He paused, then added, "Or if you had."

I scowled. I already felt bad enough for what happened to Enzo, but I wasn't about to let Alessio convince me I'd done something wrong. "We just kissed. Luca and I weren't even together when it happened."

Alessio at least had the decency to look moderately sheepish at that. "I wasn't aware of that at the time."

We both realized that didn't matter, that he still would've told Luca either way. I sighed and thought back to that week. I had been so sure of everything with Luca when we'd been in Italy, but then once we were apart, insecurities, suspicion, and doubt had nearly driven me mad. Then when someone sent me pictures of Luca with another woman, I'd snapped.

"Did you ever figure out who sent the pictures?"

He cringed. "You'll have to ask Luca."

"He's not here now."

Alessio cocked his head to the side, unwavering.

I tugged my phone from my purse and called Luca, but he didn't answer.

"He's probably with his dad," he said. "He can't answer unless it's work-related."

"You think he'd answer your call?"

He answered with a cocky grin, then tapped his phone. He

angled it towards me and put it on speakerphone, so when Luca answered, I spoke.

"Hey babe, Alessio won't tell me who sent me those pictures of you and Mila."

There was a lengthy silence and some shuffling noises. "Amore, I'm working."

Alessio said something in Italian, and Luca replied quickly, also in Italian. Then Alessio switched the phone off speaker and handed it to me. Luca detailed some very promising activities he'd pursue that evening, then disconnected.

I handed Alessio his phone, distracted by Luca's promises.

Alessio gazed at me for a moment, then blurted out, "His mom."

"What? Whose mom?"

"Luca said I could tell you, and the photos came from his mom." The cringe on his face told me he anticipated my reaction.

"Camilla? That witch! Why does she hate me so much?" I continued my rant for a few minutes, stopping only when the waiter dropped by with the check.

"Personally, I think she was looking out for you," Alessio said once I finally quieted. "She sees a lot of her husband in Luca and didn't want you to end up like her."

I wasn't sure what to say to that. Probably, we would need to put all of that behind us and start new, for Luca's sake. I decided to return to a safer subject—his adorable niece and nephew. "Has Luca met any of your family?"

Alessio frowned and nodded. "He's the twins' godfather."

"Oh. That's…" I paused, trying to find the right word. Finally, I went with the honest response. "Unexpected."

He chuckled. "Luca and my sister go way back."

My food stuck in my throat as he said that. I must've made a face because he continued.

"Not like that. They never dated or anything." Alessio grimaced as though the thought disgusted him. "Back in high school, Luca did a favor for her, and then you dumped him over it. I'm surprised that never came up."

"In high school the only time we broke up was when he blew me off to go on a date with another girl and lied about it. And that was just a temporary hiccup, not an actual break up."

He shrugged. "Yeah, well, the other girl was my sister. And it wasn't a date. Without Luca's help that night…well, I don't know if she'd have those cute babies now."

I had so many questions about that, but figured Alessio wouldn't tell me. "So I guess he knows your mom too?"

Alessio nodded. "He's basically part of the family. He used to spend some school breaks with us when his parents were back in Italy."

"How much does your mom know about his work? Or yours?"

His eyebrow jumped. "No more than she needs to."

"Well, is there anything else I should know about you?"

He shrugged. "I'm a vegetarian, a Pisces, and a card-carrying member of PETA."

"PETA," I repeated.

He nodded. "And I love puppies, but who doesn't?"

I suppressed a grimace. "Do you have a puppy?"

Alessio shook his head. "Of course not. How would I take care of a dog? Luca has me babysitting you during all of my free time." He paused, a wry smile creeping across his face. "I had a golden doodle once for a couple hours. My mom takes care of him. You'll have to ask Luca that story."

We both fell quiet for a moment.

"So what's next on the agenda? More shopping or…?"

"You can take me to the apartment. Thanks."

CHAPTER 19

Giada

After five days in Rome, Luca and I drove down to the Amalfi coast. Alessio traveled separately, taking the train to Naples to visit his grandparents before meeting us in Capri. It wasn't a short drive, but it was a gorgeous one. For the most part, we passed the time talking, but when we ran out of topics to discuss, we'd blast music. Italian radio stations played a ton of English-language songs, but also some Italian pop. I delighted in choosing an Italian station, then trying to guess the lyrics of the song. According to Luca, I wasn't exactly gifted at that game. I didn't even figure out the main theme of most songs.

When Luca and I reached Naples, we immediately boarded the ferry to Capri. Luca's beloved car traveled on the same boat as we did, but we rode on the uppermost deck. The wind was strongest on the higher deck, but the view was best. Gazing out over the water, with Luca's torso pressed against my back and his arms wrapped around me like he feared I'd dive overboard, I felt truly at peace. I was traveling the world with the man I loved, and

I didn't have to worry about a thing. Luca had my back, both literally and figuratively.

As we neared the shore, I closed my eyes and breathed in the salty sea air. Luca's breath tickled the side of my neck a moment before his lips followed.

"I love when you look this happy," he cooed, his mouth still grazing my skin. He nipped my ear then pushed away, gripping my hand to lead me down the ship's stairs. "You asked why I wanted to travel here? That's why. I haven't seen that smile enough lately."

I supposed he was right, and he would absolutely see the smile plenty over the weekend. Our trips to Palermo were always fantastic, but there was something special about Capri.

My family used to visit Capri at least one weekend a year when I was younger, and I'd always loved the island. I'd always viewed Naples as a crowded, noisy, and unwelcoming place, so having the idyllic island just a short boat ride away felt magical.

Luca clearly remembered how I felt about the location, since he planned a romantic picnic for the two of us on our second evening on the island. He looked much more relaxed than usual, wearing khakis and a long-sleeved white button-down. I'd chosen a turquoise maxi dress, not wanting to mess with sandy pants.

He'd ordered the picnic from a local shop, and they'd even included fancy clear disposable plates and wine goblets. We ate way too much food, then sat and talked for a while. The beach wasn't crowded, but as it neared sunset, it emptied altogether. Even though it was warmer than the average for the time of year, it was far from peak travel season for the island. We'd chosen a spot near a taller rock for our picnic, letting the natural barriers block the wind, but when Luca suggested a walk, I couldn't resist. We slowly made our way down the beach until we hit a spot where the water crashed too close to the rocky beach for us to continue. Then we turned and started back towards our picnic spot.

"I hope nobody stole the rest of our food," I joked.

"You can't possibly be hungry again."

I laughed. I wasn't, but it was fun teasing him.

Luca raised my hand to his lips and smiled.

"Remember when we came here as kids, and you were fascinated with those little rocks that you swore came from the volcano that formed Ischia?"

"They did!" I said, smiling at the memory. He squeezed my hand and slowed the pace.

"When we were about to leave, you gave me your favorite volcanic rock and told me to hold onto it so I wouldn't forget you."

I couldn't believe he remembered that. "Yes, and then you had to one up me by giving me that teal piece of sea glass," I added.

He nodded, grinning. "But you gave that back to me for safe-keeping because you said your brothers would just break it."

"They would have!"

"Sea glass has survived waves pounding it for thousands of years. I hardly think your brothers could've topped that." Luca's smile reached all the way to his deep, rich eyes. "I always thought it would be cool if we could somehow combine the volcanic rock and the sea glass and make some cool souvenir to remember those old trips to the Amalfi coast before everything got so complicated."

I was about to say how amazing that would've been, when he reached into his pocket. "Wait, you saved them?"

Luca nodded. "And I found an artist who could melt them together and form this," he said, holding up a breathtakingly gorgeous pendant. The glass was in the middle of the rock, its piercing blue-green color contrasting nicely with the deep gray of the rock. The stone reminded me of the actual beach on which we stood, with the rocks practically jutting out into the ocean.

"He welded a bit of iron to shape it all and hold it together, but that seemed fitting, since iron was traditionally used in Roman wedding bands," Luca continued. He held the pendant flat in his hand while I traced my finger over it. It was gorgeous, and unique, nothing like any of the other jewelry I owned.

"This isn't really the exact pieces from when we were kids…" I began.

"I swear to you, Giada, it is."

I opened my mouth to say something, but it was all too much, too romantic. The fact that he'd held onto those trinkets all these years and that he'd thought to do this, to make something as beautiful as the memories we shared of collecting the items, it was overwhelming.

"I had him put it on a longer chain, so you could wear it by your heart. You can swap out the chain for something nicer, though, or you don't have to wear it at all," he said.

I gathered my hair in my hand and lifted it off the nape of my neck. "Here," I said, turning. "Will you?"

He understood my request and fastened the necklace around my neck. As I turned back to face him, he traced his finger along the chain to the colorful center, which did rest directly at my heart. I glanced down at it and placed my hand over it as well, touching him and the necklace.

"It's gorgeous," I whispered, the waves nearly masking my words.

It was the most beautiful thing anyone had ever given me and by far the most meaningful. I wanted to tackle Luca and make love to him with the waves crashing around us. I wanted to somehow make him understand how perfect and touching this simple gift was to me. But instead, I just stammered.

"I don't know what to say, Luca. This is…"

He released the necklace and gripped both of my hands instead. "Say that you love me the way I love you, that you always will, even when I screw up over and over again. Tell me you want a future with me, not because you're scared and not because your parents want that, but because you can't breathe without me in your life."

Luca paused, but with his eyes locked on mine, his perfect words still resonating in my mind, I truly was breathless.

He raised my hands to his lips, kissed them once, then continued. "Tell me you'll stay by my side whatever happens, however hard it gets. Say you'll drop everything and run away with me to the middle of nowhere at a moment's notice if that's what we have to do. Tell me you want to have kids with me, that you can already picture them playing on these same beaches. Tell me that you need me as much as I need you."

Luca's eyes pleaded with me as he spoke, his impassioned words making my heart flutter erratically. If his speech was supposed to help me know what to say, it failed, because I was utterly speechless.

He dropped to his knee in front of me, still clutching my hands like he was falling off a cliff and needed me to pull him back to safety. "Say that you'll marry me, Giada."

And just like that, the words came to me. "Oh Luca, yes," I said, tugging him back up to stand. "Yes, to all of that."

His arms flew around my waist, tightening and lifting me off the ground with the enthusiasm of his embrace. I clasped my hands behind his neck as he set me down, pulling his face to mine so I could kiss him.

We kissed until my eyes were damp, my lips quickly were numb, and I was breathless. It was all too surreal.

"I love you, Luca," I gushed between kisses. "I love you so much."

I felt him smile beneath my lips, and then he broke away. I was about to scream and tackle him, not anywhere close to ready to end the kissing, but then he spoke again. "I almost forgot!" He said with a chuckle.

Luca reached into his pocket and pulled out a small black box.

"I took back the last ring. After you threw it at my head, I realized you weren't going to be bought, and that I couldn't show you how much I loved you just by buying the most expensive ring I could find. So I found this one instead. It wasn't obscenely over-priced, but it reminded me of you." He shrugged. "I thought you might like it."

He held the box towards me, but I didn't move.

"Luca, the necklace is better than any ring you could ever give me."

Luca pressed his lips against my forehead. "I'm so glad you like it, but I need you wearing a ring. I don't want anyone questioning if you're really mine."

I smiled, relieved that at least the sentimental romantic hadn't completely lost his cute possessive side. I opened the felt box, smiling at the platinum band coated in a row of smaller diamonds, with a large, clear round-cut diamond in the middle, and tiny diamonds circling the center stone. It was tasteful and gorgeous and reminded me of Luca—stylish and sexy and just a tad over the top. It was exactly what I would've picked out for myself.

"I love it," I said. I handed the box to him and held my left hand out flat towards him.

Luca took the hint and slid the ring onto my finger, kissing the palm of my hand before releasing it. "I can't believe you said yes without the ring," he teased.

"I would've said yes without any of this," I said. "But this has to be the most romantic proposal ever."

"Third time is a charm," he said with a wink. "I love you," he said, pulling me close for another kiss.

This kiss deepened quickly, and though I started with my hands in his soft hair, they quickly drifted down his back and onto his ass. Without breaking away from my lips, Luca reached for my hands and pulled them off of him, holding them at our sides. I groaned in protest.

"I thought this was a fairly private beach," I said.

Luca laughed and pulled back. "Alessio!" He called towards the rocks.

I turned to see the man step out and wave.

"Did you get it?" Luca called.

Alessio flashed us a thumbs up.

"Get what?" I asked, totally confused.

"I figured on the off chance you said yes, you might want a picture or two to commemorate the day I was truly slick."

I giggled. "You were very slick."

"And if you said no, it couldn't hurt to have him nearby to rescue me when I flung myself off the rocks."

"I could never say no to you."

He kissed the tip of my nose then turned back to Alessio. "Take a hike. Give us an hour or so!" he called.

Alessio grinned and walked off. Luca was smiling like a little boy.

"An hour? I'm so hot and bothered at this point that you could probably make me come twice in under ten minutes."

Luca groaned and tossed his head back. "I am not making love to you on a beach in the open, amore."

"Who said anything about making love? Your romantic speech already did that. I'm just talking about a quick fuck over by the rocks."

Luca squeezed his eyes shut. "The trouble you cause with that dirty mouth of yours," he mused. But, not wanting to disappoint, he led me by the hand towards the rocks, where we were sheltered from view of anyone who happened to walk by.

Luca

That night, when Giada finally had her fill of me, we were both exhausted. I had teased her, pretending I believed the jewelry was aphrodisiac, but really, it was me. Well, maybe not me so much as the security and comfort and affirmation she felt after hearing my words. The knowledge that my fiancée wanted me every bit as much as I wanted her was reassuring. I doubted I'd ever accept that I was the right person for her. I could never be the type of man she deserved. But I couldn't live without her. Hopefully, my need for her was powerful enough to keep my behavior in line.

I stretched out behind Giada, the front of my body curving around hers, with my arm draped over her side, pinned in place by her arm over mine. We'd partially dressed, with me in boxer briefs and her in a sleeveless undershirt of mine, but the material was thin, and I could still feel the warmth of her skin through the fabric. I waited for her breathing to slow, signaling that she was asleep, but it didn't come.

"What are you thinking about?" I asked softly, certain it had to be her mind keeping her awake despite her body's fatigue.

She made a sound in the back of her throat, almost like a kitten's meow. It was sexy enough to make me pounce normally, but even I acknowledged we needed a break from that for a few hours.

"What you said on the beach," she finally answered.

She'd already asked me to tell her again. And again. I mixed up the order of it all and kept leaving parts out, so finally we'd just written it down together, exactly as I'd said it, for her to keep forever. Personally, I didn't think it was the best proposal out there, but I had been honest, and she loved that.

"Some part in specific or…?" I asked.

"You said you want to have children with me."

"I do," I said, quickly adding, "Someday." I wasn't ready to share her yet. Just thinking about Giada pregnant, knowing my child was growing inside her perfect body, was deeply erotic to me, but also terrifying. I already struggled against being too possessive and too protective of her, so it scared me to think what would happen if she literally housed someone else I also loved. How many men would I have to assign to watch Giada to actually feel like she was safe?

And while she would be a wonderful mother—nurturing and warm, loving and capable, I wasn't ready for her to love anyone other than me that intensely. Greedily, I told myself it was okay to want a few years of her undivided attention. Besides, what kind of a father would I be? My own papà had failed me. Giada's father was probably the closest I had to a good role model, and most would hardly call him a good man or father.

"Calm down," she said, breathing a laugh. "I didn't mean now. Definitely not before our thirties. There's too much we have to do first."

I smiled, relieved we were on the same page. But then I realized she still hadn't told me exactly what was keeping her up, so I probed further. "How many kids do you want?"

She didn't answer immediately. "Two."

"No, we need at least four," I said. I was partly kidding, but mostly not. I loved the big family gatherings at Giada's. I could easily picture her with a larger brood of her own.

"Oh my, I don't think I could keep up with that many little Lucas running around," she said, giggling.

"We'll hire a nanny. Plus, the kids will all be like you, so it'll work just fine."

She sighed peacefully, and I thought that was the end of the discussion, but after a minute, she spoke again. "When we have kids, I want…" And then she stopped, shaking her head against the pillow.

I raised up to my elbow. "What do you want, baby?"

"Nevermind. We can discuss it in a few years."

"I want to discuss it now so you can relax and get some sleep.

I have big plans for this tomorrow," I said, rubbing my palm down the length of her body. "Tell me what you want?"

"I want you out," she said after a pause. "When we have kids, I want you out."

I lay back against the pillow, my hand halting mid-rub. Though her words were vague, I knew exactly what she meant, and I realized by the way she hesitated in saying it that it was truly important to her. Unfortunately, it was as likely to occur as if she'd said she wanted me to learn to fly by the time we became parents. I couldn't just get out. She didn't want me dead, and there weren't other paths out.

"You don't want our kids growing up to be just like me? Lots of adorable little Lucas running around bossing everyone around?" I joked instead of addressing her obvious concern.

"You know that's not what I mean, Luca. You can't honestly tell me you see that working out. If we have daughters, are you just going to banish them to boarding school then treat them like fragile dolls and never tell them the truth about anything? If we have boys are you going to let them grow up dreading the day when they have to take over and join this lifestyle?"

I didn't want any of that, obviously. Her questions were rhetorical, and she had made her point, so I kept quiet.

"I don't ever want to let go of you because I'm afraid you won't come back to me. I can't raise children with that same kind of fear," she said.

"Amore, I will always come back to you." I considered reminding her that the last time I was shot and "killed," I still came back to her, but decided that maybe didn't make my point.

She sighed. "I won't do it, Luca."

"I know, baby. I will figure something out. I promise. We will not become our parents."

CHAPTER 20

Luca

We'd planned to spend another day in Capri, then we would take another, longer ferry down to Palermo. We'd spend a few days in Palermo so I could check up on some business matters there and leave my car at my villa in Palermo.

Unfortunately, Matteo called the morning after our engagement. Giada's uncle Emiliano Grasso had been shot and killed. I didn't know Emiliano well, but he was both a part of the literal Conti family and also a part of the business family. He was the younger brother of Tony, Marco's brother-in-law. Emiliano and his wife Susanna were frequent visitors at the Conti mansion.

Alessio promised to escort my car to Palermo and then take care of my business matters in Sicily, so Giada and I returned to Naples to fly back to the US immediately. We didn't have many details about the shooting itself yet, but the funeral was already being planned. Of course, the official story was that it was a mugging gone wrong, but I didn't doubt that Giada understood as well as I did that Emiliano's death was a direct result of his criminal activities.

Giada was eager to share our engagement news with her whole family, but didn't think a funeral was the proper place to make a happy announcement, so her ring went back in its box in my safe when we returned home. It was only for the night, but I still hated taking it off her finger.

As we'd gotten ready for the funeral that morning, I'd tried to sell Giada on the idea of her attending the small family event before the real service without me. Maybe I would've felt more confident about joining if we were officially engaged, but without even being able to share that, I felt like I was imposing on a private party.

Still, she was insistent I go with her.

"Family only," Angelo snarled when he saw me, echoing all the concerns I'd voiced to Giada earlier. She'd assured me that Angelo's girlfriend Julia would be there and reasoned it was no different for me to come, except it was. Julia maybe wasn't part of their family, yet, but she also wasn't part of a different Family, at least not the kind that mattered.

Gathering of the Family before the official funeral had become commonplace in our world. It gave all the guys a chance to hear firsthand from the boss what had happened, where things had gone wrong, so there weren't any half-truths floating around stirring up trouble. And it built camaraderie and helped calm jitters, both of which were critical too.

"Luca is family," Giada said to her brother, brushing past him.

I took a more deferential approach, raising my hands defensively. "I won't cause any trouble. I'm here for your sister," I said.

Angelo rolled his eyes.

"I'm sorry for your loss," I added, offering my hand. He reluctantly shook it, and I leaned in, patting him on the shoulder blade with my free hand. I didn't imagine I'd ever like Angelo, but I could be cordial.

Giada wove her way through the room, greeting everyone in turn. I watched her in her element, wondering how I ever could have questioned her ability to handle this life. She was easygoing and lighthearted as she hugged each of her aunts and cousins, calming everyone with her carefree smile.

In her world, Giada clearly was the princess. In mine, she'd soon be the queen.

I glanced at my watch, noting it was almost noon. We were due at the church at one, with a two-hour window for others outside the family to come and pay their respects before the official funeral service and mass began at three. Then we'd head to the cemetery, then back to the Grasso's house for the wake. It was going to be a long day, and I had work to do. I didn't have time to waste mourning a man I'd barely even known.

I tapped out a quick text to Alessio, checking in on some of our more urgent matters, then made my way into the dining room. Giada was seated by her Aunt Sofia, with a plate of untouched miniature quiches in front of her. Looking at the table, filled entirely with women, I realized Marco must have called the men into his office. Obviously, I wouldn't be invited into that meeting.

I sat across from Giada. Sofia passed me a tray of food. I selected two, and ate them in turn, each one making a single bite. I tried to catch Giada's eye, but she now seemed distracted. Her smile was faltering, her posture stiffening. I noticed her aunt clutched her hand tightly, but nothing she was saying seemed too dramatic, at least not the parts I could hear.

I jumped as the chair beside me was dragged from the table. I turned to see Matteo sit beside me.

"Cast out with the women?" I asked.

He didn't take the bait. "I already heard everything he has to say," he explained.

Matteo was an anomaly in his house. He was a dolphin in a family of sharks. I didn't question his intellect, but he clearly wasn't equipped for the family business in any other way. He was indecisive and empathetic. Some might call him weak. He'd be well suited for a desk job, middle management even, but not for the life he was born into. God help the Conti family if something happened to Angelo and Matteo had to take the reins.

"I'm sorry for your loss," I murmured, remembering why we were there.

He nodded in acknowledgment of my statement and reached for some of the pastries. He offered me one, and I accepted.

"How is she doing?" he asked, his eyes focused on his sister.

I shrugged. "Fine." I wasn't sure why she wouldn't be. It wasn't like she had any tight bond with Emiliano.

Matteo frowned as though this was unexpected. I scrolled through my emails again, acutely aware that my screen was within Matteo's line of vision, but certain that he'd never betray my confidence even if he did see something he shouldn't. We made small talk for a few minutes, then, just as I was getting ready to excuse myself for some fresh air, Giada's expression changed.

She dropped her aunt's hand, whispering something quietly, then drew her own hand to her face. A strangled cry escaped her throat as she pushed her chair back from the table and scurried out of the room in tears.

I had no idea what had just happened.

Her aunt calmly stood, heading in the opposite direction towards the kitchen, leaving Matteo and me alone with several other ladies, all of whom were engrossed in their own conversations.

"I didn't even think she liked the guy," I said, still uncertain why Giada was upset.

"She didn't. He always stared and hugged her in a way that creeped her out," Matteo said.

His words told me he agreed with my assessment, that Giada's sudden outburst was truly inexplicable. But the way he glared at me made me think there was something I was missing.

"What?"

"Aren't you going to follow her?"

I hesitated. It was a funeral, so one more crying girl wasn't going to draw attention, and besides, it wasn't my house. Someone in her family should comfort her. I barely even knew the guy.

"She's not crying over Emiliano," Matteo said, shaking his head. "Do you not get it?" He paused again but continued when he realized I had no response. "The last funeral Giada went to was yours. Don't you think today might be a little stressful for her?"

"Shit," I mumbled, quickly wiping my mouth and rising to my feet, feeling like the biggest fool on earth. I followed in the direction she'd headed, weaving through small groups of her female relatives until I reached the bathroom just off the kitchen.

I knocked softly on the closed door. "Giada? It's me."

I heard a sniffle before she spoke. "I need a minute," she whimpered.

I jiggled the knob. "Unlock it," I said.

For once, she complied.

I stepped into the bathroom, shut the door behind me, then pulled her into my chest. She curled against me, her body shaking with tremors from her cries.

"Baby, shhh. It's okay. I'm okay." I kissed the top of her head. "I'm so sorry. I didn't even think…when you asked me to come today, well I didn't realize…" I stopped talking. The more I said, the dumber I felt for not figuring it all out sooner. Of course, she didn't want to be away from me today. She thought I died, and less than a year ago, she'd attended my funeral. That trauma was still too fresh.

"I won't leave you," I said after another minute. Gradually, her body stilled. I leaned against the door, pulling her with me, resting my chin on her head.

A sharp knock on the door interrupted our embrace.

"Occupied," I shouted back. It was a large house. There were other bathrooms.

Still, Giada pulled away slightly.

I reached around and grabbed a tissue to offer to her. She accepted, dabbing her eyes, then blowing her nose. I watched as she leaned in to the mirror, assessing the damage to her makeup.

"You will, someday," she said, quickly clarifying what she meant. "Leave me, that is. That's what happens to men in your line of work."

I shook my head. "No. Your father is still alive. My papà is still alive."

"They're young still. My grandfather was killed. Where is your grandfather?"

She already knew the answer to that question would prove her point, so I didn't respond.

"And Emiliano was only forty-two."

"That's different. He was a foot soldier, I'm more like the king watching from the safety of my tower."

A slight curve tugged her lips upward. "You need a moat," she said.

I wrapped my arms around her waist, inhaling the sweet floral aroma of her perfume before gently kissing her neck. "We could buy a house. Then we could build a moat. Our apartment isn't zoned for that."

She smiled again, but it faltered quickly. I could tell she was trying to distract herself, to focus on getting through the day. Her chest expanded as she inhaled deeply.

There was another knock at the door, this one louder.

"Occupied!" I repeated, not bothering to hide my annoyance this time.

"Marino?" A voice asked after a pause. It was Angelo. Giada clearly saw my grimace in the mirror.

"We can't find Giada," he said.

I gazed at her, needing confirmation that she was ready to rejoin the rest of the family. She nodded, so I stepped back and opened the door a crack.

Angelo stared at his sister, then turned to me, scowling. "Jesus, Luca. It's a funeral for fuck's sake. You don't take a girl into the bathroom to…" he shook his head, disgusted. "We're leaving in two minutes. Giada, you're riding with us."

"I'll drive her."

"No, she'll go in the limo with the rest of the immediate family."

Angelo reached for his sister's arm, but I was faster. I clenched my fingers around his wrist firmly.

"She's riding with me. It's not up for discussion," I said, releasing my grip on him the second our eyes locked. He didn't need another reason to hate me, but I wasn't about to leave Giada alone moments after promising I wouldn't.

Angelo held my stare for a moment, then shook his head. "You'll be at the end of the procession," he mumbled, stalking off down the hall.

~

Giada

The day of Emiliano's funeral was hard, much harder than I'd anticipated. Honestly, I hadn't even liked the guy. He wasn't super friendly, and he always looked at me in that creepy way that made me think he was picturing me naked. But still, my father's stress was palpable, Aunt Susanna's grief was heartbreaking, and my trauma from Luca's fake funeral was too fresh.

It was hard to wallow or stress, though, when Luca drove me home after the last of the guests left the dinner, slid my engagement ring back onto my finger when we reached the apartment, then kissed my forehead.

"Don't make me take you back to Italy just to see you smile again," he taunted.

I slept fitfully that night, despite feeling Luca's strong arm draped over my side every time I woke. Despite my fatigue, I went into the office the next day, proud to bring in the modest collection of items I'd found in my travels.

I'd only acquired accent pieces and other smaller items, bringing it home on my own dime, confident there'd be a client wanting each treasure. I also photographed some larger pieces. I anticipated seeing the excitement in their eyes when they saw my finds, and was smiling before I even entered the office.

I spread my treasures out on the conference table and waited for Audra and Diana, the other partner, to finish what they'd been working on. They both seemed chipper, asked me about my trip, and then their eyes had widened with excitement.

"What is that?" Audra asked, lunging forward. She gestured towards my chest, where I was clutching my new necklace from Luca in my left hand so it didn't keep clinking into the items on the table whenever I bent over.

"Oh, it's sea glass and volcanic rock," I began, pinching the necklace so they could get a better view.

"That's gorgeous," Diana said, "But I think she meant on your finger."

I glanced at the hand that was holding the necklace. "Oh! Yes, well, I got engaged in Italy, too."

As these women I'd just met congratulated me and asked me for all the details, I suddenly felt awful for not telling my parents sooner. I'd planned to wait another couple of days to be respectful of the deceased, but maybe good news was exactly what everyone could use at the moment.

The moment I left the office—having sold every item I'd brought back—I called my mom. After asking how my aunt Susanna was doing, I asked if there was a time the next day when Luca and I could meet up with my parents.

"Maybe we could meet someplace for brunch?" I'd suggested, knowing it was easier for Luca to sneak away earlier in the day. Of course, she'd dismissed that idea and invited us over to the house for brunch instead.

I'd anticipated Luca grumbling about it, having spent enough time with my family lately, but he was excited. He clasped my hand in his while he drove the next morning, casually tracing his thumb over my new ring and smiling.

"My mom is going to ask about wedding plans," I said. "And have you even told your parents yet?"

"No, I was waiting until we told your parents. I could call mine later today."

"You don't want to tell them in person?"

He shrugged. "We did that last time, and besides, my papà is in Italy."

I winced at the mention of the last time. "Can we just pretend that last time didn't happen?"

Luca chuckled.

"Audra and Diana asked about wedding plans at the office yesterday. Like I should already have some ideas."

"You don't?"

I shrugged. "I want a church wedding, obviously. And since my family is so huge, I'm assuming it'll have to be a big wedding. I'd love Gabriella to be my maid of honor."

He made a face but didn't interrupt.

"For color scheme, it'll depend on the season I suppose but I'm leaning towards magenta and black."

"Magenta?"

"Like a bold pink with a purple hue."

"I know what magenta means. I'm wondering if you're

thinking I'll wear pink."

I smiled. "I'm pretty sure you'll wear whatever I tell you to wear if you want to marry me, but no, you'll be in black." I thought about some other ideas. "I'd like to get married here, but if you want to have another reception in Italy for some of your family, we could. Oh and we have to do precana classes together."

"Pre...what?"

I blew out a sigh. For a lifelong Catholic, Luca could be pretty oblivious. "It's through the church, like religious classes on marriage. Pre-marriage counseling, sort of."

"Veto."

I chuckled. "Nope. Holding firm on this one. I'm sure we could arrange for private classes instead of doing a weekend retreat with strangers."

Luca's face had contorted into a mixture of nausea and horror, but we were nearing my house.

"We'll talk later," I said, squeezing his hand.

Matteo greeted us when we arrived, and we shared the happy news the second both of my parents came downstairs. No one looked particularly surprised at the news, but their happiness did seem genuine. They all hugged me, then Luca, then spent a minute gushing over my ring and necklace before heading to the table. We were almost done with brunch when Angelo arrived, his best friend Rico and our cousin Eddie in tow.

"Good morning," he said, sounding as annoyed with the world as usual.

"Morning!" my mom said, standing to greet him. "Luca and Giada came by to share some news."

Angelo glared at Luca then turned to me. I held up my hand, flashing the ring.

If his smile wasn't genuine, he at least faked it well. He walked around the table, so I stood to hug him. Then he offered a hand to Luca.

"It's about time," he said. "Congratulations."

Luca thanked him, and then Angelo joined us at the table. By some miracle, no one argued about anything the entire morning.

Luca claimed his parents were similarly enthusiastic when he shared the news with them. He'd gone to visit his mom—alone—and called his dad right after. Since his mom had been less than welcoming the last time we were engaged, I was okay with letting him handle this announcement alone. Luca told me they were both happy for us, and I decided to pretend that was true.

My mom dropped by the apartment the very next day with a large manila envelope. I gave her the quick tour, made some tea for both of us, then waited for her to fess up about the reason for the visit. She clearly had something up her sleeve but I was surprised when she handed me a short handwritten paragraph about Luca and me.

"I thought we could use this for the engagement announcement," she said.

"Announcement?" I wasn't completely opposed to the idea, but given who my father was…and my fiancé…and what they both did for a living, well, I didn't think we'd be going out of our way for publicity.

"Don't give me a hard time on this, Giada. You're my only daughter. I've been dreaming about doing all this stuff for decades. Let me enjoy these traditions," she pleaded.

Before I could argue, she pulled out a photo of Luca and I. It was taken over two years ago, at a black-tie event in Italy. Luca and I hadn't officially even been together at the time, but looking at the photo, I'd never have guessed that. It was a professionally shot image, but we'd posed ourselves. His arm was around me, and I was angled towards him, my hand splayed across his abdomen. I'd styled my hair myself, but the dress Luca had bought me—a midnight blue Armani sheath dress—looked phenomenal.

In the first photo, we were looking at the camera, but in the second, we were staring at each other. I distinctly recalled passionately hating him that day, but the look in my eyes was filled with an entirely different fire.

"Where'd you even get these?" I asked, not even remembering ever seeing that second picture.

"Luca. He sent it to us while you were still in Italy, saying something about how he thought we'd love seeing how beautiful you were in that dress." She shrugged. "Anyway, I realize they're not the most recent pictures, but either one is gorgeous and would work perfectly for an announcement."

I didn't disagree. "Yeah, you decide. I'm okay with either. And what you wrote looks fine too, but did you run it by dad?"

She nodded, then reached into her envelope again, her smile widening with anticipation. She retrieved a small, white notecard.

"Ready?" she asked, looking more excited than I'd remembered her being in any recent time, anyway.

She flipped the card over before I answered. It was some sort of formal invitation. I leaned forward to read.

"You're throwing us an engagement party?" I asked, thoroughly confused. I recognized the location as a nicer Italian restaurant in Bridgeport. "Wait, and it's a week from Sunday?" I felt my blood pressure surge.

She beamed proudly. "Camilla Marino said that Sal would be back in town by then, and the date works for your father too. Once you run it by Luca, we'll finalize it."

"Who exactly are you inviting?" I couldn't imagine the security nightmare that would be posed by having a big formal event involving all the key players from two separate crime families.

My mother reached into her envelope a third time and retrieved a typewritten list. The staple in the corner signifying the presence of multiple pages drove my heartrate through the roof.

"Mom!" I snatched the list away from her. "This is a billion people. I don't even recognize some of these names," I began, pointing to a few towards the end.

She glanced over my shoulder. "Those are Luca's relatives. His mom contributed to the list. Anyway, we don't expect perfect attendance with such short notice, but I'd hate to offend any close family or business associates by excluding them."

I had no idea what to say.

"Of course, you and Luca can add guests to the list."

I shook my head. It was already too big.

"Oh, come on. You have friends. And what about your new coworkers?"

"I barely know any of them. I am not inviting anyone from work," I said. "Gabriella Giordano and guest, add them."

My mom nodded and made a note. "You'll text me her address this afternoon?"

I could handle that.

"What about Luca? He's always surrounded by friends. I'm sure he'll have a few names to add to the list."

I looked closer at the printed list. Alessio Rizzo was already on the list as was Giorgio. But Thomas and Giovanni were not. "I'll ask him who else he wants to add later and text you the names and addresses. But mom, he's probably not even free that night, so don't get all excited before you hear back from me."

I spent the next hour nervously anticipating Luca's reaction when I told him about it all, but in the end, all he did was laugh. He agreed the party would be a logistics nightmare, and we mused that there had to be a bad joke about so many mobsters in a confined space, but he seemed fine with it all.

All I had to do now was secure the maid of honor.

CHAPTER 21

Luca

It had been Alessio's idea for us to track down Emiliano's killer for the Conti family. We had lucked out in that Matteo the pushover had willingly shared with me the name of the man his family believed to be responsible, so all we had to do was track him down and find an opportunity to take him out. I had zero expectations of the mission succeeding, but I didn't mind sticking Thomas on reconnaissance duty for the week.

When Thomas called the day before the engagement party, I almost didn't answer. Giada was modeling three different dresses she'd chosen for the party, and Thomas could've just called Alessio. But I sure was glad when I did answer.

"Hey," Thomas began. "He's sitting in his car alone. I don't know why or for how long, but I've got a clear shot now."

"What's the address?" I asked. I disconnected the second he answered and called Angelo. I assumed Angelo would ignore my call, but he answered, albeit in a surly, pissed off way. I motioned for Giada to wait, and I left our bedroom, shutting myself in the guest bedroom.

"One of my guys has eyes on Jonas Salvecchi right now. He's alone and in his car, and my guy has a clean shot. If you want him to take it, I'll give the order. But if you want to have one of your men handle it, he's in a metallic blue Ford Fusion." I told him the address, then waited.

He didn't respond.

"Angelo?"

I heard him repeating the address to someone.

"I can be there in five minutes. Tell your guy thanks," he finally said.

"His name is Thomas. I'll have him wait in case you need backup. Good luck."

Angelo hung up, so I called Thomas to relay the message and asked him to alert me if Jonas left. Then, I nervously awaited further news. Even though Angelo and I were now supposedly getting along, he still hated me. I didn't blame him. By stealing his drugs and ratting him out to his dad, I'd screwed him out of a lot of money, made him look bad to his guys, and trashed his reputation within his own family. If our roles were reversed, I'd hate me too.

But if I could serve this murderer on a platter for Angelo to knock out, he'd look like a hero. His father would forgive him for the drugs, and Angelo, in turn, would hopefully forgive me. Or at least start to trust me.

I about jumped out of my skin when there was a knock at the door. "Yeah," I called, still staring at my phone as if willing it to update me.

"Are you talking to my brother?"

"No," I answered, not even glancing up at first. When I did, I saw that Giada had changed into a new dress. This one was even hotter than the last, but wasn't so revealing that it would piss off my mother, either. "Well, yes. Just for a minute," I said revising my answer.

"Is everything okay? You look tense."

"Yeah, something came up, and I'm waiting to hear back from Thomas."

"Something came up with Angelo?" Concern filled her rich eyes.

"No, sorry. He's fine. I, um... Listen, can you leave me for a few minutes?"

Giada nodded, but her smile faded, showing her disappointment.

"Hey," I waited until she turned. "That's the dress. You look amazing."

Giada's face lit up, and she blew me a kiss.

It was more than twenty minutes before Thomas called back. He told me it was done, and that it looked like there wouldn't be any issues with witnesses. I'd just hung up when Giada knocked at the door again.

I already felt relieved when I answered the door. "Sorry baby, I'm all yours now," I said, leaning towards her. She stiffly pulled backwards, and I glanced behind her. Angelo's crony, Rico, was standing in the entry to our apartment.

I winced, wishing Giada would've told me before letting him in. Not that I thought he would do anything bad right now, but I didn't trust her brother's men in general, and I wanted her to get in the habit of not opening the door to them. Truly, I wanted her in the habit of not opening the door to anyone who showed up unexpectedly, especially at ten p.m.

I walked to the door and shook his hand. "Let me guess, Angelo is in the car?"

He nodded.

"I'll be right back," I told Giada.

She rolled her eyes.

"You could've just come up," I said to Angelo as I slid into the backseat of his car beside him.

"Isn't my sister there?"

I sighed. "Yes. So, Thomas said it went well? Congrats."

"I just wanted to check what your game was."

"My game?"

"Yeah. Why'd you tell me where he was? How did you even know?"

"Dumb luck," I said, lying in response to the second question first. "And I told you because your father wanted him dead, and I figured he'd get over that situation with the drugs a lot faster if you served up Grasso's killer."

Angelo narrowed his brows. "So you want me to take credit for it?"

"I mean, you did it. Or one of your men." I shrugged. "As far as I'm concerned, Thomas was never even there. I don't know what you were up to tonight."

Angelo took his time considering my words. "Why?"

I struggled not to roll my eyes. "For starters, I'm a nice fucking guy. Plus, there's a lot of potential benefits for both of us if we can get along." I paused. "And I like your sister. I need you to be less of a dick to her."

He leaned back against his seat. "That's it—I have to play nice with Giada, and you erase all of your involvement in this?"

I raised my hands. "It's already erased, regardless of what you do next."

Angelo extended a hand reluctantly. "I appreciate it. Emiliano was a good man. He didn't deserve what he got."

I started out of the car. "I'll tell your sister you said hi. We'll see you tomorrow, right?"

"Couldn't miss it if I tried," he said, smiling slightly. "And believe me, I tried."

I laughed, waved at Rico, then jogged back into the building where my gorgeous fiancée was waiting.

~

Giada

I had told Gabby the engagement news over the phone days before, and she'd offered me a polite but insincere congratulations. I invited her to join me for manicures, pedicures, hair and makeup styling the day of the engagement party, bribing her with expensive champagne and the opportunity to try and talk me out of the engagement.

Unfortunately, my mom had dropped several not-so-subtle hints about wanting to be included in the first part, so our twosome grew. Gabby wasn't crazy enough to talk shit about Luca in front of my mother, so I enjoyed the brief respite. My mom headed home after her nails dried, and by the time we transitioned hair and makeup, Gabby launched into her spiel.

"Giada, I see why you like Luca," she began. "He's charismatic, he gets along with your family, he's rich, and of course he's hot."

I giggled at her final inclusion.

"And if you tell me he's never hurt you and you're sure he's not cheating on you, I'll believe you," she said.

I sensed a 'but' coming, so I hurried to comment. "He's not. I know what it looks like, and I admit he has a less than ideal track record, but Luca is absolutely not cheating on me. And he'd never hurt me, I swear. He's bossy and almost as sexist and overprotective as my brothers, but he loves me so much. If you want me to be happy, you have to understand that he's the one who does that for me. There's not a doubt in my mind that he will love me and keep me safe for the rest of his life."

She nodded but still looked unconvinced.

"A lot of the things that probably seem off about him to you are cultural. Growing up in Italy and being Italian is so different than living here and having Italian heritage. And his business is insanely time consuming now, so he does get calls at all hours.

But it's all work related, usually from Alessio. He's a private person, but he tells me everything. I know what he's up to when he's not with me, I just can't share it. And he wants to get to know you better," I added. The last part was a total lie, but I wanted them to spend some time together and was determined to make it happen.

"Okay. I'm sorry for being such a downer. I just want you to be happy."

"I appreciate that," I said. "So…I have a favor to ask."

She grinned. "Does it involve a hideous dress and bache-lorette-party planning duties?"

I laughed. "Yes. Will you be my maid of honor?"

"Of course!" She leaned in and hugged me.

The makeup artist scowled. "Don't mess up your mascara!"

Gabby and I both giggled.

"So what plans have you guys discussed so far? Any timing?" she asked.

"We haven't picked an exact date yet. I told Luca he can have final say in the reception location and the rehearsal dinner, but I'm planning the menu."

"Definitely."

"And I think we might have a reception in Italy down the road too, just so his family there still can celebrate with us. We're starting the pre-cana classes soon."

Gabby looked surprised. "He agreed to that?"

I nodded. "He's insistent I have my dream wedding. It's all surreal though, because, in a way, I've been dreaming about this since high school. But then, I haven't come up with much in terms of concrete plans since then."

My friend smiled. "I'm happy for you, Giada."

Luca

*A*s we drove up to our engagement party, it felt like Giada and I had been engaged for a lifetime, but also just a matter of days. I couldn't fathom how our mothers—mostly Giada's—had pulled together such an extravagant affair with such little notice, but they had. That fact gave me hope that maybe, this time, we could truly pull it off. Maybe at the end of this engagement, I'd walk away with the wife of my dreams.

I gazed at Giada, still taken by her beauty. At some point, I figured that would fade. Not her beauty, but my surprise every time I noticed it. Over time, surely I'd get used to it, grow immune to her exquisiteness. By some miracle, I hadn't reached that point yet. Quite the opposite, actually. As cute as Giada had been in high school, I could now say with confidence that she woke every single day even more gorgeous than the prior day. And her beauty wasn't just on the surface. Giada was the type of good person that most people only aspired to be. Giada was as close to an angel on earth as one could get.

I'd never know what I did to deserve my very own angel.

Our ride slowed to a stop, and I unfastened my belt, shifting to stand.

"Wait," Giada said, blocking my exit from the vehicle. She'd said almost nothing during the drive from the apartment, but apparently now that our SUV was idling at the curb in front of the restaurant hosting our engagement party, she needed to talk.

I raised an eyebrow expectantly, ignoring Alessio's eyerolling from the front seat.

"Do not leave me alone with your mother. She hates me. Or your father, actually." She paused. "And please don't speak Italian in front of me. Or at least translate if you do. I need you to be nice to me tonight. Like, really nice."

"Like oral sex in the bathroom nice?" I interrupted, eliciting a giggle from Alessio.

"No, like try to show Gabby that you aren't a controlling narcissist."

"You want him to lie?" Alessio piped up.

She ignored him.

"Giada, relax. This is a party, for us. You're supposed to have fun."

She wasn't normally the worrying type, so her current panic-mode stumped me. I pressed a kiss to her forehead, then nudged her out of the car.

The restaurant wasn't busy yet. As the guests of honor, we'd arrived a few minutes early. Mrs. Conti rushed up to greet us the moment we stepped inside. She gushed over how handsome we looked, and then I walked Giada to the bar before greeting my own mother. I ordered her a white wine, then watched her sip tentatively. By my calculations, Giada would start to calm down after the first glass, and by the time she finished her second, she might be relaxed enough to have fun.

I'd only downed one sip of my drink before my mother approached. She greeted me in Italian, then dragged me close for the traditional two-cheek kiss.

"You look lovely, sweetheart," she said to Giada, almost sounding sincere. "May I?" she reached for Giada's hand, inspecting the ring. "Very pretty. What happened to the last one?"

"I like this one better," Giada piped up.

I wrapped my arm around her waist. "We should probably say hi to our fathers before the guests arrive."

My mother stepped aside, so I walked Giada to the table in the back. My papà and hers were seated adjacent to each other, each of them with their backs to a wall so they had an excellent view of the room. They were alone at the table, but each of them was flanked by two guys on foot serving as security. I almost chuckled at the sight. It was like an image from an old-fashioned mobster movie.

They both stood as we approached, politely greeting us. My

papà congratulated us, then made awkward small talk. After a moment, he nodded to me, then asked in Italian if we could speak in private.

Mr. Conti spoke Italian too, so I wasn't completely sure why my papà felt the need to switch to his native tongue, but I quickly declined in English. "Our guests should be arriving any moment now, so Giada and I should stay out here to greet everyone," I said.

I guided Giada back to the bar for a refill, grinning smugly.

"Well played," she said, and it was. I was a master of many roles, and doting fiancé certainly wouldn't be a challenge.

As our close friends and extended family members arrived and congratulated us, Giada and I stood together, my arm tightly wrapped around her waist. I certainly didn't mind the close contact, but as an added perk, the guys who normally would want to talk shop or, worse yet, ask for a favor, didn't. Having Giada at my side ensured the conversations stayed strictly social.

There were appetizers positioned around the room, so at a break in the action, I tugged Giada to the corner and fed her. We'd have dinner in another half hour or so, but I didn't want all the alcohol hitting her on an empty stomach. After a moment, Gabriella came over and joined us.

"This food is amazing," she said, still chewing.

"Thanks. We had nothing to do with the menu," Giada replied.

"Can I get you ladies a refill?" I offered, getting the impression Giada wanted a moment alone with her friend. Gabriella gave me her drink order, then I leaned in and kissed Giada before starting to the bar. I gazed out the window as I walked, noticing several men outside who were trying to appear casual but obviously were plainclothes officers.

"She seems happy enough now," Alessio said, sidling up to me at the bar, his eyes on Giada and her friend.

"Yeah. My family makes her nervous."

"Your papà makes everyone nervous," Alessio pointed out. "But your mom is awesome."

I agreed with that assessment, but also understood why Giada felt differently about my mother. "You say that because my mother loves you. She's not so friendly with Giada." I ordered another glass of wine for Gabriella and an Italian soda for Giada to give her a break from the booze before the toasts began.

"How many cops are outside?" I asked him.

He shrugged. "Five. Maybe six."

I considered my options. "Keep em fed and happy," I said, pulling a few crisp hundred-dollar bills from my pocket.

I turned to the manager, who was standing beside the bartender. "Can you see that the kitchen prepares some extra food and takes it to our friends outside?"

The manager accepted my money and nodded politely, as though there were nothing odd about my request. I didn't have to ask Alessio to oversee it all.

"Anything else you want me to do while I'm here? Anyone I should talk with?"

I thought about it, then shook my head. "Just enjoy yourself. Make friends with some Conti men."

Alessio raised an eyebrow, and we both laughed.

"Okay, not that kind of friend," I clarified, shaking my head as I delivered the drinks to the ladies.

Giada's father called everyone to their tables after a little while, and champagne was passed around. Mrs. Conti thanked everyone for coming and made everyone chuckle by talking about how, back in high school when we were dating, everyone had hoped we'd end up here. My papà gave a much less personal toast, followed by another quick word from Giada's father.

I squeezed Giada's hand, then stood. "I'll be brief since I know everyone is hungry, but I wanted to say that we appreciate you all taking time out of your busy schedules to come wish us support. As you all know, I've spent years trying to pin down this amazing woman, and I don't know what miracle has finally convinced her to agree to marry me, but I am now a very happy man. I'm sure I have many of you to thank for that. I am also very grateful that the Conti family has welcomed me and my family so warmly, and I look forward to a growing partnership between our two families."

I gazed down at Giada, whose cheeks had flushed a bright red, and mouthed "I love you," before turning back to the crowd. "If you'll all raise your glass with me, I'd like to toast my bride-to-be. She is the most generous, thoughtful, sweet, patient, and beautiful woman I've ever met. We are all better off for having her in our lives. To Giada," I lifted my glass then took a sip amidst cheers of "aww" and "salute."

"Alright, well, let's eat!" I said, sitting down with Giada.

"You are so dead," she whispered, pulling me in for a kiss. "I love you."

I grinned, pleased to have successfully embarrassed her, but also certain that was the exact reassurance she needed for her friend and anyone else who doubted us.

I continued piling on the attention the rest of the evening, even later, when Alessio pointed out that the police seemed to have tripled their normal patrol outside the restaurant. Tonight was only about love, not any conflict between the families, and certainly not any illegal agendas. As far as I could tell, Giada didn't even notice the cops outside. For once, she could just enjoy the upside of being the true mafiosa princess.

CHAPTER 22

Giada

The engagement party was perfect in every way. I'd expected a disaster, since that was what always occurred when I spent time with Luca's parents or Angelo, but nothing had gone wrong. Everyone got along, the food and drinks were all fantastic, and I'd enjoyed simultaneously mingling with all the various parties in my life that I'd kept separate up to that point.

It had been two days since the engagement party, and I was still reeling with happiness. Luca had pulled out all the stops and exceeded my every expectation in the doting fiancé department. Even now, I couldn't stop smiling, even though I felt like a fool grinning through a series of afternoon meetings at work.

It was almost dusk when I neared my building. My mind had been on various living room arrangements for a client Diane had discussed with me, but I immediately noticed the familiar man sitting on the steps in front of my apartment building.

I slowed my pace, but Adrian stood and walked closer when he saw me.

"I guess my invitation to the big party got lost in the mail," he said, shifting his weight back and forth from his heels to his toes.

"It seemed disrespectful to invite you."

"Disrespectful," he repeated, clearly biting his tongue to avoid saying more.

"I'd love if we could get to the point where we could be friends again, Adrian. But I didn't want to hurt you by inviting you," I said.

"When were we ever friends?"

I didn't have an answer for that. I supposed, really, we were never friends. In my mind, he'd been my best friend for years, except he was a friend I slept with often. In reality, we were a couple, and then we were nothing, and then we were a couple again, and then nothing, and then... I'd treated him badly, and I knew it.

He deserved more, but it was in the past. I could see now that my feelings for Adrian had been different than they should've been. I did love him, but as a friend. It was never the same as it had been with Luca.

"Well, I guess I didn't have anything to say. I thought I should come congratulate you."

"Thank you," I said awkwardly. "I'm really happy."

"Yeah, I heard the celebrations were pretty festive. I guess for your...what is it now, fourth engagement to the same guy, you gotta go big or go home."

It was our second engagement, but Adrian already knew that, so I said nothing. We were silent for a full, painful minute. I tried to think of what a friend would say.

"How's the dog? Um, Scruffy is it? Did the shelter find him a good home?"

He narrowed his gaze. "Like you care."

"Why are you here, Adrian?" I dared him to say that he wanted me back. If we got it out in the open, we could address it.

I could convince him I truly loved Luca, and we could move on once and for all.

"I don't know. I felt like I needed to check up on you, to see if you needed saving from him. Again."

He was goading me, and I knew it. I should've just thanked Adrian for his concern and gone inside, but, of course, I couldn't. "I've never needed saving from Luca, not really."

Adrian rolled his eyes so dramatically that people a block away probably saw.

"He's loved me for years, Adrian. He would never hurt me."

"Except he has."

"You know what I mean," I said. Sure, Luca had hurt me on an emotional level, but I had hurt him too.

"You're a smart girl, Giada. You have to see that this pattern isn't healthy. This relationship isn't healthy."

"I'm not doing this with you, Adrian. I made my choice, and I'm sticking with it. I'm sorry."

"Sticking with it for how long? Until he cheats on you again? Until you find a body in his trunk?"

"Shut up, Adrian!"

But he didn't.

"Maybe when Father Ryan disappears to a new church too? Or maybe he'll have some bad accident?"

"Fuck you," I spit. "Luca had nothing to do with Father John.

"You sure about that? Because I heard differently from a reliable source."

Before I could answer, he shook his head and continued. "Jonas Salvecchi, the guy your father thought killed your uncle, Emiliano Grasso. He turned up dead. His body washed up on the shore. That's convenient."

"What are you talking about? How would you know that?"

"The news, Giada. Murder victims tend to make the news." Adrian rolled his eyes. "Police believe he was killed the night before your big party. But I'm sure Luca was with you the whole time that night."

"He was," I said, and it was the truth. Although he had seemed tense. And there were several "urgent" phone calls and a visit from Angelo that seemed out of place. "Luca had nothing to do with that. He didn't even know Emiliano."

"Sure. And he had no interest in making his new father-in-law or brother-in-law like him, I suppose." Adrian paused. "There were police around your engagement party. Did you know that? Maybe you should skip the middleman and just invite the whole SWAT team to your wedding."

"I'm not hashing all this out with you, Adrian. You're drunk. You should just go."

"Fine." His head drooped, and when he gazed back up at me, there was a newfound sorrow in his eyes. "I just don't get it. I was good to you. I took care of you. I always did right by you."

"Yes, Saint Adrian, I know. You were fucking perfect. And you probably always would've been."

"Then it is true, nice guys finish last?"

"No, but did it ever occur to you that I couldn't live like that, always knowing you were better than me and just waiting for the next time I messed up to prove it to you? Next to you, I'd always be the screw up."

"What?"

"Not all of us came out of the womb knowing what we wanted to do with our lives and always doing the right thing. The rest of us mere mortals mess up from time to time. We screw up, we say the wrong thing or do the wrong thing, and we hurt each other. You don't even seem to understand that it's not easy or even possible for the rest of us to be selfless and good all the time."

"So you're happier with Luca because he makes you feel better about doing bad things?"

"He accepts me for who I am. He loves me even when I'm not

perfect. He's not constantly judging me and everyone I love. I don't always feel inadequate next to him."

Adrian scowled. "You should spend your life with someone who challenges you to be a better person, not with someone who teaches you how to hide bodies and smuggle drugs."

He was trying to get a reaction out of me, and he had. I slapped him and was about to say something else when someone flew between us, shoving Adrian back several feet. As soon as I got a good look at the situation, I panicked.

"Shit! Thomas, stop. It's fine. We're just talking." I ducked in between them before either of them could throw punches.

Adrian raised his hands in the air, but didn't even glance at Thomas. His eyes were locked at me, his expression clear that he thought this somehow made his point.

Except it hadn't.

If anything, the fact that Adrian telling me what I should do drove me to violence proved *my* point. I wasn't good enough for him, and I didn't need that constant reminder of all my short-comings.

"Go home, Adrian," I said.

He opened his mouth to say something, then closed it and took a step backwards. "Congratulations on your engagement," he finally said before turning and walking off.

I watched him go, then turned to Thomas.

"I didn't realize I had a babysitter today," I said.

"You don't. I was waiting for Luca."

"I didn't need your help."

Thomas scowled. "If Luca heard I was there and let that guy put a hand on you, my ass would be on the line."

"Adrian didn't touch me."

Thomas shrugged, probably thinking I should thank him for that fact, when in reality, nothing could've ever made Adrian lay a hand on me.

"Are you going to tell Luca about this?"

Judging from his face, that was a dumb question. I blew out a sigh then started to the door. "I'm going inside," I said. I paused in case he expected to be invited in, but he said nothing, so I left.

Once in the apartment, I poured myself a drink and then texted Luca. "Adrian came by. He's hurting over the engagement. I don't think we'll see him again, but if we do, be nice." I reread my message then clicked send.

I assumed we'd still talk about it later, but at least this way he heard it from me and not his minion.

~

Luca

When I got home that night, the first thing I noticed was an open bottle of pinot noir on the counter. I heard the familiar sounds of a home renovation show playing from the bedroom, so I grabbed the bottle and made my way down the hall. Giada was perched at the head of the bed surrounded by a sea of decorative throw pillows. A near-empty jar of olives rest on the nightstand beside her.

She had changed out of the sophisticated tailored suit dress she'd worn to her office earlier, and was now wearing a pair of yoga pants and one of my hooded sweatshirts. She turned as I stepped fully into the room, smiling sheepishly then tugging the strings of the sweatshirt to tighten the hood around her face.

I breathed a laugh then leaned over her, kissing her nose, as it was practically the only part of her still visible.

"Refill?" I offered, holding up the bottle.

She nodded grimly. I filled her glass to the brim, downed a gulp, then handed it to her before squeezing onto the bed. We'd bought a king-sized mattress and Giada had found some custom headboard she loved, so I wasn't sure how it already felt like we didn't fit on the bed. Perhaps it had something to do with the pillows, which seemed to multiply daily.

"Sorry," she mumbled. "Yours is softer."

It took me a moment to realize she was talking about the sweatshirt. "You don't have to apologize for wearing my clothes. You look adorable." I paused, eying the olives again. They were her favorite food, but also her go to for stress eating.

She gulped a few ounces of wine, then handed the glass to me. "I probably shouldn't drink more. I think they expect me in the office tomorrow."

Giada usually loved going into her office, so I wasn't sure why that had her so frazzled.

"They invited me to their client meetings today and to a budget meeting. It was so dull. Like is that what normal jobs are? A bunch of boring meetings, one right after another?"

I shrugged. "I'm not exactly the best person to speak about normal jobs."

Giada snickered at that.

"So, are you stressed about work or about Adrian?"

She groaned at the sound of his name, effectively answering my question.

"What did Thomas tell you?"

I briefly debated not telling her, but decided that might stress her out even more. "Pretty much what you said, except he added that you punched him."

Giada wrinkled her nose. "I didn't punch him. It was more of a slap."

I bit back a laugh. "I wish I'd been there."

"If you'd been there, it wouldn't have happened."

She was probably right, but I was still envious that Thomas got to witness it all. "So do you want to tell me anything else?"

She chucked a pillow onto the ground and snuggled up against me. "Not much else to tell. He just seemed to be thinking you were going to hurt me again. He said you'll cheat on me and murder people and that you're making me a worse person."

"I will never cheat on you," I said.

Giada peered up at me through thick lashes. "Really? That's the only part of that you want to clarify?" She settled back against my chest and sighed. "Adrian said you had something to do with some guy dying, the guy that killed my uncle."

She paused, but no question had been asked, so I kept quiet until she pushed further.

"Hmm, so judging from your silence, he's not completely wrong about that?"

I sighed. "Not completely. The guy is dead. I didn't pull the trigger. I wasn't even there. And that's all I can say."

"Was it Angelo?"

I started to repeat that I couldn't tell her, but realized I could answer honestly. "I don't know."

She inhaled slowly through her nose, then exhaled. "Adrian used to tell me my family did bad things. I didn't believe him. And now..."

"Giada, you are not your family. And Angelo is hardly representative of your entire family," I said. "Plus, for what it's worth, I wouldn't be so sure that Adrian would be any different from Angelo in the same circumstances."

Giada didn't speak for a few minutes. "Adrian also said Father John was dead. He blamed you. He said he had a reliable source for that info."

"Father John is fine. I don't know who would've told Adrian..." I stopped midsentence. I knew exactly who would've told Adrian, and Giada most likely did too. "I'm sure he said that before. Angelo and I are on good terms now, okay? Nothing for you to stress about."

Giada stretched and turned to me again. "You can't just tell me not to stress and expect me to comply. I need a distraction."

I nudged her off my lap, closed the blinds, then turned on

some music. And as soon as the beat dropped, I commenced the most ridiculously bad strip tease ever. But a half-hour later, as Giada lay sprawled out on the bed debating whether gnocchi or ravioli sounded better, I realized I'd served up the most successful distraction out there.

CHAPTER 23

Adrian

I'd never been so grateful for my insane school and work schedule as I was the weeks after Giada's engagement party. I couldn't believe I'd shown up at her apartment, drunk, of course. I couldn't believe half the shit I said. I also couldn't believe she'd actually hit me. Well, no, that I could believe. She'd always been feisty, just not usually with me.

What I couldn't believe was that I hadn't heard or seen a damn thing from Luca since the incident. Even if Giada hadn't told him, surely his minion would've. And if he learned I'd antagonized his precious princess to the point of violence, he would've come after me, right? Unless I truly wasn't worth his time anymore.

Giada had texted me the day after. I hadn't expected an apology, but I was also surprised by what she did say.

"Be careful around my brother. He's blaming Luca for things he himself did. He doesn't care about anyone. You don't want to get in his way," was all she wrote.

I didn't reply.

But maybe she had a point. Maybe the way to get back at Luca wasn't by joining forces with Angelo. Luca was not a good man. I didn't need to falsify bad acts to pin on him; he'd done enough crappy things on his own. I just needed proof.

In a matter of weeks, I found it. Well, technically, Claudia deserved all credit. I'd used resources through the law school research system to investigate the records of Luca's stupid strip clubs. I assumed I'd easily find evidence of money laundering, accounting errors, or tax fraud. Instead, the books were pristine. I moved on to employees. Surely they employed illegal citizens, or at least minors. They probably had teens serving drinks and stripping.

I didn't find any evidence of that, either, but what I thought of next could be even better. The last time Giada had dumped Luca because she thought he was fooling around with strippers. Apparently, he later told her he wasn't, but that was beside the point. If I could prove that he had cheated on Giada with a stripper, that would almost certainly be the nail in the casket for their engagement. And Luca would be alone and miserable, just like he deserved.

When my search yet again came up empty, I happened to think of Claudia. She had mentioned how she'd become gifted at cyberstalking during her intern year at the newspaper, so I figured it was worth a try. I called her up and casually mentioned that I was trying to prove that this jerk in New York had an affair with an employee and asked her how she would go about that search. She'd laughed outright at my goal, but then offered to look into it for me. All she needed from me was his name, the clubs, and the years I was interested in.

Claudia texted me two days later. She detailed a few several sexual favors I owed her the next time I was in town, then included the name of one of Luca's former employees. Claudia didn't offer me details, so I didn't expect much when I called the woman. As luck would have it, she was just as desperate as I was, though her immediate desire was money, not revenge. Regardless, after one follow up phone call, we had devised a foolproof plan that would achieve both of our goals.

And the best part? I could prove Luca was a cheating asshole without anyone knowing I was involved.

~

Luca

Giada had launched full speed ahead into the wedding planning, and within a few weeks of the engagement party, she'd turned our guest room into a twelve by fourteen three-dimensional Pinterest board. Inspirational pictures covered the walls, sample stationery cluttered the desk, and swaths of fabric occupied the bed. It was overwhelming, to say the least, but she was so happy that I could hardly interfere. Besides, she was excited about marrying me. That was what mattered.

She'd also begun decorating the rest of the apartment, starting with our bedroom, which now resembled something out of a magazine. Next she'd moved on to the primary bathroom, turning it into a veritable spa. She'd begun work on the living room, but that project was taking longer. And between her actual design job and the wedding planning, she didn't have tons of time.

I was keeping busy enough with work, but was still riding the coattails of my success with the Marco / Angelo plight. My papà was actually proud of me, and for the first time in my life, he seemed to trust me enough not to micromanage my every task. The Porsche had been a gift from him, but the greatest gift was his return to Italy. Leaving me alone to handle all of our East Coast business was exactly what I needed.

The new guys were working out well. Business was booming.

Angelo seemed apologetic for ratting me out to Adrian, and for the time being, we were getting along. Marco treated me with respect and gratitude, and I started to envision a true partnership between our families.

Everything was going so well, in fact, that I was acutely aware that it all was about to turn to shit.

~

Giada

On Sunday night, Luca had just returned from the gym and was changing after his shower when the doorbell rang. I groaned, assuming it was Alessio or someone else coming to drag him away from me for the evening. We had homework tasks to complete from our pre-cana class, and then we'd reward ourselves in bed. My plans would be ruined if Luca had to do more work.

I certainly wasn't expecting to see a woman and a baby when I gazed out the peephole.

I opened the door, pretty certain Luca's over-protective rules about not letting strangers inside didn't apply when the stranger held an infant in her arms. Besides, she looked harmless enough. She was probably about my age, with hazel eyes and fiery red hair.

"Can I help you?" I asked.

Her eyes locked on me for a moment, as if trying to recognize me, and then she turned to the ground, suddenly nervous. "I'm sorry, I must have the wrong address. I was looking for Luca Marino."

The boy in her arms dropped his stuffed animal, and the woman quickly bent to pick it up.

"Um, this is his apartment," I said. "What's your name?"

"Carla," she said. "I, um, I can come back at another time. I didn't mean to interrupt your evening. We're just, old acquaintances. I mean, I used to work for him."

"It's fine, he's here," I said. Suddenly, the boy looked up at me through thick, jet-black eyelashes, flashing me the most hauntingly beautiful deep brown eyes. I smiled at him and reached for his finger.

"Giada?" Luca's voice startled me. I turned to let him know he had a visitor, but was momentarily distracted by the fact that he was only wearing a ribbed tank top along with his jeans. Luca's stare was focused past me, squarely on Carla. By the look on his face, he definitely wasn't expecting her to drop by our apartment.

Not surprisingly, he got over his surprise quickly.

"What are you doing here?" he asked her, frowning. "How did you get this address?"

"I, um," she swallowed audibly. If I'd thought she looked nervous before, now she looked terrified.

"Are you going to introduce me?" I asked, trying to lighten the mood.

"No," he said, pulling his eyes off the visitor just long enough to turn to me. "Can you give me a minute? I'll be right back."

Luca didn't wait for my answer, instead brushing past me and dragging the woman outside. He shut the door behind him, leaving absolutely no question in my mind that the woman was someone Luca had dated. Well, maybe not dated so much as screwed. What I didn't know though, was how long ago it had ended. Or if it really had.

I chided myself for that stupid thought. Just because Adrian and Gabby both had made comments about Luca cheating didn't mean he would. He wouldn't. Still, something about the way she'd looked at him, or maybe the instant anger he'd clearly felt when he saw her talking to me, seemed...off.

I spied on them through the peephole. Luca kept his voice quiet, but judging from his hand gestures, he was furious. I couldn't tell what Carla was saying, but Luca clearly wasn't having it. He motioned for her to go away, but she stood her ground.

Then she spoke, her words so clearly enunciated that I could read her lips. "Just look at him," she said.

Luca reached for the door, and I jumped back.

"I really don't see it," he said to her. He came inside, slammed the door behind him, then kicked the inside of the door lightly with his toes. "Fucking whore," he mumbled. He looked out the peephole again, then apparently satisfied she had left, he went into the kitchen.

I watched warily as he plunked a few ice cubes into his glass then filled it with bourbon.

"Everything okay?" I asked.

He blew out a sigh. "Yeah. Sorry about that."

I waited for him to say more, certain he'd a least recognize he owed me some explanation. He didn't.

"Old…friend of yours?" I asked.

Luca shook his head. "No. She was a dancer at Rize. I haven't seen her in a while. We were never friends."

"So what did she want?"

"Money."

I supposed that explained his mood, at least. But it didn't fully explain the visit. "Was that her son?"

"Yeah, I guess so."

"Did you know she had a kid?"

He shook his head. He sunk onto a barstool, staring into his nearly-empty drink as if it held the answers to my questions.

"Why would she bring her son with her to ask you for a job?"

He swore in Italian. "I said she wanted money, not a job. And I don't fucking know why she'd bring him. Maybe she didn't have a sitter. Maybe she thought he'd make me feel sorry for her. I don't know, okay? You could chase her down and ask," he snapped.

I sighed. Twenty minutes ago, Luca had been singing in the

shower. Now he looked angry. Violently angry. He wasn't the sort of guy that many people would visit at home to ask for a favor. Carla must be really desperate. Or maybe she had nothing left to lose. I considered the way she cowered when I'd answered the door.

"You didn't...hurt her ever, did you?" I asked. "Or someone close to her?"

Luca tipped his glass, letting the ice clank against his teeth as the remaining liquid drained into his mouth. Then he stood and glared at me, a disgusted look on his face.

"Are you really asking me that, Giada?" he shook his head. "If that's what you think of me, I don't know why you're marrying me."

I watched as he refilled his drink, then stomped back into our bedroom, slamming the door behind him.

I picked up the packet of questions from the church and filled out my portion of the homework as best as I could without his help. Then I dropped the packet on the table and went into the bedroom to see if Luca had calmed down.

The room was dark, and Luca was sitting in a chair by the window, gazing out at the river in the distance. He held his glass close to his lips, but wasn't drinking. The light from the street beneath us illuminated his face, casting an eerie glow.

Even tense, Luca was truly beautiful. His prominent jawline, straight nose, and full lips met every standard of male beauty. But his most striking asset was his eyes. They reminded me of shots of espresso, smoldering hot, accented with thick, black lashes.

Just as he turned to me, my breath caught in my throat.

Something else I'd seen that night reminded me of Luca's eyes too, and now I realized why he was so upset.

The End

Thanks so much for reading! If you enjoyed this story, please take a moment to leave a review. If you're reading the digital version, this link here should take you directly to your retailer site to review. Review Mafiosa Princess-Trust here

You can also review on Goodreads and Bookbub.

Thanks so much, and keep reading for an exclusive excerpt from the fifth book in the Mafiosa Princess series!

SNEAK PEAK OF MAFIOSA PRINCESS- OMERTA

Giada

On the last night of our trip to Florence, exhaustion flooded my bones. Yet somehow, I still couldn't sleep. I supposed it didn't matter. I could sleep on the flight. And once we were home, I didn't anticipate leaving bed the next few days, so I could catch up on rest in between other, more entertaining, activities.

My mind kept drifting back to something the Father had said, about how we should love our partners even more when they're struggling to love themselves. At the time he'd spoken the words, I'd smugly disregarded the tip. I assumed I already loved Luca that way, but perhaps I was mistaken.

To a casual onlooker, Luca oozed confidence. He didn't doubt himself or his abilities for a moment.

But I knew him better. I understood that the cocky man everyone else saw was merely putting on a show, playing the part of the strong leader, filling his role perfectly. In reality, Luca's self-hatred bordered on crippling some days. I'd thought that by marrying him, I'd show him I loved him despite his lie about sleeping with Carla.

Maybe what he'd needed wasn't for me to love him in spite of the perceived fault, but to believe him when he said he hadn't cheated.

The waxing crescent moon shone through the oversized windows, casting a gentle glow on the room. In our post-lovemaking exhaustion, we hadn't remembered to shut the curtains. As soon as the golden rays of sun lit up the room, we'd surely wake, but I didn't dare risk disturbing Luca early by sneaking out of bed to close the drapes. He'd fallen asleep on his back, with one arm bent behind his neck and the other arm on my hip.

From my side-lying position, I had the perfect view of my lover's face. Few experiences in life were as satisfying as watching Luca sleep. It was a rare occasion that he actually fell asleep before me—or stayed asleep when I moved. Luca was an impossibly light sleeper, so every time I caught him sleeping felt as magical as a unicorn sighting.

I relished the stark contrast between sleeping Luca and wakeful Luca. When awake, Luca was always alert, on guard, and analyzing everything. Even if he seemed relaxed, he wasn't, and there were subtle signs that would betray his attempts to appear at ease.

But in his sleep, Luca lost all traces of tension. His facial features relaxed, making him resemble the young teen I'd had a crush on back at boarding school. He still had those same lips I'd kissed in the library, and that same adorable nose I'd dotted with powdered sugar in the dining hall. And those eyelids...agh. Luca's eyes were stunning—mysterious, deep, and dark, but even when he shut them, something about his eyes still mesmerized me. Maybe it was his impossibly thick, long lashes, or maybe it was just the memories of catching him napping in the courtyard in front of the science building that captivated me.

Whatever it was, I could watch Luca sleep for hours. Unfortunately, his calm appearance and even, smooth breathing also relaxed me, and I usually fell asleep within minutes of gazing at my sleeping beauty.

Tonight, I was determined to stay awake longer, to fully absorb and appreciate the man beside me. Not just the smooth curve of his ears and the masculine cut of his jaw, but the parts of Luca I couldn't see. His courage, his grit, his generosity. Even his loyalty.

No matter what may or may not have happened with some stupid dancer years before, I didn't doubt the man beside me was wholly devoted to me. He'd sacrifice everything for me, stop at no lengths to protect me. His desire for me was steadfast. Luca was even tenacious in his drive to improve.

Did I think Luca was perfect? No, of course not. But more than anyone else I'd encountered, Luca tried. Every day, Luca fought the instincts his father had so deeply engrained in him. Luca's line of work forced him to teeter along the line between good and evil, but he was making progress. Making it better. Making himself better. I didn't doubt Luca would ever cease striving to be a better person. Maybe he wouldn't do it for himself, but for me, he absolutely would.

I shifted my hand to his face, appreciating the contrast between the scratchy stubble beneath my palm and the smooth flesh of cheek against my fingers. For a breath, I thought he might've slept through the contact, that I could touch Luca without disrupting the sleep he deserved. But in a flash, his hand flew from my hip, his fingers tightly circling my wrist. I nearly giggled at my naivety in thinking I could thwart Luca's cat-like reflexes.

"Need more sleep," he mumbled without opening his eyes. "No part of me is ready for round three."

I breathed a soft laugh against his neck. "I just like watching you sleep."

He lifted my hand to his lips, kissed it softly, then flipped onto his side, shifting me along with him. His arm roped around my waist and his legs pressed against my own. "Get some sleep, Princess," he whispered, burying his face in my hair to kiss my neck, then promptly stilling.

The fifth book in the Mafiosa Princess series will be out later in 2022. In the meantime, make sure you've subscribed to my newsletter and follow me on Goodreads and Bookbub so you get updates about all my new releases! If you haven't already reviewed *Mafiosa Princess- Trust*, I'd be so grateful if you did so.

If you're reading the digital version, this link here should take you directly to your retailer site to review. Review Mafiosa Princess- Trust here

You can also review on Goodreads and Bookbub.

https://www.LizaMalloy.com/registration

FAMILY TREES

Having trouble keeping track of all these hunky mobsters? Here's a quick guide:

Conti Family Tree

Giada's Grandparents, Giuseppe and Illaria had three children.

1. Marco married Martina, and their children are Angelo, Matteo, and Giada.

2. Sofia married Antonio G, and their children are Gabriel, Giulia, and Giacomo. Gabriel married a woman named Nicole and Giulia married a man named Carlo. Antonio has a younger brother, Emiliano Grasso, married to Susanna, who also works for Marco.

3. Vincenzo married Bianca, and their children are Vinny, Edoardo, Diego and Mia. Diego married a woman named Brittany.

Other Conti "Family"

- Leonardo Ricci ("uncle")
- Giovanni Romano (brother of Bianca Romano-Conti)

- Stefano G. Bruno (Marco's cousin)
- Antonio Ricci (son of Leo and his ex-wife Noemi)

Marino Family
- Salvatore Marino, married to Camille
- Samuele Marino (Salvatore's brother), deceased

Luca's "Crew"
- Alessio Rizzo, Thomas Verratti, Giovanni Costa, Roberto Carbone

Angelo Conti's "Crew"
- Cousins Eddi Conti, Antonio Ricci, Giacomo Grasso
- Friends Federico "Rico" Regio, Giorgio Lomba, Nicolo "Nico" Controni, Tony Violi, Mike Monti

ACKNOWLEDGEMENTS

The Mafiosa Princess series has been so fun to write and even more fun to share with readers. I love every email I receive about the series—even the ones where you're frustrated over my treatment of your favorite character. I'm so grateful for my loyal fans and for all of the bloggers. I couldn't keep delivering books in this series if not for those of you buying the books and leaving reviews.

I'm so grateful to the team helping deliver high quality books. Sarah P., thank you for catching all my random typos and other errors that my eyes have glossed over. J.D. Designs, thanks for your patience and willingness to tweak cover versions over and over to meet my vision.

Thank you also to my beta readers and ARC team. With millions of great books out there, I'm always flattered when you spend your time helping promote my stories!

ABOUT THE AUTHOR

Liza Malloy writes contemporary romance and women's fiction. She's a sucker for alpha males, bad boys, dimples, and muscles, and she can't resist a man in uniform. Liza loves creating worlds where her heroine discovers her own strength and finds her Happily Ever After. When Liza isn't reading or writing torrid love stories, she's a practicing attorney. Her other passions include gummy bears, jelly beans, and the occasional marathon. She lives in the Midwest with her four daughters and her own Prince Charming.

Visit her website at www.LizaMalloy.com

Join her email list at http://eepurl.com/gnuROD

ALSO BY LIZA MALLOY

Sixty Days for Love

For Love and Italian

Forbidden Ink

The Brothers' Band

The Brothers' Band: The Next Track

Hollywood Endings

Hollywood Beginnings

Supporting Roles

Legacy: The Awakening

Legacy: The Revelation

Legacy: The Reckoning

Mafiosa Princess

Mafiosa Princess: Sacrifice

Mafiosa Princess: Honor

Love-All: A Steamy Sports Romance (exclusively on Kindle Vella)